No Mercy~ A Darker Continua

# NO MERCY

A Darker Continuation

By Lucian Bane

**© 2015 by Lucian Bane**

**All rights reserved. No part of this document may be reproduced or transmitted in any form or by any means, electronic, mechanical, photocopying, recording, or otherwise, without prior written permission of Lucian Bane or his legal representative.**

To all the readers, fans, and or reader's clubs. Thank you for supporting my work. I'd also ADVISE you not to pirate my work. I've hired Karma to hunt down the cheap mother-effers who can't spend 2 or 3 effing 99 to buy a good effing book, and put some smack down on their asses. You've been duly warned.

And if you know of anybody that can't afford a copy, just let me know. I'm a nice guy. ☺

Also, if you need a different format, please contact me, the author.

### Dedication

This book is dedicated to my beautiful, amazing, gorgeous wife. I love you forever. Thank you so much for putting up with me, for believing in me, for loving me.

### My Dark Erotica Group Acknowledgements

Gina Terribile Enge ~ Abraham's car (hearse)

Linda Kidwell ~ Harpoon gun

# NO MERCY

A Darker Continuation

By Lucian Bane

© 2015 by Lucian Bane

**All rights reserved. No part of this document may be reproduced or transmitted in any form or by any means, electronic, mechanical, photocopying, recording, or otherwise, without prior written permission of Lucian Bane or his legal representative.**

To all the readers, fans, and or reader's clubs. Thank you for supporting my work. I'd also ADVISE you not to pirate my work. I've hired Karma to hunt down the cheap mother-effers who can't spend 2 or 3 effing 99 to buy a good effing book, and put some smack down on their asses. You've been duly warned.

And if you know of anybody that can't afford a copy, just let me know. I'm a nice guy. ☺

Also, if you need a different format, please contact me, the author.

### Dedication

This book is dedicated to my beautiful, amazing, gorgeous wife. I love you forever. Thank you so much for putting up with me, for believing in me, for loving me.

### My Dark Erotica Group Acknowledgements

Gina Terribile Enge ~ Abraham's car (hearse)

Linda Kidwell ~ Harpoon gun

No Mercy~ A Darker Continuation

Maria S Brownfield ~ Secondary Character name: Norris Bartley (Crayz Legs)

Tammy Singleton Burch ~ Mechanical limb and name

Tammy Singleton Burch ~ Liberty's hand Gun: modified hand rifle and Hello Kitty

Angela Peters ~ with our very own Roxie Phelps for face and personality.

Treena Ross ~ Media Center pic

Nan DeVore-Lindsey ~ Drink Name: "Slow Screw" for Mercy

Linda Kidwell ~ Drink Name: "Screaming Orgasm" for Sade

Kelly Mallett ~ Funniest Gun: TRAIN GUN

Tami Czenkus ~ Mercy's Black Party Dress

Karen Lowry ~ Liberty's Red Party Dress

Penny Prentice Lusk ~ Mercy's new hairdo

Brandy Michele ~ Mercy's heels for the party

Roxie Phelps ~ Mercy's jewelry for the party (necklace and earrings)

Sandy Hammond Ambrose ~ LMAO Jewerly


To my ever wonderful PA, Jan Kinder for working around the clock in helping make everything perfect. You're my HERO. My angel. And a great friend that is now part of our family.

To Kim Poe, Kristi Collins, and Lo for keeping that ship full speed ahead.

To Kimie Sutherland, who made herself and every resource imaginable, available at all hours to help with the beta process of No Mercy—thank you!

To Carol Hall for standing by for that final look at No Mercy that never happened because Lucian was LATE! But you were there and ready, and for that I am grateful.

A HUGE THANKS TO THE FOLLOWING KICK ASS WOMEN THAT BRING THE BOOM, LEADERS IN BOLD!

Amanda Craig, Amanda Reiter, Angela Peters, Annamaria Folkerts, Antonella Ciarico, Ashley Anne Applebee, Babel Td, Barbara Danks, Carol Ann Sonnet- McCall, Carolina Mamos, Catherine Byrley Coffman, Cathy Passwaters Brown, Cathy Schisel Knuth, Cati Estelle Gentry, Christi Lynne, Christy French, Danielle Wittenberg Fulton, Des Yearning, Donna McManus, Doris Hires Collins, Edith Dubielak, Elaine Kelly, **Elena R. Cruz**, Ellie Masters, Emma Dulin, **Felicia Welch-Reevers**, Fran Brisland, Fran Jones, Frida Friberg Pedersen, Gina Terribile Enge, Heather Holland, Heather Witherell Ray, Heather Young, Hilary Suppes, Holli Gronas, Jackie Lemay, Jami Tamblyn, Jan Brassell Fink, **Jan Kinder**, Jan Wade, Janna Crowley, Jennifer Conken Capizola, Jennifer Gallucci, **Jenny Mckinney Shepherd**, Jessica Bush, Jessica Gallagher, Jessie Baldwin, Julie Hanna Kolt, Karen Lowry, Karen Shortridge, Katherine DiLauro, **Kim Poe**, Kim Urichuck, Kimber Leigh, Kimberly Burden, **Kimmy Johnson**, **Kristi Widner Collins**, Kristin Cox, Lauretta Gomes, Lilian Flesher, Lilli Collier, **Lillian H Snyder**, Linda Baldwin Martin, Linda Hansen Buie, Lindsay Odom, Lisa Campbell Dean, Lisa Jamison-Loyd, LJ Knox, Lori Garside, Lorraine Campbell, **Lorraine Campbell Darcy**, **Louisa Gray**, Louise 'loppy Lou' Bailey, Maria Ria Alexander,

Mary Forster, Melissa Ann, MiChelle Brown Fortress, Mishelle Evans, **Nan DeVore-Lindsey**, Nanci Lopez Bryson, Nanette Magers Stewart, Natasha Weir, **Nathalie Pinette**, Nichole Vincent, Nina Stevenson, Pernella Rodriguez, QuiMo Monica, Rebecca Kummel, Renee Marquis, Renee Mills Henson, Robin Cornelius, **Roxanne Cooper**, **Roxie Phelps**, Ruby Hinkleberry, Sara Prevendoski, Sarah McKenna Ferguson, Stacy Anderson Mraz, Stacy Lewis, Stella Martin, Suzanne Inzana Gangarosa, Tammy Singleton Burch, Tammy Sommervold, Tammy Stearns Sauld, Tangie Byrd, Teresa Jorgensen Winter, Teresa Travnichek, Terrie Meerschaert, Tina McClay, Treena Ross, Vicky Darnold, Wendy Tucker Wignall

## Chapter One

"Abraham." Sade's heart hammered as his brain recollected details about the demented legend before him. The sad clown mask, dark blue coveralls, and gun wagging next to his leg had Sade's blood at a slow crawl.

Vague memories rose to the surface about the man's connection to the family business. Something about how he took his name seriously, that it played a part in his kink even.

Sade didn't recall ever being afraid of the rumors, but with the nightmare only ten feet away with the woman he loved slouched unconscious against his leg and her hair clutched in his meaty fist—he was terrified.

"Don't worry." The man waved the gun loosely. "I'm not a killer. I'm a healer."

The scenario suddenly spelled sick. The kind of sick that would possibly allow you to buy more time but then regret you had.

"Good to know." Whatever reality he had going on in his head, Sade needed to play it. "We can all use a little healing."

"Yes!" The happy muffled words with the sad face added to Sade's dread. "I was hoping to kill a little time while waiting for my son to arrive."

Sade picked up a hint of British in his accent as he contemplated the man's angle. *Kill time.* "Your son?"

"Kane, of course. The lost sheep. I have many children—I'm Father Abraham. Kane is a wayward boy and in need of... a bit of discipline."

*Discipline?* "I see," Sade nodded slowly while using his peripheral vision to locate some type of weapon. "He's certainly been a bad boy. That I can vouch for."

The sad face stared back, and Sade waited to see how his words would play on him. "Bad indeed. Not like you, though. You're still fresh. Open to healing. As she is." His urgent low words came with a brief drop of his head at Mercy, making Sade's stomach clench with an urge to kill.

Sade opened his arms wide, the feelings inside him stranger than he'd ever known. Lust, fear, longing, sadness, and guilt wrecked inside him. "I'm as broken and sick as they come, Father. If you could… maybe heal me first. Please."

Distant thunder rumbled outside just as Abrahams's low laughter mixed with the growling for a demonic sound effect. "Now see?" Excited joy edged his words. "It's nice to find a child *eager* for healing. I don't understand the world these days." He angled his head a little. "I pin it to the end times as God wraps up the age like a dirty garment. So many lost lambs without a shepherd, wool dirty and matted." He tilted his head the other way. "I think that is what we will do first. I was debating on ceremonial styles and shearing," he made buzzing sounds over his bald head, "is indeed the perfect way to prepare with a clean slate." He held up his gun in a show of safety. "Not a killer. A healer." He wagged the weapon a little. "This is merely the pen or corral to keep the sheep from attempting to escape the inevitable. I mean why would I kill you?" he cried as though the idea baffled him. "What good is killing the defiled? Won't their stains be forever uncleansed? What kind of a father would ever do such a merciless thing? How can one be cleansed and purged of sins when *dead?*" The final word gnarred with disgust and the contradiction said the argument had been made before, no doubt with somebody in that fucked up steeple behind the mask.

Sade shrugged slowly. "I agree, it doesn't make sense."

He nodded for a while. "I like you," he finally said, sounding genuinely pleased. "I do think there is much potential in you. I am very eager to see what a thorough cleansing will produce." The gun tapped rapidly on his leg in his excitement. "You know…maybe you're the disciple I'm procuring in this mission." He shot out a breath like he might be smiling behind the mask. "In the vision, I was told that. I have visions and dreams. Do you have those?"

"Sometimes." Middle ground seemed like the thing to go with as he felt his way through the halls of his demented mind. A proper show of deference occurred to Sade and he slowly lowered to his knees, crossing his arms over his chest with a bow of his head. "I am willing to be whatever you want, Father Abraham."

Sade prayed that his game would buy him what he wanted. Not time, but opportunity. To drive his thumbs through both eyes of that sick fuck.

"Fantastic," he said, sounding genuine. "Do you mind keeping an eye on her while I grab my ceremonial supplies? It won't take me long. Come."

Sade looked up to find he'd laid Mercy on the floor and held a chair out for him to sit in.

"Oh, she's fine. I didn't hurt her. Just some chloroform." He glanced down then back at Sade. "I think I used too much, she's been out for so long. Such a delicate flower. Unlike your little friend. I had to use quite a bit, and boy, did he put up a valiant fight."

"Bo is a fighter." Panic surged through Sade as he slowly approached the man standing behind the chair. "I hope you taught him a lesson."

He let out an eager laugh that made Sade sick. "Let's just say, he's being trained in becoming a fisherman."

"A fisherman?" Sade chuckled, sitting. "That dumb shit never fished once in his life."

"Oh, well, he's not really fishing." His humored tone said he was either buying Sade's game or playing another one far better. He was too sincere to tell. "He's my little naughty Jonah. I'll deal with him later, but for now…" Standing at Sade's shoulder now, he drew a finger along the back of his neck. "…I'll focus on you."

"And Kane?" Sade clenched his eyes at the sensual glide of those fingers on his skin still. "He's made my life very hard over the years."

"You like the ink I see."

The idea he was tracing his tattoo made him feel only a little better. "I like the pain." Sade fought a shudder from his continued caress, gliding along the column of his neck.

The smell of sour sweat thickened the air as his breaths turned shallow. "You like pain." His eager whisper trembled like he either hated that or loved it more than Sade wanted him to.

But whatever would keep Mercy safe. "Very much."

The man's fingers roamed up into Sade's hair now, the act of a lover. "Did you know," he whispered, curious. "That there is neither male… nor female… in the body of Christ?"

Sade grit his teeth as Abraham stroked over his lips. "I didn't know."

The large fingers left his mouth and moved to roam over his skull. "An innocent lamb you are. Once I cleanse you and purify your vessel, I think you will make a fine disciple. Would you like that?" He closed his hand over Sade's throat. "Go on," he whispered, his mouth at his ear now. "Tell me."

A trickle of sweat rolled down Sade's face. He knew there was only one right answer to give the predator shifting on restless feet as he assessed his prey. "I would love that, Father."

"I see your body has been pierced." He stroked his hand eagerly over Sade's chest. "That is a grave sin, my son."

The eager words said that was a turn on in some sick way. "I'm dirty, Father." Sade barely managed to resist the full body shudder rolling through him.

"Indeed." He slid a finger over his nipple. "I'll inspect your body later. After the ceremony. I have many tools to heal you and seal all your wounds."

Sade's cock jerked at the idea of sexual pain just as he leaned to his ear again. An elbow to the face nearly overcame Sade in that second.

"This will be your first test as my disciple. A Master must be able to… trust his servant." The sour breath brushed Sade's cheek. "Don't disappoint me, son. Please."

Abraham's beg held an orgasmic tone, shooting more sadistic desires through him—eye-gouging being the strongest and immediate. "I promise, Father." He kept his voice to a whisper, not trusting it. His heart hammered furiously with the effort to appear calm as the man finally walked away, his steps hurried. "I'll only be five minutes."

Sade nodded at the sad clown mask staring back at him from the door. His pause could mean he was fantasizing or having second thoughts. He finally turned and walked out, leaving the door open.

Sade jerked at the feel of a touch. Mercy knelt next to him, tears in her eyes and a finger on her lips *shhhhing*.

He dropped to his knees and pulled her hard to his body with a gasp then looked toward the door. The guns. Did he have time? "The bedroom," he whispered, pointing.

Crouched, Sade and Mercy hurried across the living room, dodging the windows. "I was waiting for the right moment," she barely whispered, clutching his shirt. "When he said he'd let you watch me, oh my God I couldn't believe it. I decided to wait. He's fucking crazy, I'm scared," she gasped, her voice shaking.

Gripping her hand tight, he shot a glance out the window before dashing into the room and hurrying to the closet.

He yanked the door open and felt around for the bag.

"Oh my God! I moved it upstairs!" Mercy whispered. "I'm so sorry!"

A sudden boom made them jump. *The front door.* Fuck, he was back.

Sade flew to the bedroom window and unlocked it. "We'll run to the truck," he hissed, grabbing and helping her out quickly.

"Son?" The bellow sounded confused.

Sade climbed through the window and dropped to the ground right as thunder rumbled louder. The smell of rain thickened the air as Sade grabbed Mercy's hand and raced to the front of the house.

They made it to the vehicle and climbed in. *Oh fuck, no keys.* Ten feet in front of them sat a black antique hearse. "Lock your fucking door," Sade ordered, searching beneath the seat for a weapon.

"Oh my God, he's coming, he's coming!" Mercy shrilled.

Sade eyed the sad clown face hurrying toward the truck as he opened the glove box. Mercy screamed as the maniac banged on the driver window.

"Son!" he bellowed, yanking off his mask and glaring at Sade. The blue eyes were nearly brilliant in the darkness. "How could you?" Agonizing betrayal twisted his face before he turned and paced next to the truck, holding his head.

Sade jumped at feeling something buzz under his ass. *His fucking phone*!

"I trusted you, son," Abraham muttered.

"Look for a weapon, anything!" Sade wrestled the phone out of his pocket.

"I don't understand…" Abraham looked up and searched the sky. "I thought you said I was getting a disciple? Have I not earned that?"

Sade's heart stopped when he looked at the phone. *Zero battery.*

Fists hit Sade's window shaking the truck making Mercy shriek. "I'm not happy about this, son!" he growled, heaving. "I'm very upset! Really upset!"

"Call the police! Call the police!" Mercy screamed.

Sade looked at the text blaring on the screen. *LEAVE NOW!!! ABRAHAM IS COMING! HE'S CLINICALLY INSANE!* Sade's fingers trembled over the keypad, hitting 911.

"Where's he going?" Mercy gasped. "He's leaving, he's going to his car. What's he doing? Oh my God!"

"911 what's your emergency?"

"We're stranded at--"

"623 Fallen Lane Prairie City!" Mercy screamed. "Oh God, he's got a gun!"

"623 Fallen Lane, Prairie City! There's a psycho with a gun!"

"You're breaking up. Are you in town? What town are you near?"

Abraham stalked back to the truck and stopped in front aiming the shotgun at them. Sade shoved Mercy on the seat, covering her. A jolting boom rocked the fucking truck when he fired. "Fuck!" Sade gasped, finally glancing up to find Abraham stalking to the rear of the vehicle. Sade ducked as the back glass exploded. He put the phone to his mouth and screamed, "623 Fallen Lane!" He fought to cover more of Mercy. "Can you fucking hear me!?"

Mercy screamed and covered her head as her window shattered next. Sade looked at the phone. *God, fuck no! Dead!*

Two more shots took out the windshield. Then Sade's window blasted into the vehicle, pieces hitting them.

"Goddamn!" Abraham muttered.

Sade shot his head up to see the animal storming back to his car. Sade opened his door and dragged Mercy out. "Don't look back!" he gasped, running with her down the driveway. "To the highway!"

The sound of a vehicle door slammed and a low engine growled. Light beams soon bounced behind them with the demonic rumble of the engine screaming toward them.

They wouldn't make it, they wouldn't fucking make it. Sade remembered the boathouse. "This way!" He shot into the woods and headed in a diagonal direction back, making sure Mercy stayed on his heels. There had to be something there he could kill him with. He'd use his bare hands as a last option. Fucking that up and risking Mercy wasn't a gamble he could take.

"Where are we going!" she cried.

"The lake," he gasped. "There's a boathouse."

"Where is he? Why isn't he following?"

"Just keep running," he said between huffs.

They dodged trees for another five minutes then finally the lake came into view. Looking around, they ran across the open grassy area near the boathouse just as headlights lit up the road beyond it. "Jesus!" Mercy gasped.

"Behind the boathouse, hurry."

They raced down the short pier leading to the shack on the water, then carefully navigated around to the back. "Oh my God, what's that?" Mercy pointed in the water.

Something white caught Sade's eye near the pier. Pain tore through his chest as he realized it was a body. "Fuck! No!" he gasped. *Bo.*

"He's coming! What are we doing, what are we doing?"

Sade stared at the body in the water and his heart lurched at seeing something rise. He tore down the wood planks and jumped into the water, grabbing him.

Bo made painful bellowing sounds, pushing at Sade. Oh fucking God, his face.

"Something's in his face!" Mercy cried.

Bo's hand trembled, pointing to whatever it was as Sade made his way closer. "H-hook," he whispered, his voice frail and shaking.

"Oh my God, he's coming, Sade!" Mercy knelt on the pier by them. "Help him, hurry!"

"I got you," Sade whispered to Bo, grabbing his trembling hand while following the multiple fishing lines from his mouth, tied to the pier. His stomach tightened at finding it wrapped a hundred times around a giant nail that was beaten and embedded into the wood. Sade tried to bite his way through the thousand-pound line, making Bo whimper in pain.

"He's here, he's here," Mercy gasped.

"Stay with him!" Sade pulled himself back onto the pier. "I'm getting something to cut him loose."

"I'm here," he heard Mercy say as he ran to the boathouse, glancing back in time to see her dropping down into the water with him. Good. Hide.

He reached the worn white structure under the near starless sky just as the rumble of Abraham's engine shut off with the headlights, leaving Sade to stumble around the garage-sized shack in total darkness, searching for their salvation.

## Chapter Two

"Johnny?"

The booming voice sent Sade racing faster in the inky dark for a weapon—anything. He drew his hand back at encountering something sharp. He pulled on it, but it didn't budge.

"I'm really upset," Abraham bellowed, his heavy steps thonking with urgency along the pier. But it was the wobble of agony in his deep voice that said his insanity was at full throttle. "Father didn't want to hurt any of you. You've forced my hand." The last words seethed like a madman pushed beyond his limit.

Sade refocused his efforts and jerked on the object in several directions. Finally, it gave way and Sade quickly felt along the strange piece. The sharp tip seemed attached to some type of barrel with a handle. Could it be a speargun? Fucking *please* be that.

The heavy steps stopped just outside the boathouse and Sade quickly felt for something that could cut Bo loose. His frantic blind search produced loud clanging as he knocked things over. Too late to worry about noise, he needed to find something *now* and get the fuck out. Engaging that psycho needed to happen never if possible. Because he was sure about one thing—Karma had it in for him. Whatever he wanted, Karma denied. He wanted death? No can do. He wanted life? He wanted Mercy? Bo? A fucking chance at happiness? No can do. He had to be smarter than Karma for once. On his self-destruct missions, Karma played the role of his straightjacket. What would she play now that he was on a survival mission?

Sade crouched down, making his way back to the rear of the building, his hands gliding desperately through the dark as he went.

The front door scraped along the floor just as Sade made it to the back. His hands slid over the wall, and metal clanked. Stilling his shallow breaths, he felt at the objects and worked at freeing one.

"Johnny?"

Sade nearly gasped in shock that he'd found a knife. He waited for a few seconds to see what the man's intentions were, what direction he was moving in.

"I just wanna help you, son," he finally said. "That's all." He gasped several times and then chuckled. "I see you found your friend? Are you going to help set him free? Of course you are. Be careful with that treble hook—it's a one-way street. But without a doubt, a tool of *mercy,*" he whispered, sounding reverent as he got closer. "I have the tool to remove it without too much damage. But he really *needed* that wound, son." His voice broke with empathy. "His beauty blinds him. This will help him see."

Sade angled his head, still unable to discern where he was in the dark. Just closer.

"God has shown me he has great plans for all of you. Aren't you excited about that?"

With those final hissed words, Sade grabbed hold of a shelf and shoved with all he had, sending shit crashing to the floor before he slipped out the back and sprinted down the pier. Reaching Mercy and Bo, he plunged straight into the water. "Hold this!" He thrust the spear contraption into Mercy's hands and sliced the fishing line carefully with the knife.

"He's coming!" Mercy tapped her hand rapidly on his shoulder. "I think he's coming!"

"Fuck! Bo, can you swim?"

He nodded, the whites showing all around his eyes.

"I got you," Sade put his hand on the back of his head. "We'll swim under the pier back to the boathouse."

Sade took the speargun from Mercy and held the knife between his teeth. He went from post to post beneath the pier, making sure they stayed close behind him. Fucking pier was three times longer in the back of the boathouse, making the trip agonizing.

Erratic footsteps clonked just ahead, accompanied by light singing just ahead of them. "Father Abraham… has many sons…. Many sons has Faaaaather Abraham. I am one… and so are you… sooooo let's all praise the Lord!"

Gunfire blew a hole in the pier ahead and Sade halted them, his heart racing.

Abraham worked his way toward them, shooting craters in the pier with every step and cheery whistle.

Sade signaled to Bo and Mercy that they stay put then he swam his way toward Abraham. When he was close enough, he went under the water and swam far enough to get behind him. He surfaced slowly, his heart booming in his ears.

"Johnny? That you?"

Sade swam away from the pier, putting himself in the open. "Father?"

Abraham jerked around and Sade shot the speargun. The man roared and Sade swam hard as gunfire ripped through the water around him. Swimming behind him, he jumped back on the pier and yanked the knife from his pocket. He gave a roar and ran at him.

Abraham spun and gave Sade his target. In one swing, he sank the blade as hard as he could into his upper torso, the momentum sending them both into the water. Abraham yanked the knife from his chest and Sade power swam back to Bo and Mercy. "Go, go!" he yelled shoving Mercy onto the pier then launching Bo up next.

"Johnny!" Abraham roared. "I'm coming, I'm fucking coming," he growled, coughing and splashing water. "Father is *very. Very.* Upset! You shot me, Johnny! You stabbed me! The Lord has protected his servant! And shall pour… his wrath on you!" His words cracked and wailed as Sade prayed he'd bleed out quickly.

"His car," Mercy cried, running toward the boathouse.

They raced to the ugly vehicle as fast as Bo could run, and got in it to the surprise of a lifetime. Fucking Batmobile. Sade looked around frantically at all the gadgets and equipment springing out of the dashboard and doors.

"No fucking keys," Sade said, looking and feeling around.

"Hot-wire!" Bo bobbed a trembling finger at the steering wheel.

Sade fought with the panel under the steering column only to discover more electronics. Fuck. "We'll go back to the house. I stabbed him in the chest and shot him with a fucking speargun. That should at least slow him down." Sade slammed the butt of the gun into every electronic he could get to, praying it damaged something important. He felt around for the hood latch not expecting to find it. But there it was, the old fashioned lever on the left.

He pulled it and the deep metal *plonk* sent Sade racing to the front of the car and opening the hood. He blindly felt around and yanked every wire he could reach.

"Hurry, hurry," Mercy whispered next to him.

Sade gave one final glance at the eerily quiet boathouse and the three of them ran up the road toward the house. He'd only been to the lake once when he purchased the place years ago and didn't remember how far it was from the home.

Not ten steps in and Bo's harsh breaths drew his gaze. He was limping with stifled grunts, black hair clumped over his forehead now furrowed in seven kinds of agony. The sight of that giant hook in his mouth with the three spikes sticking out his cheek made him sick. The entire side of his face was swollen, making Sade worry that the sick fuck poisoned it.

Sade lifted Bo's arm and put it around his neck. "Mercy, help me. We'll carry his weight."

She quickly got under his other arm and they half ran the entire way back, keeping a constant eye behind them. Fucker had to be too injured to do much, if anything. But with the bends in the road, Sade didn't feel safe. Felt like he could hear Abraham's lusty breaths right behind them.

Seemed like an hour passed before they finally made it to the clearing that came with the view of the house. Sade's body ached and his lungs burned as they hurried to the backyard. Eyeing the darkness all around, he wished again he'd gone there more often. He barely knew the place.

"What was that?" Mercy whispered as they set Bo down at the back door.

Sade listened and finally heard it. Somebody was in the house. He put his finger to his lips, praying it was Kane while he pointed to the corner of the house. They all made their way to the side and stopped. With the house on piers, they didn't need to duck at the windows but he couldn't see inside them either. Sade led them slowly to the front corner of the house, Mercy right behind, nails biting into both his shoulder blades.

Another vehicle sat in the yard, right in plain sight. Sade's heart raced as he stared at the older El Camino, waiting for something vaguely familiar to pop into his mind about it. The fact that they parked in the open said they weren't trying to hide. Could it be some kind of property maintenance he didn't know about? Surely not at this hour.

"Who is it?" Mercy whispered.

Sade shook his head and turned to face them. "Here's the plan. I'm going to sneak in and figure out how many people we're dealing with. Hopefully, just one. If so, I'll distract them while you both enter the back way, go upstairs, and grab the bag with the guns." Mercy nodded while Bo darted his wide eyes around. "Stay put while I go look."

Sade made his way to the car and hid next to it. First thing he needed to know was if the keys were in it, and if not, could it be wired. Problem was, he didn't have shit for a single tool.

He peered inside the car window and saw the door was unlocked. Glancing at every part of the house he could see, he carefully lifted the handle and opened it. Sade pulled the door and froze when it creaked loudly. He eyed the house again for signs of movement, especially the edge of the house for that psycho. He didn't know how, but he was pretty sure that fucker would round the corner any minute.

Once in the car, Sade looked around, the remnants of smoke mingling with sweet and sour odors. The smell of an overworked liver. Maybe they were older. He felt around under the seat for anything that might serve them in some way. He pulled out a metal something and realized it was a long screwdriver. Fucking miracle.

The door to the house slammed and Sade quickly got out of the car and laid on the ground, looking for feet. Dark boots headed for the car. Shit. Sade waited to see exactly what direction they were taking to the vehicle. When it was obvious they were coming to the driver's side, he hurried on his haunches to the rear. Were they leaving? He couldn't let that happen.

The driver door opened and the car bounced a little with the person's weight. Sade lowered back to the ground, waiting.

"No, I didn't," Sade heard them say. "I checked everywhere. Looks like there was a struggle, a trail of blood and a blue truck in the yard shot to shit, that's it." The deep gravelly voice said he was a big man. Or a skinny dude with half a lung. "No. His car's not here. Well I don't know what to tell you. Wait here? How long?" Whatever the answer was to that made the man sigh. "I'll have a look around the place, maybe they're still here. Yeah well they don't pay me enough to go that far. I know that too. I'm just saying if I find that sick fuck with his dick cut off and shoved up his ass I won't be heartbroken." He paused a moment. "I know that," he spat. "I know that too. Yes, I get it, find them. No shit asshole, that's my job." More silence before his voice boomed, "Well tell the moron you can't clean if there are no bodies to fucking clean!"

Cleaners. Sade's stomach clenched. Was the cleaning job connected to Abraham? The maniac didn't seem the type to work with others while running his own kook factory. His operation was its own world and domain. But if not Abraham, who was supposed to kill them? Had to be him.

Sade waited in the silence, not sure if the phone call was over yet. The flick of a Bic lighter, the smell of smoke, and the door opening answered that. Back to watching the ground under the car, the man's large feet headed back to the house after the car door clonked shut.

Sade crawled back to the driver's side and his breath caught when the size twelve boots stopped half way to the house. They shifted and aimed in the direction of Mercy and Bo. Shit. Sade's mind raced with possibilities as he waited to see what he'd do. When they headed in their direction, he felt along the ground and picked up a rock. He darted up long enough to throw it hard toward the opposite side of the house.

Back to watching the large feet under the car, the rock hit something metal and Sade again held his breath as the feet paused. Crouched, Sade made his way to the front of the car, peeking around it. Finally a visual. The man was burly and tall, another fucking mammoth.

No doubt he was armed too. Sade needed his weapons. Did the dude find their bag in the closet upstairs was the question. Gripping the screwdriver tight in his hands, he debated. He could chance trying to kill him, but that could go seven kinds of wrong, putting Mercy and Bo at risk. At least he seemed to be alone. He needed the guns first.

The second the man disappeared around the corner of the house, Sade made the dash to the other end. Pressing his back against the wall, he took Mercy's hand and held it tight before giving them the news in barely a whisper. "No keys in the fucking car. I think he's alone, probably armed. He's here to find dead bodies—my guess ours. So we get the guns and the keys to his car and get the fuck out of here."

"We can take 'em," Bo whispered around his swollen mouth.

"I'm not fucking risking it!" Sade hissed. "He's probably armed and I'm not getting anybody killed if I can fucking help it. I want you and Mercy to hide under this house while I go find the bag. Do *not* come out until I return. You both *fucking* understand me?"

"Got it," Mercy nodded and turned to Bo. "You and me. Let's do it." She pulled him down to the ground and Sade peeked around the front of the house. At seeing the guy looking down the driveway, Sade ran to the back door and entered. Ducking down, he hurried to the stairs in a crouched position. Glancing at the front windows, he realized half of the staircase was visible to them. Sade counted to three then shot up on all fours.

Hurrying into the dark bedroom, he felt his way to the closet. Breathing heavily, he searched every inch and came up empty. *Fffuuuuuck!*

A bang below shot him back to the door. Opening it a crack, he listened. Where was the fucking bag? Had the dude found it? Taking the screwdriver out of his back pocket, he slowly made his way to the stairs, hearing steps. He was in the house. Fuck.

Crouching low, Sade made his way down the stairs very slowly. He froze and crept back up when the dude carefully headed into the downstairs bedroom with his gun raised.

Once the dude entered the room, Sade had a split second to decide if he should make a run down the stairs or back up and leave out a window. Not remembering any safe way to the ground from the second floor, he quickly ran down and raced for the kitchen.

"Freeze motherfucker!"

Sade dove behind the couch and gunfire exploded behind him, tearing through the wall above his head. Another shot followed as he quickly crawled around the couch.

Glass shattered with an oomph and a barrage of thuds came with Mercy's distinct grunts. Panic shot Sade up in time to see her roundhouse kick the gun from his hand. All three of them dove for the weapon at once, the giant hitting the floor first. Sade was right behind him with a body slam. He pummeled the meaty hand covering the gun with his fist, but the dude was latched on. Sade pinned his hand to the floor. "Get something!" he roared, fighting to keep him down.

"I ain't your enemy," he huffed and grunted.

"Who the fuck are you?" Sade slammed his forehead into the man's head, aiming for his temple.

"Move!" Mercy yelled.

Another shatter of glass came, followed by Mercy's face hitting the floor. Sade flipped and pulled the guy onto his body as a shield.

"Johnny!" a muffled voice roared. "Hold him still, I'll get that maggot!"

Sade's vision swam and his muscles weakened. He peered up at a man with a black mask and his stomach turned as a metal pipe slammed down onto the man covering him.

"Get off of my servant!"

Oh God. Abraham.

Sade fought the haze tugging at his brain and muscles while the man's body jolted with blow after blow.

"I got you. Father's got you." The words sounded far away behind the gas mask. Chloroform. Odorless, tasteless. All around them.

Abraham kicked the dude off and the room spun as Sade's feet were lifted and he was dragged across the floor.

"Don't worry, I got you. Redemption is here, son."

Sade waved his lead weighted arms, hoping to grab onto something, anything.

"You were dirtier than I thought. That was all my fault, I'm far too optimistic and empathetic, always have been. I just believe in the goodness in people. That light. You know that light I'm talking about?"

Sade's hand latched onto the edge of something, but one tug ripped whatever it was from his fingers. He blinked and looked around, struggling to clear his cloudy vision. Mercy. She slowly rolled onto her side. Fuck. Get up. Run.

A strangled roar split the air behind them and Sade's legs hit the floor as Abraham crashed into the wall. More animalistic screaming followed with repeated sounds of hitting. Sade barely managed to turn onto his stomach. He finally looked up and his adrenalin surged.

Bo. Bo swinging something at the now fallen monster. Abraham rolled left and right, shielding his head. The gun. Sade fought to orient his mind as he dragged himself in the direction he remembered.

"Sade," he heard Mercy gasp.

Behind him, the whacking slowed and something shattered on the floor. Soon there was another clatter just as Sade's vision went darker. More chloroform. Fucker had endless glass vials of it.

## Chapter Three

Mercy slowly pried her eyes open.

"Mercy!" a voice cried, sounding relieved. "Finally, something goes right!"

That voice. Stark terror sent her heart pounding hard. Abraham. That sick Abraham. She managed to look to her right and blinked until her vision cleared a little more. But what was she seeing? Several people were there. Laying? Or was she laying? She didn't feel like she was laying. She gave up for a moment and closed her eyes, pain spearing her head that felt bloated. She assessed the damage in her body. She'd been hit in the head and drugged with the same thing from before.

"All of you are awake right on time," he said with a calm excitement. "The ceremony is all set, I was just waiting for my children to wake up." He chuckled like an excited boy. "I can't perform a cleansing while you're asleep, now can I?"

"Mercy." The croaked voice shot fear through her and she jerked her head toward the sound.

"Sade? I'm here."

"Mercy," he barely whispered again.

His desperate tone made her heart hamme. "I'm here, I'm here." That's what she meant to say, but sluggish blather came out. "Here," she fought to say, "*Here*!"

"Mercy," he gasped, sounding heartbroken before croaking, "Bo… where…" he grunted several times, his breath coming faster. "Mother… fugger you…."

"Now, now, stop that," Abraham chided softly. "Stop using your strength for silliness. Bo is fine, he's with us. As is our new friend. Our rude intruder. Or so I thought that at first, but that's not at all what he is," Abraham said, his voice muffled, moving around like he was busy doing things. "He shall serve as the sacrifice. I'm rather glad for that since I wasn't fond of using your Bo. See what I'm saying, Johnny?"

"Get... off me," Sade whispered, his words breathless.

Fear helped Mercy pry her eyes open. Her vision swirled on two blurry figures. One standing one... sitting. They both seemed naked. Terror sparked through her at why they would be.

"It's a sign really!" Abraham's excitement rose with his voice. "Just like with Abraham and Isaac. He was supposed to sacrifice his own son you know, but it was a test," he hissed then giggled. "Abraham passed and so have I. I was prepared to give the offering required, and look," he squealed in utter joy. "The Lord has provided a *ram* to take the place of our sweet lamb. God is *good*."

Terror pumped through Mercy at the sickness behind the tirade.

"The clouds in your head will soon pass. Do we have a name for our little ram?"

Mercy watched through slitted eyes as Abraham stood before the man who had attacked them, face between both hands.

"He looks like a Rick to me. Is your name Rick?"

"Fuck you," the man barely croaked, sounding half dead.

Abraham's laughter boomed with a wheeze before he angled his head toward Mercy. She gasped at the realistic skeleton mask staring at her. "Perfect response from a ram, don't you all agree?" He regarded the man again and tapped his swollen, bloody face.

Mercy looked around again, her sight clearing. The horror grew at seeing the nightmare around them. They sat tied to chairs in a circle, an old wooden table between them. The silver objects on top made her look away. She couldn't handle the confirmation of what she already knew in her gut. Basement. They were in the basement.

"Alright then." Abraham clapped once and rubbed his hands together. "I see no point in waiting any longer."

Mercy fixed her gaze on the monster, her eyelids no longer closing on their own. He was naked and aroused, his manhood swinging and bouncing as he moved around comfortably. She didn't want to look at Sade or Bo, and yet needed to. She was afraid of what she'd find and what it'd do to her already strained psyche.

A chill hit her body and she realized her skin was exposed. Looking down, she saw her own nakedness. Heart hammering, she looked quickly around. They were all naked.

Her stomach burned with the need to heave. There was something different about the horror of it and tears surged. She gasped in effort to keep the weakness back. She couldn't break. God, please, no breaking.

"First of all, I'd like to welcome you all to Mount Sinai. Right here in this room, God has transcended—through me." He palmed his naked chest. "Entered this broken realm to perform this… transbobulation." A shot of hysterical laughter followed as he slapped his leg. "I'm kidding, it's not really called that but it's a funny name."

Giving in to the desperate need, Mercy allowed her gaze to crawl along the floor to where Sade sat on her right.

"It's important to maintain your humor in these dark times, you know what I mean?" he said in all seriousness. "Father Ass taught me that—not *the* Father Ass. This Father Ass was a genuine *ass* who loved all things ass—" more laughter shot out "—if you get my drift. He was one of *those*, yes. That's not what I am, I hope you know. I find the concept truly insulting and wasteful. A man of the cloth is more than his flesh." He flicked his hard penis, making it bounce. "I used to wish the Lord had chosen me to clean his house, but it's the children he's assigned me to."

She finally made it to Sade's feet and her breaths came too quickly as she stared. Nails stuck out of the top of them. Oh God. Blood leaked from the large heads and pooled on the floor around them. He'd nailed him to the floor. Mercy's breaths turned shallow until she grew dizzy. He'd nailed him to the fucking floor.

"I'm going to keep this very simple. Black and white as it actually is. And don't worry, I'll let you know what I'm going to do before I do it," he said easily. "And most importantly boys and girls, if you must address me during this process, you *will* do so by my ceremonial name—Purgatory."

Mercy realized she couldn't move her legs. Or feel them. Her gaze swerved to Bo's hanging head on her left then shot down to his feet. Sickness gripped her stomach at seeing them nailed to the floor too.

"I just find that guiding the children as I go is the most merciful way to conduct this. I'm too soft, I know. But I've learned that a little tenderness goes a long, *long,* way. Who wants '*oh my God, what the hell'* moments? Not I."

Her teary gaze slid to the man's feet across from her and found the same nails through his feet.

"Starting with our ram—and thank you Lord again, for such a miraculous provision," he said reverently at the ceiling before gesturing to the man. "I'm going to sacrifice him and use his blood to purify the threshold that the Lord shall perch upon in my spirit." He slid his hands along his body in an elegant show.

Mercy's gaze fixed on Abraham's hand now hovering along the torture instruments on the table. He paused and picked up a dark knife with jewels on the handle, wagged it briefly, then waltzed over to the man, humming as he went.

"There is no need to torment or torture the ram." He stood behind the man, stroking his greasy gray hair with one hand. "Simple. Black and white." Abraham placed a hand on his forehead and forced it back against his chest.

The man grunted and fought his hold. "Please… please don't," he rasped.

"Don't look!" Sade whispered harshly.

Mercy's eyes refused to disengage as Abraham brought the blade to the man's straining neck.

"Black. And. White." He slid the knife slowly across the skin and the jolting man began to gurgle and choke on his blood.

"Ah, damn!" Abraham hurried to the table and returned with a dirty looking cup. He pulled the thrashing man's head back again and caught the spurts of blood. "That's okay," he said softly, his scary mask angled at her. "Any of the life force is fine." He looked back down at the man, his breaths sounding excited behind the mask. "Don't fight it little ram." He gripped his head tight as the man battled for his life. "Swing loooooow, sweet chariot… comin' for to carry me home."

Abraham's soprano voice mixed with the nightmarish sounds of gasping and choking, making Mercy's stomach sicker.

"Oh don't cry little darling," Abraham cooed. Mercy realized her tears were pouring. "He's a hero, really." The man finally went still and Abraham let the limp head slowly fall forward before leaning and kissing it. "He spared our little Bo-Peep." Abraham raised the cup in the air with both hands and muttered some words before downing the blood. He strolled over to the table and set the cup gingerly down then picked up a pure white cloth and dabbed at his mouth over the hole in the skeleton mask.

"And now… the cleansing can begin," he sang lightly. The red tint of bloodied teeth showed from behind the mask as he looked around at them. "Starting with…" he swirled his finger then pointed at Bo. "My heart is saying the little lamb."

"Me first," Sade gasped. "Please. Me first! Me first!" he roared and jerked.

"Oh no, no, no." Abraham clicked his tongue. "That's not how it works, Johnny. As the spirit leads, that's out of my hands, I'm sorry."

"Please," Mercy begged.

The skeleton mask jerked to her. "You don't even know what I'm going to do and you're all '*please, please,*'" he wailed. "Show a little faith, honey. I'm not a monster. God is not a monster."

"W-what are you going—"

"Glad you asked that." He cut her off with a jab of his finger then hurried to the table and picked up a small silver scalpel. He held it up for her to see. "Two rivers. One flowing out…" he began to dance and twirl before her, waving the blade through the air. "...and one flowing in." His sick dance ended at Bo who whimpered and thrashed his upper body around.

"Stop, stop!" Mercy cried. "Don't, please, please don't!"

"Do me!" Sade roared. "I fucking *hate* God! Do *me,* I hate that sick fuck as much as I hate you! I will never be clean no matter how much you make me bleed, you sick fuck! Your God is a prick just like you, he's *weak* and sick and can't clean a *fucking thing!*"

Abraham stormed to Sade and aimed the blade at him. "Take it back," he roared right in his face. "Take it *back* or I cut *her* tongue out!"

Sade's body heaved with visible hatred twisting his mouth as he looked at Abraham for many seconds. His mouth trembled with fury and disgust before he gritted, "I. Take it. Back."

"That's. What I. Thought!" Abraham nodded a few times then hurried back to Bo. "He took it back, didn't he?" The man used the blade to turn Bo's face, hissing like he'd not seen the hook in his cheek. "That looks so *nasty*. And painful."

Dread tightened the knot in her guts. There was no escape. There was only surviving somehow. They had to survive.

"You know..." Abraham let his face go. "I'd remove it, but there *is* a window of opportunity involved in this process. So it will have to wait. Now..." He straddled Bo's knees and grabbed a handful of his hair from behind, tugging his head back a little. "First, I'm going to carve a river from here..." he touched the blade to the right side of his head then traced along his body, "...down to the sole of your foot. That will be the river going out, the sewer drainage if you will, draining all that nasty sin congregating in your soul. And then..." He aimed the blade at his left foot. "Starting from your sole..." He moved the knife back up his body. "I'll carve a second river all the way up to your pretty little head." He angled his ugly mask their way. "River of sin out. River of life in." He turned back to Bo. "Simple, see? Black and white. Sin out, righteousness in. All clean."

"We're here, Bo," Mercy gasped. "Focus. Focus your mind."

Bo's fingers strained white where he gripped the edge of the chair while Abraham wasted no time and put his blade on his starting point. Beginning to lightly hum another hymn, he slowly dragged the surgical instrument down.

Bo growled and gasped.

"Focus!" Mercy yelled when he let out a small sob.

His body shook as the monster continued to hum and cut so very slowly. The blade reached his hip and Bo screamed.

"Oops," Abraham hissed in apology. "May have gone too deep. Easy sailing from this point out though." He lowered to his knees and continued. "Unless that shot is wearing off, then maybe not. Think it might be, since he's feeling it here. Ah well," he muttered, dark gaze angled intently on the job before him. "No pain, no gain."

Once he got to the bottom of his foot, the maniac stood. "Now we let the waste bleed out." Abraham held the handle of the knife between his teeth and took hold of his penis. Yanking it a few times, he aimed it at Bo and muttered around the knife, "Eye for an eye. Tooth for a tooth. Waste for waste." He urinated along the incision letting out moans and wails as though it burned him as much as it did Bo who screamed and fought to jerk away from it.

Sade roared and pulled uselessly at the restraints, and Mercy felt his agony and hunger to kill.

"It burns," Abraham's words rasped as he wagged his tick shaped body until he was done. "That should do it." The skeleton mask shot from Mercy to Sade then back to Bo as he took the knife from between his teeth and lowered to the floor for the second river.

"God doesn't want this," Mercy whispered.

The monster began cutting at his foot and Bo's screams escaped between his growls. "Sorry if I go too fast," Abraham whispered, ignoring Mercy. "I'm just so excited about this."

Bo jerked around when the blade cut along his upper thigh.

"Be still and take it!" Sade growled.

"He's right," Abraham muttered with a carefree tone. "All this dancing around isn't helping in this delicate operation."

"Bo, think about something," Mercy hurried. "Remember fishing? I'm going to show you how to fish."

"Ohhh, that sounds like a lot of fun," Abraham said happily before hissing when Bo let go of a sharp scream. "That hip does it every time. You need some meat on those bones young man."

Bo roared in response, before screaming, "You sick fuck!"

"Don't say that," Abraham warned with a near delicate whisper. "Not that. I don't like that. I'm your redemption, I'm not sick. Now Father Johnson, he was sick. Putting his cock into little boy's asses for funsies. I won't have any part of that unless it's sanctioned by a higher authority. See, Kane is a lot like me, he's a rebel with a cause, disbanded from the family of which he was born. He understands purpose and reason even though he misunderstands my purpose and reasons. Technically, we're on the same side. He wouldn't agree but see…" He stopped cutting Bo to aim the knife at Sade. "That so-called prophetic dream Father Peters had that put me in line to be an eternal guardian of the abyss?" His scary mask shook. "I called bullshit on that even at ten. Then I had my own prophetic dream." He gave a low, eager chuckle. "Ohhhh, Father Peters didn't like that. Of course he didn't." He went back to work, putting a hand around Bo's neck while cutting along his side. "He didn't think I was holy enough to have dreams and visions. The nerve, right?" he muttered, focused on his demented job. "He especially hated my given name. Blasphemy!" Abraham hissed, then chuckled. "He wasn't saying that when God made him my first assignment, now was he. What a champ. Now that cleansing was *messy*. I'd never known a person could live that long without that much blood. But the Spirit assured me it was fine, so I pushed on in obedience. It was my first true act of faith and not too shabby for a lad of sixteen. And lo, the man did survive. Of course he'd live the rest of his days blind and mute and unable to… you know… enjoy the little boys the way he loved. Almost done little lamb," he said to Bo's increased whimpers.

"Father Peters was very dirty. He'd have spent eternity in hell if it weren't for God's merciful purging while here on Earth." He jerked that mask to them. "Contrary to what they think, there is *no* purging in the afterlife. Ohhh-ho-ho-hooo they did not like that one. But God told me so. This is it. Right here, right now. This is the only purgatory and his servants are like his little scrubbing bubbles." He giggled and nodded before standing back abruptly. "And we. Are. Done!"

He put the knife on the table behind him and turned. "And now for the transfusion." His words wisped in excitement as he planted his feet apart before Bo. "God, yes," he whimpered, grabbing the base of his erection and stroking the length with his other hand. His masked breaths huffed loud and shallow as he yanked on himself with hisses, gasps, and grunts. He cupped his balls and squeezed, letting out a lusty half roar as he inched his way closer to Bo. "Fucking hot, so fucking hot when the spirit enters the tree of life. Ohhhh, are you ready?"

Abraham let out a long eager hiss. "I'm going to rain righteousness all over you, little lamb." He moved close enough to rub the tip of himself along the incision. "Ohhh yeah," he whispered heatedly. "Now it's coming." He yanked on his penis faster. "It's fucking coming!" he roared, bobbing his body and squirting semen in the open cut.

Bo screamed and thrashed until the horrific sound tore Mercy's mind and heart apart. She screamed with him, screamed with all she had. Then Sade's thunderous roar joined in until the room filled with the deafening mixture—humiliation, agony, fear, pain. But it was terror's dark intentions yet to come that crawled through the stifling basement and raced like black spiders all over her skin and mind. Please God. Please help us.

## Chapter Four

Mercy became aware that Abraham was now licking along the incision. "Has to be properly mixed. An even penetration." His gaspy tone said he loved this part and the taste even more. Mercy's stomach revolted finally and emptied onto the floor next to her with loud gagging and coughing.

"I'll take that as ignorant applause," Abraham said, strolling to the table while Mercy fought the urge to vomit again. "And now to seal the doorways." He brought several things to the floor next to Bo, and Mercy's breath came faster as she tried to decipher his intentions.

"What are you doing?" she couldn't stop from asking.

"Oh!" he said. "Cauterizing is the quickest and most complete closure. I call it the triple C: Concise, complete, closure." He poured alcohol on a white cloth and began swiping in long strokes along the incision, making Bo scream.

She gasped as low constant sobs escaped her. "Can't you give him something for the pain, Abraham?"

The skull face snapped to her.

"Purgatory," Sade gritted.

"P-Purgatory," she gasped.

The skull face remained on her for agonizing seconds before going back to what he was doing. "Pain, my dear, happens to be a probiotic against sin." Again he cleansed in long, rough strokes while Bo growled and panted with his eyes clenched tight. "Without pain, one can't come to the crossroad of repentance.

Without pain, we continue to do that which kills the spirit. And I already removed more than I should have."

He lifted up some kind of pen tool and clicked a button that brought a light buzzing. "This here is a blessed little tool, got it for a great deal on E-bay, something like thirty-five bucks. I just love a great bargain. It uses electricity to do the job." He pointed to the handle. "Set at sixteen, it heats the flesh to the perfect temperature, melting the surface together for that concise, complete closure that we want and need."

Bo began breathing faster as he approached his temple with the tool. Mercy sobbed as the maniac hummed and burned his incision closed while Bo fought to be strong and take it, his screams and groans escaping when it was too much. Mercy no longer cared that she cried, she wailed nonstop as the smell of burning skin made her gag and dry heave through her sobs.

"Goddamn, Bo!" Sade roared. "Fucking take it! You take that fucking pain, you hear me?"

Bo stifled his sobs and gasped for breath.

"You're my brother," Sade yelled at him. "You're my fucking blood, pain won't kill you!"

He wailed lowly now. "I'm sorry. I'm so sorry, so sorry, I'm not strong."

"Don't be sorry," Sade gasped, his voice shaking like he was the one sorry. "I'm your brother. I love you, I'm right here. I'm here with you," he gasped then roared, "Nobody can take that from you!"

Abraham paused a moment, shaking his head. "Wow." The skeleton eyes looked at Mercy. "Did you feel that? The power? In his *words?* I felt the foundation of *hell* shake with that!" He aimed the little tool at Sade. "You have so much potential Johnny, I knew that," he hissed excitedly. "I think God is going to make a way to redeem you from your sins, I do," he muttered softly, back to burning Bo again. "I know it hurts little lamb, I'm going as fast as I can."

The nightmare proceeded in slow motion as Abraham chattered and burned Bo's mile long incision closed. The sound of slow pouring liquid drew Mercy's gaze and she began to cry when she realized Bo had peed.

"I'm sorry," Bo wailed.

"Fucking nothing to be sorry for!" Sade yelled at him. "Piss all you fucking want, take a fucking *shit* if you need to man. Purgatory doesn't care, do you Purgatory?"

"Not at all," he said. "I'm rather impressed you haven't yet, little lamb. Most would have by now."

"Five more minutes," Sade heaved. "That's all you got, then you can rest, okay?" Mercy heard the restraint in Sade, heard the murder lacing each syllable and word. "Remember what we've been through, this is *nothing*."

Bo was wailing now, sobbing without restraint. "Sorry, I'm sorry." The hook swollen cheek made the words barely intelligible.

Sade's body heaved and Mercy could feel his agony and fury building.

"Done!" Abraham announced like he'd just won the gold and they should all applaud him. "How do you feel? All clean? Like a new person?"

Bo's head remained lowered before him, a steady fragile wail putting a dense rock in Mercy's chest that she couldn't breathe around.

"And now for our next lucky lamb."

"Me," Sade growled. "Me. Do me."

The skeleton face angled at him for several moments as though thinking. Then it finally shook slowly. "Afraid not, Johnny. Seems like part of your purging requires you to go last."

"Don't do this. Don't you fucking do her next, do me, just do me, you can make that decision."

"I can't," he gasped. "If I could I would!" He went before Sade and knelt, his filthy large hands on his thighs. "Do you think this was a game to me? A cruel joke? Do you think I'm doing this because I *get off* to hurting people?" The squealed words reeked of hurt insult. "I'm not a monster, Johnny." Mercy followed the sensual stroke of his hands on Sade. "I would very much like to give you what you want, I would. And I will. I promise. And when I do… I know you. I know that you…" the skull face lowered to Sade's groin, "…are going to really like it." He looked back up at Sade. "Don't be ashamed." He shook his head and ran his hands over Sade's chest. "I know it makes your cock hard to have pain, it's not your fault. It's part of who you are now. But I can help cleanse you. I can help you be clean," he whispered fervently. "You do want to be clean, don't you, Johnny?"

Sade finally turned his head right and lowered it and Abraham stood and made his way before Mercy. She fought to remember her survival training but it came in erratic mixed up strands. She watched the skull face angle left for several seconds, then right, as though contemplating what to do.

"What are you going to do, talk to us," Sade ordered.

"Shhhhh," Abraham said, finger to skull lips. "The Spirit is speaking to me now about it. The fact that she belongs to my brother Kane makes her very special. Even though the blood relation isn't there, the spiritual one is strong." His body slowly began to move in sensual swaying, leading with his erection. "Ohhhh," he said, sounding slowly shocked. "I think the Spirit wants to join us. My seed in Kane's vessel."

"You can't do that!" Sade said, his voice trembling. "She belongs to another man."

The skull face regarded Sade then her. "Always exceptions to rules, Johnny. The spirit takes precedence over the flesh." He nodded more. "Yes, my seed in her body, a merging of two lights to become one." He was stroking his penis now while Mercy latched on to hope. He'd have to undo her to manage that, wouldn't he?

"Too bad I can't take a chance on untying you. We'll have to make do with her swallowing it." He said it like they were all in agreement.

But the only thing Mercy could think about in that second was Sade's mother, and what she'd done to that man. And whether or not she could manage to bite this motherfucker's nasty penis clean off.

\*\*\*\*

Sade's hatred had reached lethal sadism. He saw seven different deaths in a blood red haze, seven different ways to make Abraham suffer long and brutally. "I have a confession!" Sade roared as Abraham approached Mercy. "I need to confess, Father. Please." Sade gazed at the monster's face frozen on him, giving his best remorseful and desperate act, praying that the psycho's obvious fondness for him would make some kind of difference in his sick decision.

Abraham hurried to him and knelt down. "What is it my son," he whispered, the lust in his tone causing Sade's skin to tighten with repulsion.

"I can't say it in front of them," Sade whispered, lowering his head.

Abraham grabbed hold of Sade's neck and pressed his forehead to his. "Tell me my son," he whispered. "Say it quietly. What is in your heart? I'm listening."

"I..." Sade hadn't anticipated needing something to confess, he'd anticipated having a six-inch space to ram his forehead into his nose. But his sadism was not lacking ideas and another one presented itself eagerly. "I have to see you when I confess."

Abraham yanked off the mask so quickly that Sade again lost the opportunity for a head butt. Forehead to forehead again, Sade lifted his head just a little so his lips could graze the bridge of Abraham's nose. "I just... I want you. I want you first." Sade leaned enough to press his lips against his cheekbone.

Abraham's sour breath came warm and shaky on Sade's mouth while his eager fingers massaged his neck. "Me too, I can't wait to have you. Shhh. I'll do her quickly."

Sade turned his head an inch and opened his mouth, sliding it along his sticky face. Abraham gasped, letting him. "I want to taste you," Sade said, opening his mouth more.

"Yes," Abraham nearly whimpered, allowing Sade his way just long enough.

With the speed of a viper, Sade opened wide and bit as much of his fucking nose as he could. Abraham roared and adrenaline shot through Sade as he took orgasmic punches to his head. Bellowing in shock and pain, Abraham wrapped lethal fingers around his throat. Sade jerked his head right with a hungry roar, taking a large piece of his nose with him. Before the monster got too far, Sade rammed his forehead into Abraham's and knocked him back. Murder burned a furious path through Sade as he ripped his feet free of the nails. He didn't feel anything but the hunger to kill, fueled by Mercy and Bo's screams to *"Kill him! Kill him!"*

Still tied to the chair, he spun to hit Abraham with it, only his legs refused to move the way he needed them to. The room spun as the floor raced up and slammed into his face.

"Move! Move!" Mercy screamed above Abraham's insane roaring.

Sade tried to roll out of the way of what was coming, but the chair prevented any real movement. A large object rushed down and Sade managed to put the chair between him and what was coming. His body and brain jolted from the jarring hit and he blinked away the dizzy suddenly swimming in his head. The screaming pain in his shoulder and feet saved him from being sucked into darkness. He focused on it and let it fuel his adrenaline—anything to keep him conscious.

"He's coming! He's coming!" Mercy screamed. "Move!"

Abraham had officially flipped and was a raging lunatic, throwing things, slamming them into the wall before clobbering Sade with any and everything.

Mercy let out an ear splitting painful scream just before she dove for Abraham. Panicked, Sade squirmed along the floor, managing to turn enough to see Abraham pick her up, chair and all.

"Noooooooo!" Sade roared as Abraham threw her into the wall.

Bo screamed and Sade watched in horror as Mercy hit the floor like a rag doll still tied to the chair.

"You made me, Johnny!" Abraham screeched, coming for him. He grabbed Sade by the head and threw him. Sade's only thought while airborne was, *please don't let me land on Mercy.* His head slammed into the wall and he fought for air as his vision tripled, making it look like three wide-eyed lunatics raced for him again.

"Me, me!" Bo screamed. "Come get me you fat bastard with your stupid fucking god! Your god is a whore bitch!"

Abraham spun with a roar and stormed to his little brother.

Sade fought to yell or move but managed only grunts and gasps as he watched the monster raise both hands in the air, clasped together like a fucking sledgehammer.

A vision of red crosshairs danced on the back of Abraham's head like an angelic apparition. Sade's heartbeat slowed in his ears as sounds faded in and out. It seemed like slow motion when blood and chunks exploded from Abraham's head. Sade watched in a daze as the monster fell slowly backward onto the floor.

His line of sight blurred as the door banged open and the real Angel of Mercy raced in. His blood smeared face and terrified blue eyes were suddenly before him. "We're leaving…."

Sade wanted to hear what else he said as he stared into that immaculate gaze. But darkness passed a soft hand over his mind and turned out the lights. Something about they were coming, and they needed to hurry.

## Chapter Five

Sade's eyes fluttered open constantly from the chatter coming and going in his head.

"I need you to wake up, Sade!"

He fought to wake up, turning his head. A face kept flashing toward him. Kane. Panicked Kane.

Sade jolted awake as the memory hit him. "Mercy!" he tried to say.

Kane put his palm on his chest. "Shhhh! She's fine, Bo's fine. Liberty has them in the back. We're headed to a safe house. I need to know what you know, I need to know what's happened."

Sade's vision crossed and he blinked and gasped as pain shot through his shoulder, head, and up from the soles of his feet. "Abraham," he hissed.

"Abraham is dead. Was there anybody else besides the other man?"

Sade thought and shook his head. "I don't… I don't think so. Abraham… he's…"

"Clinically insane. I tried to text you."

Sade groaned and held onto the van door when Kane flew around a curve. Morning sunlight streamed through the passing trees and he squinted in pain. "I got it. The text. Too late."

"What happened to Mercy?" he asked.

Sade shook his head, knowing exactly what her father wanted to know. "Nothing sexual. Thank God," he barely managed. "Bo... Bo's hurt." A flash of Mercy hitting the wall jolted him forward again. "She's hurt!" He fought with his seat belt, adrenaline turning him into a mad man. "He threw her into the fucking cement wall," he gasped.

Kane grabbed his arm. "Stay put!" he yelled, startling Sade enough to make him stop. "She's as fine as she can be, Liberty's got her. She's our best medic. I'm taking you to a safe house. It has supplies—everything you could need. Mercy's strong."

Sade covered his face with both hands, his body trembling. "Not that fucking strong," he rasped, his chest suddenly too tight. He roared to get the pain out of him and a loud banging erupted on the metal door behind them.

"He's upsetting her!" a voice yelled.

"She's awake?" Kane nearly yelled back.

"Negative. Reflexive, please keep him calm!" she hollered.

Kane's face was drawn in silent agony as he sped to wherever they were going. "This was my fault," he whispered. "Thank God you were with her."

Sade's mouth tightened. Thank God *he* was with her? He *caused* all of this. Being who he was and daring to be with a fucking angel. "What's going on, who's after us?"

"I had to call in my old team." Kane shook his head. "I tried, son. I tried to make a new life, I did. I was so close too. I mean I got one more move in this game and it's such a fucking long shot but at this point, I don't think it could go more wrong."

Sade wanted to stop him right there and introduce him to his best buddy, Karma.

"You'll hide at the safe house, heal there until I execute plan Z. All or nothing. What do you know about Abraham, I have to figure out how deep the shit is I've stepped in."

Sade regarded him and let his head rest on the seat. "He mentioned people at the Vatican."

Kane glanced at him several times, confused. "Vatican?" He checked all his mirrors then muttered, "I need every detail you have."

"I don't think he was *with* the Vatican. He thought of you as his brother."

"Sick fuck. Everybody is family to him in some way or another."

"He saw you as his equal, working for the same cause."

Kane shot out a derisive laugh. "Did he tell you by any chance where his Garden of Eden is?"

"He mentioned a Father Peters." Sade thought harder through the flashes of the nightmare. "A Father Johnson. Some psychobabble about an eternal guardian of the abyss."

"It may be psycho but it wasn't babble. The man believed every word, and now I fucking killed the one lead we might have had in that nest of evil. I've been trying to crack that nut for years while staying out of his all seeing eye."

A cold shiver passed over Sade. "Well, it doesn't matter now?"

"I wish, son. But usually with all seeing eyes come many devils. I don't think I'll ever not look over my shoulder where that sick fuck is concerned."

"He called himself Purgatory."

Kane regarded him a few times. "I don't want to know, not right now. Later I'll get the details. Having all the dirty pieces on the board doesn't hurt a thing in the big scheme of things, but let's save that for another day, we've had enough for one."

They soon drove up a winding dirt road for miles it seemed before they stopped. Sade looked around for anything besides trees.

Kane pointed right. "See that hill? That's the backside of the entrance to the house. I'm going to help get you all settled in, then I have to go work plan Z." Kane regarded Sade's body. "I'll carry Bo in first and come back for you. Liberty will take care of Mercy."

"She'll see you," Sade said.

Kane sighed and looked around. "Nothing I can do about it."

Sade was happy about that. He thought Mercy needed to know her father was alive at this point in her life. She could sure stand some good news.

Sade watched Kane carry Bo in and then the woman who was apparently Liberty, carried Mercy. His stomach tightened at the blood matted in her hair and the fact that she was out cold still. He gasped for air, unable to breathe, needing to touch her, hold her. Fuck. Please let her be okay.

Kane returned for him and Sade was prepared to walk in. "I'm carrying you in, deal with it," he muttered.

"You can't—"

But he fucking could and did. "You sure do eat your Wheaties, don't you son?"

"So do you, I see."

Liberty met them at an old rusted door half buried in a hill and held it open.

"Go take care of my daughter," Kane said. "I want an update immediately."

"Yes sir," she said, all military before heading out.

Sade's eyes closed intermittently as Kane half ran with him down a long dark tunnel that he was apparently familiar with. The bright light made him squint in the next second as they entered a large room with furniture. They hurried through the space that looked like something carved out of slate. The strange walls suddenly closed in to form a wide hall. Kane stopped and fought a door and hurried Sade to a bed with a gasp.

"God, you're a heavy bastard," he muttered before hurrying out. "I'll be back, don't walk," he called as he went.

Sade sat up on the bed, knowing he was going to check on Mercy. Sade also knew it was stupid to try and do the same. He made himself lie down, taking the pressure off his throbbing feet. And just when he was sure he'd never sleep, he was suddenly being shaken awake.

"Shhh," Kane said, helping him sit up. "Mercy still hasn't woken up."

Panic slammed him. "What? How long has it been?"

He gave a quick shake of his head. "Not long, don't worry. But we took her to the med room and ran a scan. There's swelling on the brain, not uncommon with that kind of knock on the head. Liberty gave her Mannitol and by tomorrow we should know more. I can't stay. I wish I could. I'll be back as soon as I can and will keep in touch by Satellite SMS Mobile. It's set up as a one-way communication so don't miss my calls. Take care of her."

"Absolutely," Sade said, fighting the panic in his muscles, ready to go see her.

"Liberty is bringing you crutches to get around while your feet heal. Stay off of them as much as possible, I don't know what is coming, but I need you healed. Do you understand?"

"Yeah, when can I see her?"

"She's sleeping."

"I don't care, I need to see her."

The door opened and Liberty entered with the crutches and Sade reached for them. Kane helped him stand and he grit his teeth from the agony. Once on his way, his body trembled from fatigue and something else he didn't want to think about.

He made his way out of his room and crossed the hall to Mercy's. By the time he made it to her bed, a sheen of sweat covered his body. He stared at her until he had to look down and steady his breaths.

He wasn't going to cry in front of Kane, now standing next to him. "You hold down the fort. I have to go," he whispered.

"I got it," Sade said. "Where's Bo?"

"He's in the next room," Liberty said behind him. "I sedated him. He was in a lot of pain. If you don't mind, I'll need to ask a few questions so I know how to best treat him."

Sade reached out and stroked Mercy's brow, unable to keep his fingers from shaking. "I'll be back, Angel. Just going check on Bo."

"I'll say goodbye now," Kane said. "Just need a few moments with Mercy before I go.Sade nodded and followed Liberty out of the room and into a studio sized living room. He realized it was the same room they'd first passed through. Wow. It hadn't just looked carved out of slate, it was.

"I know right?" Liberty said as she went into the adjoining room that appeared to be a large kitchen embedded in rock, too. "Fucking Bat Cave. Getting you something hot to eat and drink, to help get your strength back. Have a seat while I find my way around, sure it can't be that hard," she muttered.

Sade made his way to a black leather couch, taking in his surroundings. He couldn't help the giddy feeling of being in one of the hideouts of his childhood hero. He eyed the floors, ceiling, walls… all various shades and textures of gray rock. The floor reminded him of glass while one wall looked rough enough to rock climb. The media wall before him appeared three-dimensional. Two feet of that shiny gray floor material sat on top of a long slab of rougher slate below the theatre sized television.

"Check out that ceiling," Liberty mused, heading his way.

Yeah, it was hard to miss. Three trays held hidden lights that cast their glow toward the giant abstract chandelier hanging in the center. For him, the most impressive was the wall of glass. Judging by the tint on it, it was one way. You saw out, but you didn't see in.

Liberty set down steaming food and Sade wasn't sure he'd be able to eat it. But once his stomach smelled sustenance, he devoured every drop of what could be called vegetable soup. He realized she was watching him, and for the first time he allowed himself to assess her without actually looking. She had large mocha eyes that held a calm fearlessness, telling him this was definitely not her first rodeo. How skilled was she, was the question. The casual black slacks and black dress shirt said professional, minus the jet-black shoulder length ponytail. The leather gloves seemed a bit overkill, but the fact she was with Kane allowed whatever the fuck dress code she liked. He'd have been happier with a small army anywhere Mercy and Bo were concerned.

"What happened to Bo?"

Right to business, good. He leaned and set the bowl on the table before him, hoping the food in his stomach stayed put while he answered all her questions. "How's he doing?"

"I sedated him as I said."

"Abraham happened to him."

"The hook in his cheek?"

"He did everything to him that you see done."

"The cuts on the body, how did they get there?"

"He cut him with a scalpel. After nailing his feet to the floor. After putting a fucking whale's hook in his mouth. After beating him to manage it all. Then he pissed and ejaculated semen onto his incisions and licked them up nice and clean," Sade said, wanting to make sure she got the exact trauma he'd been through. "He did all this in the span of I'd say... ten minutes. The only thing he had for pain was given at the time his feet were nailed to the floor. Which wore off by the time he was cut."

"Alright," Liberty said. "That's enough recollection for now."

"I'm fine. It's him that won't be fine, not for a long time." Sade looked down, his chest burning. "Not for a long time," he muttered, remembering how he'd peed and wailed like a lost, abandoned boy. "Sick fuck broke him. I'm only sorry I hadn't had the pleasure of killing him with my bare hands." He looked at her. "Slowly. Piece by fucking piece. You know what I'm saying?" His sadism burned white hot as his gaze bore into hers.

She angled her head a moment and held his gaze with her own empty looking one. "I do." She got up then and went into the kitchen, ponytail swishing. "When he wakes up," she called back, "he'll want to see a face he's familiar with."

"I'm his brother."

She returned with a steaming drink and handed him the mug. "Kane told me."

He took the drink and eyed it. He only trusted her because Kane seemed to. How much did she know about him? About Mercy? About his family's sick little operation? He didn't like not knowing that. He was in the dark again, and he was a little tired of that disadvantage. "What did Kane tell you?"

She sat in the matching leather chair next to the couch again. "Everything I needed to know. Which is everything. Your life history since you were born, up until I met you. Same for his daughter and your little brother." She looked around then, showing a sharp jawline. "Didn't know about this place though. He kept this one tight." She gave a tight smile that was purely superficial. "Place is loaded with everything. Self-contained city in a home. Something you'd want in an apocalypse. Or long term hiding."

Sade was suddenly curious with what she knew about Bo and Mercy than him. But he'd keep it on Bo for now. "So you know Bo's had a bad life." Sade looked down into his drink and lifted it, sipping carefully while the bite of steamy herbs saturated his sinuses.

"I do," was all she gave back with ease.

The sound of a straining voice crackled nearby and she shot up, grabbing a device off her hip. "I'm coming, don't try to move," she said into what looked like a walkie-talkie before calling over her shoulder, "Our young Geronimo is waking."

Sade fought his way standing. He used his bad shoulder to keep the weight off his feet, making it scream. Definitely would pay the price more than anything during this healing.

He peeked in on Mercy as he passed by, the sight of her in the same position putting his insides in knots.

"Help," he heard Bo mumble.

"I'm here, I'm here," Liberty said like she was all the salvation he could ever need. "What are you up to in here, causing trouble for me?"

Sade paused at the door while she made quick work checking his incisions, mumbling mundane things as she pulled her light out of some pocket and shined it in his eyes. Her soft tone was a stark contrast to the tough façade, but he was grateful for it. The kid could stand a little tenderness in his life. Because God knew Sade had never shown him a fucking ounce of it.

"S-Sade, where…"

She waved Sade over. "Hey, bro," Sade announced. "Last thing you need is more beauty rest. Any prettier and I might marry you."

Bo turned as Sade made it to the bed on his crutches. At seeing him, he let out an audible gasp and closed his eyes seeming relieved.

"How's his pretty face?" Sade asked.

Bo raised his hand up when Sade stopped at his bed. At seeing a slight tremble in it, Sade took it in both of his and squeezed, not sure how to show the feelings suffocating him. "No more fishing expeditions for you."

Bo gave a light chuckle and met Sade's gaze with a worried one. "Mercy…"

"She's fine. In the room next door. We're all safe now. You hungry, our maid here cooks a mean soup."

"Maid my ass," she muttered. "I'm getting him better so he can be my maid. I'm due a vacation."

Bo lowered his eyes and leaned his head away as she pulled one side of his face bandage off to inspect. "Wow," she said, impressed. "I am *good*." She shut the bandage gently in place and pulled his covers up a little. At catching her fly by caresses in her hurried movements, Sade relaxed more. In fact, seeing with his own eyes that Bo was okay and in good hands brought weakness to his knees. All that was left was Mercy waking up and showing him she was okay. Until then, he'd be a silent wreck.

"I'll go get your lunch, you keep him company," she said hurrying out.

When she was gone, Sade grinned and muttered, "Yes ma'am Nurse Liberty who likes Bo." He winked at him and Bo gave a barely shy grin that made him chuckle.

"I'm sure she's so impressed," he said.

"Hell yes she is. You're alive, aren't you? I'd say that's pretty impressive."

He gave a small nod and looked up, the shame shadowing his dark blue eyes bringing Sade's fury. "Guess so. Mercy is really okay?"

"She got a nasty bump on her head, but she's fine."

Bo looked at him for several seconds, that terror in his eyes again. "He's dead?"

The tremble in his voice said he'd be needing endless confirmation on that. "I didn't bury him personally, but I did see his brains splatter out of the back of his head if that's any consolation."

He gasped and nodded. "Yeah. It is. All I saw was…" He paused for a few seconds.

"How are you feeling besides like shit," Sade asked, moving him away from that ledge.

"That's about it." He looked up at Sade then. "Can you ask her not to make me sleep anymore? I want to be awake, get stronger."

Sade's gut tightened as he sat next to him. "I can try, but she's pretty bossy. You having bad dreams?"

He shot out a gasp. "That too."

Fucking needed painkillers for his feet. Felt like the nails were still in them and he wasn't in the mood to get off to pain. "I'm having them too. Sure we all will for a while."

"Well, I'd like a short break from them if you don't mind."

Sade angled a grin at him. "I feel you my man. I'll make sure she helps keep you awake until you're so tired you won't give a fuck. Maybe she can read to you."

He laid his head back and closed his eyes with a sigh. "Don't think I'll ever be that tired."

Liberty entered with a tray of food. "You wanna feed him or am I?"

"If you need me to I can," Sade said.

"I don't." She set the tray down on the other side of the bed.

"I'll go check on Mercy then. You good with that, Bo?"

He nodded but Sade knew he wasn't good with it. Which was odd since he'd always been a lady's man. Fucking Abraham had broken more than skin on his little brother.

"There's a sauna and a whirlpool tub next to the workout room at the end of the hall," she said. "I'd advise you to take a nice hot soak with a cupful of Epsom salt, get those feet all clean and ready so I can properly treat them and prevent infection. I searched around and found a ton of supplies in the closet next to it. Towels and robes, whatever. In fact if you don't mind, do it now so I can take care of Bo's. I'll need to sterilize the tub when you're done, the sooner the better.

"Yes ma'am," Sade muttered, eyeing Bo's tense face. "I can help you with that. I mean I can do it. Take care of Bo."

She pffed. "I've bathed plenty of patients in my days, this tiny chump is nothing."

Of course she'd miss the whole problem. "I can bathe myself," Bo said.

"You damn well can, don't be thinking I was going to wash your manly parts." She yanked off one of the leather gloves she wore and wagged mechanical fingers with a half-smile. "Not really qualified for gentleness, I'm afraid. But she was certainly a helping hand with that hook in his cheek."

Holy shit. His curiosity made a mental note to ask *what the fuck* later. Meanwhile, all the color left Bo's face. Sade grinned, unable to help himself. "I'll leave you two love birds then."

She shot her middle mechanical finger up at him. "There's your love bird baby," she muttered.

"Yeah, and here's another one," Bo said, flicking him too.

Sade laughed and turned to go. "I'll kick your handicap ass."

"Not on my watch you ain't," Liberty warned as she sped past him out the room.

Sade glanced back and raised his brows at Bo, who double birded him. "Better watch your cock-a-doodle-doo around that one," he said, glad to have something to distract him with.

"No need to, she's not my type."

"Right, right," Sade chuckled. "Mr. Loverboy."

"I don't do GI Janes," he hissed.

Sade laughed lowly. "I don't think you'd need to, my brother."

## Chapter Six

He walked out, anxious to finally see Mercy. Once, at her door, he stared in on her. Same position. When was she supposed to wake up? He needed to drill Liberty about that. He hobbled his way to her bed and sat slowly then leaned the crutches quietly next to him.

"How's she doing?" Liberty whispered as she zoomed in and went straight to the trash can next to the bed, putting in a bag.

"You tell me."

Without stopping or looking she shook her head. "Gonna run another scan tonight to see how much help that Mannitol was. We'll know a lot more then."

"What do we know now?"

She leveled her gaze on him while tying the trash bag to the can. "Not much. But I've seen worse, if that helps.

He wanted to know more but he didn't really want to ask or beg for the fucking details. "What time are you doing that scan?"

"After dinner."

"Which is?"

"Six o'clock sharp, I guess. Thirty-minute chow then scan our sleeping beauty at seven. Work for you?"

Her tone said it'd have to. "You're the doc." He carefully took Mercy's hand in his and immediately everything fell away, but feeling her. Her warmth soothed him as he stroked her skin with his thumb, silently hoping Liberty would leave so he could speak to her.

He finally got his wish and as soon as he did, inadequacy and fear restrained the urge to lean in and kiss her. He stared at her hand in his. So small. And yet so strong. He stroked each digit reverently, sliding his index finger over the tips of her fingernails. Their jagged edges made his heart ache, knowing how they'd gotten that way. He stroked her forearm next and lifted it, resisting the nightmare images that already haunted him. Especially what nearly happened to her. Kissing the top several times, he then turned her hand and kissed her palm. He closed his eyes just feeling her with his lips. Smelling her.

He needed her so bad, but he also knew he needed to let her rest. Leaning in, he kissed her cheek and rubbed his nose softly against her skin. "Angel," he whispered, bringing her hand to his neck and pressing it tight to him. "Get your beauty sleep. Bo's fine, he's awake and eating. I'm fine too. Following the doctor's orders and taking a hot soak. After that, we'll peek in that pretty head of yours, see what's going on. Take all the time and rest you need baby. But hurry and fucking wake up, okay? I miss you." The words strained on a hot whisper and he wiped his eyes on his shoulder before pressing several kisses to her cheek and pulling back.

Felt like forever for six o'clock to get there. While waiting, he did as told, soaked in the giant whirlpool for an hour, willing his body to heal quickly so he could be ready for whatever might come. When he returned to his room in the white terrycloth robe, he found a basket of clothes his size. GI Jane was right on top of things.

Sade decided to eat supper with Bo just to help him get his own food down. When he entered Bo's room, his handsome face lit up. Hard to believe polar opposites could be related. Bo could pass for a sweet angel, and Sade... Satan's prized vagrant spawn.

How the fuck did he end up with the Angel of Mercy was the question. He still couldn't help feel like the joke was on him and any minute reality would slam him into his highly elusive grave.

"Want company?" Sade asked.

"Yes, please. About to go crazy. No TV, no radio in here?" He held up a book. "She gave me this. To read," he whispered exasperated.

Sade chuckled and sat on the chair Liberty must've placed next to the bed. "You forget how to read?"

He held the book up. "*The Land That Time Forgot*? Double dose of valium right there."

Sade laughed for real at that and looked down, smiling. "Mercy read to me when I was tied up."

"Well that's a big difference."

"Maybe Liberty will read to you."

"Or crush my balls in her iron claw. Holy shit," he shrilled quietly. "You see that thing?"

"Ohhhh," Sade hissed at that idea even while his cock jerked in response. It had become reflexive when ball crushing was mentioned.

"Wonder what happened to her," Bo whispered.

"You could ask her."

"Ask her what?" Liberty said, coming in with a large tray of food.

"Nothing," Bo shot out while Sade bit back a mischievous grin.

"Keep your secrets then, fine with me." She set the tray on the foot of the bed and handed Sade a plate with a TV dinner on it. Sade noticed the plate she gave Bo looked like a professional chef had prepared it. The steamy food with fancy garnishing made him hide a grin. He was glad she was taking extra good care of him.

"Wow, this looks good," Bo said, grabbing the fork and digging in.

A few moments later, Liberty got up. "Eat as much as you want but don't gorge, you'll get sick. And I'm not cleaning up vomit because you're too stupid to pace yourself."

"Yes ma'am," Bo muttered, woofing his food down.

By the time she returned with a small cup of his medicine, he was moaning. "Oh my God," she said, "you *ate* all that already?"

"It was sooooo good," he said. "Did you make that?"

"Of course I did, you see anybody else around here? Here's your vitamins and something to help you sleep."

Bo's head came forward. "I'm fine on sleep."

"What does that mean, 'he's fine on sleep'?" she asked Sade.

"Means he doesn't want to sleep so much."

Liberty quirked her brow at Sade and he quirked one back, hoping she got it. She looked at Bo, who took his vitamins. "Suit yourself, but don't be crying later when you're in pain."

"Yes ma'am," Bo muttered.

"Stop calling me ma'am, do I look like your mother?"

"No ma'am. Oops. Sorry."

She shook her head and walked off. "Sade, Sleeping Beauty is in the med room waiting if you're ready."

Sade grabbed the crutches and got up, hurrying after her.

"Let me know when you're done?" Bo called.

"I'll be right back."

"Is there some kind of wheelchair for me? I'd like to see something besides the same four walls," he yelled after them. "I don't like boring books!"

Liberty shook her head as they headed down the hall. "He's cruising."

Sade would've found that funny except he was too worried about Mercy now. "How long does this take?"

"Only a few minutes. I'll need your help moving her from the hospital bed to the table, to be safe."

Thank God. He stood next to the table she lay on and looked around at the room. All this shit they had. She wasn't kidding about a city in a home. The supply closets scattered here and there were packed. He stroked the top of Mercy's hand and along her arm while Liberty turned on the machines. When Liberty was ready, Sade stepped into the side room with the window to watch.

\*\*\*\*

"So it's better?" Sade asked.

"Yes, the swelling is nearly all gone," she said, sounding relieved. She went on to show Sade the results of the scan in medical gibberish before ending with the one thing he was waiting to hear, "So, I think she's going to be fine."

He let out half a breath with that. He wanted to hope. But with his track record, it would only worsen the odds. And not hoping… just made him feel like a useless piece of nothing and nobody.

Sade followed Liberty as she navigated the hospital bed back to Mercy's room "If you don't mind, I'd like to stay with her."

"Figured you might want to. Fine with me. You need anything, call for it, don't try to get it. I need your feet healed. I need all your feet healed," she muttered pulling the door closed. "Be hell if we all had to run," she said as the door shut.

The idea struck him with fear. That would be bad, very bad. So much for feeling safe there.

Sade climbed carefully into the bed with Mercy. It took him five minutes to get in a position that he was comfortable and close as he could be. He wanted to pull her to him but wasn't sure where she was hurt. They'd done a scan of her head and neck and hadn't found anything, but that gave him little comfort. And nothing showed up in the x-rays either but only a couple were done. It seemed the chair and her head took most of the hit on that wall. He let out a shaky breath and stroked her face, putting his mouth to her ear. "Come back to me, Angel."

Sade fell asleep finally, only to have nightmares that ended with him jerking awake. He realized he was next to Mercy and gasped. Had he hurt her? Fuck, he wasn't safe to sleep around.

He sat up in the bed for several seconds before making his way to the bathroom. Each room was stocked like a hotel. All except TV's and electronics. He passed the mirror and stopped but couldn't bring himself to look at the face in the reflection. Not until Mercy was safe. Until then, he didn't want to see or know the one responsible for getting her hurt.

Unable to sleep, he went to check on Bo and found him staring at the ceiling. He jerked his gaze to the open door when Sade knocked softly.

"What are you doing up?" Sade asked, making his way to the bed.

He shook his head and looked at the ceiling. "Can't sleep. Can't close my eyes."

"Me either," Sade said, sitting on the bed. "That was one fucked up ride, huh?"

Bo nodded and looked right. Pain stabbed Sade when his chin trembled and a tear rolled down his cheek. "Sorry bro," he said trying to sound strong, wiping it off.

"Don't fucking apologize," Sade ordered. He realized his tone was way too harsh and took Bo's hand, staring at it. He'd planned to give him a stern speech about being strong but… he suddenly could only focus on drawing his next breath. "I'm scared too."

He felt Bo's gaze on him. "You?" he asked in quiet shock.

He shook his head slowly, hating to voice the words but needing to. "Mercy won't wake up."

"I thought you said she was okay?"

The panic in his voice didn't help and Sade had to turn his face away from him. "I want her to be."

"Liberty said she was gonna be fine man," he assured, covering Sade's hand with his other one. "I know she'll be fine."

"How you fucking know, man?"

"Cause she's Mercy!" he whispered heatedly. "She's like… God's own angel dude."

Sade couldn't breathe and he covered his face with both hands. "Why would…" he gasped in several gulps of air "…God… do this to her? Why would he let this happen?"

"Aw man," Bo shook his head. "She loves you. She chose you. Don't insult that gift with that unworthy bullshit." He gave a soft laugh. "You deserve her."

Sade shook his head. "Never."

"Always," Bo argued, stubbornly.

Sade jerked at the sound he heard. He took his crutches and hurried to the hallway and looked down, listening. He quickly went into Mercy's room and froze at seeing her twitching in her sleep.

Fuck. He rushed as fast as he could to her bed and stared at her. The furrow in her brow said she was dreaming and it wasn't anything good.

He wasn't sure what to do and then her condition grew more violent. He sat on the bed and shook her shoulder. "Mercy. Mercy wake up." She whimpered and became more frantic, so Sade took hold of her hand, tapping it hard, ready to snatch her from the nightmare.

She finally woke with a huge gasp, like after being submerged in water too long. She snatched his wrist and pulled him down in a headlock that would put him to sleep in ten seconds.

"Mercy!" he yelled, panic rushing through him. "Mercy, you're ok! Liberty!" he roared, fighting to move into the lock.

The door banged open. "Oh shit, live wire."

Mercy screamed, pulling on his head like she changed her mind about choking him. Now she was going to fucking rip it off.

He growled, working his hands up under her arms while she screamed and added iron legs into the assault, slamming her foot into his kidneys.

"Liberty!" he growled.

"I'm hurrying, fucking cheap ass syringes! Sweetheart, wake-up, look around you. I need you to hold her Sade," Liberty ordered.

"Fucking trying! She's strong!"

"She's running on adrenaline, I need you to step it up or I'll have to hurt her."

Mercy screamed again, tightening her hold, bringing patches of darkness into his vision. "Fuck!" He worked his body onto the bed, fighting for leverage.

Mercy's foot stopped jabbing him long enough to kick at Liberty. "Get the fuck away, bitch!" she roared.

"Got you sweetheart."

"Help me! Help meeee!" Mercy screamed.

Whatever Liberty stuck her with took effect almost immediately, and Sade crawled out of her limbs, shaking and staring at her.

She sat up in bed on her knees, looking around, blinking back the drug taking effect. She looked down and spied the catheter and gasped before the non-stop screaming and wailing erupted again while searching around her in confusion.

Sade held his hand out and she crawled backward on the bed shaking her head. She nearly fell off and Liberty was there to catch her only to have Mercy fight against her with sluggish limbs.

"Mercy!" Sade called. "Wake up, you're okay!"

Her eyes closed and she mumbled incoherently as Liberty laid her down.

"Get some restraints. In the closet."

Sade stared at Mercy in confusion.

"Hurry up! Anything, get that bathrobe tie until I can get something better."

Sade half ran and brought it to her. "What the fuck?" he whispered, confused.

"She's just got a bit of post-trauma amnesia, not uncommon with a knock on the head like that."

Sade watched Mercy kicking weakly around, fighting the drugs as she looked all around still, her survival mode hanging on. "Help," she kept saying.

"Mercy, it's me Sade," he called louder to her. "You're safe now, you're safe. Tell her she's safe," he yelled to Liberty.

Mercy looked from Liberty to Sade, brows furrowed. Tears suddenly rolled down her cheeks and Sade lost it.

"Tell her she's okay," he yelled, slamming his fist into the wall before turning to Liberty.

"You're not helping, you're scaring her. Her memory will return, now calm the fuck down, hero."

Sade limped on his feet, gasping for air, looking at Mercy who was barely conscious now. "How long?" he whispered. "How long before she wakes up and I can talk to her, make her understand?"

Liberty pulled the covers over her and looked at him. "Let her sleep this off for a couple hours. We'll know more when I talk to her."

He rubbed his head with both hands nodding, fighting to be calm. "Okay."

"We're going with best-case scenario, I'm warning you now."

Best-case scenario? What the fuck did that mean, scenario? "How about you tell me what you mean by that, exactly."

"I'm saying one to four hours and she'll be fine."

He didn't want to even ask worst-case. He wouldn't.

"I'll wait till she's calm and run the tests that will tell us what we're looking at, the amount of amnesia."

Sade covered his face with both hands and bent over. "She'll be fine," he said before pacing again.

"You need to get off those feet."

"Fuck my feet," he muttered, holding his head as he continued pacing like an animal. "Let them fucking bleed."

Liberty was suddenly blocking his path. "Listen to me," she whispered pointing to the bed. "She doesn't need you doing this. She needs you being smart." She grabbed his upper arms and shook him. "I mean it, buck the fuck up, I'm not going to let you cost this operation. How about you go right now and assure that boy in there that everything's okay before he screams a lung up."

Bo had been calling both of them, demanding they tell him what the hell was going on. Sade reluctantly nodded and took the crutches she fetched from the floor. Before leaving the room, he glanced back at Mercy, sleeping peacefully again. His stomach knotted with a thousand fears. He couldn't handle this. He could handle a lot of things but not fucking this.

## Chapter Seven

Sade stared at Liberty from across the small kitchen table. He'd barely managed a wink of sleep. "I need to know what to expect with this."

She widened her eyes, indicating he was fucked in that department and she was sorry for that, but he'd need to deal with that like a big boy. "It really all depends."

"I want all the possibilities then, no surprises. What can I expect?"

She sat back and crossed her arms before laying it all out in a monotone voice. "Standard symptoms come with confusion. Feeling dazed, clumsiness, slurred speech, nausea, vomiting. Headache. Balance problems," she added with slow nods. "Blurred vision." The list dwindled as she recalled off the top of her head. "Sensitivity to light and noise. Sluggishness, ringing in ears. Behavior or personality changes. And of course, concentration difficulty and memory loss to varying degrees."

Sade gasped and leaned back in his chair looking at the table. "Wow."

"She may have only a few of those symptoms. I won't know until I test her."

"When?"

"After breakfast I guess. I need to talk to her, help her understand what's going on so she can help us."

"What are you going to do?"

"Tell her what happened and what she's going through and why. Just the basics though, anything more in depth needs to come from you."

"I think I'll let you test her before I talk to her, so I at least know what to expect."

"She could regain everything in a couple hours. She seems healthy and strong."

"Something tells me healthy and strong doesn't have a damn thing to do with this."

"It always does. Look…" her voice lowered while keeping that sharp edge, "…I'm not going to soften the blow but I do need you not losing your shit, remember? And let's face it, when it comes to her, you are not the most in control individual. I don't mean that as in insult, just the facts that I'm stuck dealing with in a delicate situation. So, please do your best to keep that in mind while you are *dealing* with everything." She made it very clear she meant for him to deal.

He knew all about dealing. Taking a deep breath, he let it out. "I can deal once I figure out what I'm dealing with." But something said this was different, this wasn't going to be like the other demons he'd dealt with. This one was new and big. Bigger than anything he'd ever dealt with in fact.

"Did Kane say when he's coming back? Any word on that?"

She gave a *no clue* shake of her head with raised brows. "And we need to talk to Bo about this no sleeping nonsense I see he's up to. He needs rest. No rest isn't going to help him. I get that he's having nightmares, I understand that. My thought is, he needs something that puts him beyond the reach of dreamland."

Sade nodded, knowing she was right. "You're the doc."

"You'll need to talk to him," she ordered.

"Yeah, sure, whatever."

"I don't mind telling him, hell I don't mind giving it without his cooperation, but I'd like him to trust me. That'll happen faster if I'm not force-feeding him shit that leads to his worst fears."

"I got you."

"Good. And I need to bathe him, he stinks. I'm taking him to the whirlpool after I test Mercy. I let him get out of his last bath, but I have to take care of his feet before he gets an infection. I'd let you do it but you *really* need to stay off your fucking feet more than you have. At this rate, you'll be healed never. And that is unacceptable." The word *soldier* hung unspoken in the air, loud and clear.

"Yes ma'am," he muttered, hating the limitation his injuries put on him.

"And we have one wheelchair in this outfit and one set of crutches. You guys will need to share. I'll work on a makeshift pair of crutches."

It was the least of his concerns, but he remembered to nod his appreciation. "You deal with Mercy, I'll go deal with Bo. Can you bring more reading material to him? He's not happy with his selection."

"Well pretty boy needs to deal too, this isn't the fucking Ritz. I'll bring him paper and pencils, he can get creative. I brought the wheelchair to his room but told him under no conditions is he to walk on those feet without me there to help. You better let him know I mean it. If he crosses me, he'll find himself bed-bound. Literally."

"Got it." Sade grabbed the crutches and turned to go.

"And it's not Alzheimer's," she called as he left. "Don't make this worse than it is."

Sade didn't even go near Mercy's door as he headed to Bo's room, knocking before entering.

"Come in." Bo's tone said *why bother knocking, it's not like I can do anything that would require it.* It was only day four at the Batcave and already Bo was showing signs of cabin fever. It was hardly the contributing factor to his problems, but it was something Sade could blame it on. All of them could.

"Long time no see," Sade muttered.

"How's Mercy?" he asked right off. It was surely the wrong foot to start off on.

"We'll know more after Liberty bathes you."

His eyes rolled hard in his head as he groaned and muttered, "Jesus Christ."

"She's a medic."

"She's scary!" Bo hissed.

Sade welcomed the distraction from his problems. "I'm sure she'll be gentle with you."

"Very funny man, verrrry funny."

Sade let his chuckle go. "You might as well enjoy it, it's all the fun you'll be having for a while."

"Did you talk to her about finding something besides these books?" he shrilled quietly like she might hear him.

"Yep. She's bringing you some paper and pencils so you can get creative."

An exasperated huff blasted from him. "Are you kidding? Paper and *pencils?* They still *have* those? Who the fuck uses that? There's got to be a TV around here, some kind of video console? Man, I'm a Legend on HR, I could be working on my rank while laid up!"

Sade could only shake his lowered head and grin. But at the same time, he loved that Bo cared about those things, those childhood thrills. Even though he was technically not a child, he deserved that kind of life even now. "I'll dig around and see what I can find."

He let out a huge sigh, laying his head back. "So what about Mercy," he said, like he needed something else to think about. "What she's got?"

It was Sade's turn to sigh, not wanting to think about it. He ran down the brutal symptoms that could come with PTA until Bo gasped, "God stop! You're freaking me the fuck out!"

"Yeah," Sade barely managed.

"Well... isn't there like... shit you can do to help? Her remember?"

He attempted a shrug and found the feat nearly unmanageable. "Whatever I can do, I'll do it, you know that."

"Yeah I know," he said matter-of-factly. "I'll help you think of things, we'll have her back to her old self in no time."

Sade froze at the sound of Mercy's voice raising.

"Uh-oh," Bo said, hearing it too.

They listened in the silence for more, but nothing came. Liberty was on the scene. "Can you imagine," Bo whispered. "Those two going at it?"

No he couldn't, nor did he want to. They sat in silence for a while and a knock preceded the call, "Bath time pretty boy."

"Fuck," Bo hissed, bolting forward. "Tell her you'll do it!"

"I'm on Mercy duty, sorry."

"Come on, man! Please, really."

At hearing the fear and shame in his voice, Sade gave in. "I'll ask again."

"Beg her. I'll owe you big."

"Fine, it's a deal."

Sade walked out just as Liberty headed his way. She halted abruptly and looked down. "Sade!" she whined.

He followed her gaze down to the blood seeping out of his bandages, through his tube socked feet. Bo was officially fucked.

"In. Bed. Now. I will dress them as soon as I'm done," she said with a tone of *thanks a lot Mr. I'll help.* She shook her head and headed to Bo's room, leaving Sade to stare at Mercy's closed door.

He wanted to know what Liberty had discovered, and yet didn't want to ever know. Everything in him said it was bad. Bad, bad, bad. It whispered with every boom in his aching head. He went to his room to wait for Liberty, only to realize waiting was nowhere in the vicinity of his ability. To avoid a confrontation with the doc, he went to his bathroom and cranked on the hot water, rummaging through supplies in the closet next to it. He'd get the foot doctoring started.

When the bath was full, he sat on the edge and slowly sank into it, keeping his feet out. Fucking shoulder didn't like that. He gritted his teeth at the pain.

Fuuuuck. Was Bo's and Mercy's feet this bad? He hated to think they hurt like this.

As he laid there, he made himself deal with what was about to come. No matter how he spun it in his mind, it always landed on the same dreadful thing. Mercy not remembering him. For some reason, somehow, that filthy idea was dangerous. Dangerous for him. But that's what he was up against and he needed to be ready. He slowly closed his eyes and sank lower into the hot water.

Fucking ready… he'd be ready. He'd help her however she needed. Always. It was his turn to play healer and angel. He couldn't fail her.

God, he was fucking terrified.

## Chapter Eight

Mercy's insides jolted at the sound of a knock on her door. All she could think was, *is it him?* She'd been unable to get the huge man out of her mind. She tried to remember things, order things in her head. They wouldn't stay put. Everything was running together. Whoever it was knocked again, and she stared at the door trying to remember what she should say. Even common words evaded her. "Hello," she called, her voice breaking. Not hello. "Come in."

The door opened and her heart raced at seeing it was him. On crutches. She felt herself become a little… less something. But as he got closer, the less something changed to something else that made her grip the covers tight. He was so big. She waited for her brain to remember him. Anything about him, something to ease her fears. Why did she feel like that? Her body seemed to be that with him, and she was sure it had a reason. But the lady said they were… a couple. Mercy hadn't even known what that meant when the lady told her. She found out it meant intimate. How could that be if she was scared? How did that woman know that? She didn't know the woman, not now or before. So she wasn't even sure how much of what she said was true. Or accurate. There could be things the woman thought she knew and didn't.

She needed to ask more things. Questions. Mercy had been given the gist and this guy would give her the rest. She felt like a puny human asking Nimrod the details.

"Is it okay if I sit?" he asked.

His voice made her stomach flip. She remembered nodding meant yes, and gave a small one. She watched his every move. Especially the ripple of muscles in his arms and shoulders, promising strength she didn't want to see in action. The clingy black muscle shirt left nothing to the imagination, and between his body and the tattoos covering it, she was riveted.

She glanced at his face and found his eyes locked on her, making her jump inside. His eyes were gray and bright. Maybe silver flecks in them. She wanted to glance away but needed to stare longer. Study. That's what it was called. She was gaining word memory at least. But so much was still just… blank. It was really, really strange.

"I'm sorry I scared you," he said.

Again his voice spoke to her body in ways she didn't like. She clutched the pillow tighter in her lap and remembered she was supposed to answer him. "I'm sorry… I don't remember."

Concern marked his brow. "You don't remember the incident?"

It was her turn to be confused. "Incident?" She shook her head not remembering what that word meant. "What's… a fucking incident?"

"It just means something that happened," he said cautiously. "It's okay that you don't remember. It'll return any minute."

"I meant… I'm sorry I don't remember you. I know that I should. She did say it'll come back."

"Yes, it will."

Her gaze got stuck on his mouth. Something about it. She waited for a memory, but she felt like it wouldn't be a good one, by the way her body felt. Erratic. Confused. The tip of his tongue swept over his lower lip and she gasped from the surge of feelings it gave her.

"So I was thinking…" he said.

She looked into his eyes now.

"Maybe… I can help you remember."

"How?" she barely managed, afraid of his answer.

"If you… let me touch you."

Her head shook of its own accord before she could even think.

"Okay," he hurried. "No rush. She just said touch might help."

"My body… is…" She swallowed, searching for the right words that matched what she felt. "Is not… connecting you in a… good way." And the *fuck* word seemed to spring to mind a lot. Was she a foulmouthed person before?

His gaze narrowed. "What do you mean?"

"I just…" Her heart raced at the hardening of his tone. "… you…"

Somebody knocked on the door and she jerked her head to it.

"Who is it?" Sade called. The bite in his voice made her stomach race with energy.

"Bo."

He sighed and closed his eyes. "Come in."

The door slowly opened and he came through in a wheelchair. "Mercy!" he smiled brightly. "You're awake. It's about time."

She stared at him. She obviously knew him and yet didn't. Fear and disappointment slithered through her at how much she didn't remember.

"It's okay if you don't remember me," he said, seeming happy to see her. "I'm sure you will, in like five minutes after you see how awesome I am. I'm Sade's brother."

He stopped next to Sade and she was aware of those intense gray eyes on her, watching her reaction. "Bo," she said, wishing something would come. "I feel like… we were friends."

He gasped a happy laugh and pushed on Sade's shoulder. "She remembers me!"

Mercy was sure it was a joke, but the way Sade lowered his head said he either didn't get it or didn't find it funny.

"I'm sorry," she said, but wasn't sure why, only felt it. For something.

He raised his gaze to hers and shook his head barely. "Nothing to be sorry for, Angel."

Her heart pounded her chest at the *angel* term and how it made her feel… weird. Scared? Out of breath.

"I think you… scare me." She was immediately sorry she said it, remembering some things shouldn't be said out loud. "I'm… I'm having trouble knowing what things are okay to say and what to call them. I feel them but I don't know exactly what it is and why. How long have we been together?" she asked, wishing she could make her mouth stop.

He sat forward with that. "About… a month. Give or take a few days."

Alarm hit her with that. "A fucking *month?*" That's it?"

He suddenly looked like somebody who didn't get a joke. "It doesn't sound like a long time but... it was a good month. A lot happened."

A month? She couldn't get over the short time. How could intimacy possibly develop so soon? "Maybe... you can tell me about it."

"How's our sleeping beauty?" The lady called Liberty came in with a tray of food.

"I feel good."

"She looks fucking amazing," Sade muttered.

Mercy looked at Sade, her stomach jerking hard at the way he said *fucking*. Like she'd heard it before during... something that made her feel light headed. She parted her lips to get more air, not liking the way he made her feel. Something had happened. Something not good, she was sure. A month and they were intimate? Not possible. No way.

Liberty set the tray on the bed and picked up the notebook on the table. "You still adding to the list of everything you remember?"

She chanced a look at Sade, feeling him staring. "Yes." His eyes were burning into her. She looked at Bo and he gave her a half grin that made her insides relax a little. He was nice. She felt that. Her body seemed to remember him, just not her mind. Same with Sade. Her body remembered just not her mind. Yet.

"Oh, nice. You remember most of your childhood, I see."

Mercy looked at her. Most? She only recalled from thirteen to her early twenties and stopped at her going to nursing school. She couldn't remember anything else. Did she have a family? Sisters? Brothers? Aunts, uncles? Mother, father, grandparents? Her stomach knotted at all the possible things she didn't remember. She flicked her eyes toward Sade, only letting him in her peripheral vision. *One month. Give or take.* No wonder she didn't fucking remember shit.

"How do you know me again?" she asked the woman.

"It's my job to know you."

The odd answer made her feel more lost and scared. "I never did find out what that job was?"

"To watch over you."

"Why?"

"To keep you safe."

"From… from what? Do I live here? And where is here, did you tell me that? I don't remember if you did. Is-is my memory getting worse or better, can you tell yet?"

"Whoa missy. Some questions aren't for me to answer."

"You're not allowed to answer some? Am I in trouble or something?" She looked at Sade, her fears raising. "Have I done something bad?"

But all she got from him was that pensive look that made her need to ask him to leave the room.

"Is this normal?" Sade asked Liberty now. "She remembers, she forgets, she remembers?"

Emotion slammed Mercy until tears stung her eyes. "I'm fucking trying," she gasped.

He jerked to her, concern on his face. "Baby, I'm not saying you're not trying," he said softly. It was like he'd walked over and touched her inappropriately. Jesus she didn't understand this.

"I don't...." she closed her eyes and rubbed her forehead. "I feel things and... I don't like them. They make me feel bad."

"Like what?" The lady asked.

"Can I... can I talk to you?" She looked at the woman with silent pleading. "Alone?"

"You heard her guys. Out. Girl talk."

When they were finally alone, the woman sat on her bed. "Talk to me."

"He scares me," she whispered, feeling like she needed to be quick.

"Sade?"

Mercy nodded. "How do you know we were intimate?"

She seemed to think about that and sighed. "Listen, I can't answer a lot of your questions right now but don't worry, they're not bad answers. Just not answers I can give."

"I don't care about that so much, I care about him," she glanced at the door. "Every time he's around me, I get... scared."

"Sweetheart, listen. There's a lot going on with your body and mind, remembering connections while forming new ones. I wouldn't put too much trust in how you feel at this point. Sade is a good guy, he'd never hurt you." She put her hand on Mercy's arm, reassuring. "You're safe here, I know that. Ask him whatever you want. If he's a problem, I'll deal with it. But he's not."

"You'll deal with him?" She flicked a thumb at the door. "Did you see him? He's Goliath."

After a few contemplative moments she said, "I tell you what." Her dark eyes darted to the door then back to her. "You keep notes on all those feelings. You remember anything you think I need to know about, let me know on the down-low, okay? But until then, I want you to trust me."

Would be hard when she didn't even know her.

"How do you feel about Bo?"

"I like him, I think he's good."

"Then maybe you can talk to him about memories?"

She nodded, biting her thumbnail. "You think he would?"

"He does seem to dig you."

"Can you ask him to come in?" She grabbed Liberty's arm. "Don't... don't tell Sade what we talked about. Until I can sort through everything. I don't want to upset him if I'm wrong." That wasn't entirely true. She didn't want him knowing, in case her hunch was right about him and he might go whacko on her.

"You got it." She got up and left the room and soon after, Bo came in.

"Heyyyy Mercy," Bo said happily, rolling himself in.

She waited till he stopped and looked him over, taking more time than she did before, now that Sade wasn't there to distract her. Dear God, what fucking happened to him? Despite the large bandage on his cheek and the cuts down both sides of his face, he was very handsome. The easy kind of handsome that made you happy and want to smile. Not like Sade. He had the kind of look that sucked you in so hard, you forget how to breathe and think, forgot what words ever meant.

"You remember everything?" she asked.

He gave a slow smile like he was getting her unintended pun. "I have all my memory, why?"

"What do you know about… Sade?"

His brows shot up with a kind of surprised joy. "Everything pretty much."

"What about… me and him?"

He gave a chuckle. "Aw man, he loves you. A *lot*."

She waited for the words to do something good, but they didn't, they only gave her all those feelings that made her scared. And confused. How could he love her in one month? "How did we meet?"

"You and Sade?"

"Yes."

It was his turn to furrow his brows and glance at the door. "Well… you stopped Jay from beating him up."

"Who is that? Where?"

"Just a friend. It was at the Black Velvet, a nightclub Sade's father owns."

Nightclub. What was she doing at a nightclub? "So he was glad I saved him?"

Bo grinned. "No. He was pissed at you."

Pissed? "Why?"

Again he looked back at the door and rolled closer to the bed. Mercy was glad no alarm bells went off with the close proximity. "See, every year he makes one of us beat him up. On the anniversary of his mother's birthday," he whispered. "She died when he was four and for some reason that none of us really know, he blames himself. Well that's my theory. Why else would he do that?"

She suddenly felt like she was crossing lines. "Are you supposed to be telling me this?"

He shook his head with wide eyes and Mercy glanced at the door again before barely whispering, "What else?"

His face softened as he went on. "Sade's had a really bad life. After he lost his mother, his father was a ruthless motherfucker to him, raised him to fight and kill. Sade isn't your average man, he's… well he's sadistic."

She drew back, trying to remember that term. "Sadistic… he likes hurting people?" Her heart raced into her stomach. Something about that jogged her memory, her body's memory at least.

"I can't say he likes it, he just does it. He also likes *getting* hurt." Another quick glance at the door before he leaned in. "Anyway, after that incident behind the Black Velvet, you showed up at his tattoo shop."

"He does tattoos?"

"Yeah, and so you came in to have a tattoo done."

"I did? Where?" She looked down on herself.

"You never got it. I found out you were the one who had stopped him from getting beat up and so we thought you were an undercover cop."

She stared at him amazed and confused, waiting for memory. "Am I?"

He shook his head with a smile that said the event had been humorous to him. "Not, hardly."

"Then what was I doing? Did I actually like him?" She couldn't believe she'd do something like that, even if she did like him. Had to be a legitimate reason. She was pretty sure she wasn't that kind of person, judging by the memories she did have.

A loud knock on the door made them jump. "Bo, can I talk to you?"

"Shit," he whispered, wheeling in reverse.

"Are you scared of him?" Mercy asked.

"Uh, kinda, yeah."

"Why?"

"Coming," he called before looking at her. "He's killed a lot of people—"

"He has?" she gasped alarmed. He'd said that, but she hadn't taken it literally.

"I gotta go. Ask Sade what you want to know, he'll tell you anything, I'm sure. He loves you, I know that much."

He gave her a wink and rolled out while Mercy drew her legs up and held them tight to her chest, willing the vomit down. The giant came in then. Even on crutches he was scary. *My God, killed people?* She believed that. Easy. What the hell had she gotten herself into with this man? She tried to remember if she'd been on drugs or something. She suddenly froze, her spine turning ramrod. "Oh my God," she whispered.

He stilled a few feet near the bed. "What?"

"My dad! My dad died!" Her mouth hung open and she gasped several times as the horrific memory avalanched through her. Tears filled her eyes as dense pain stole her breath. She grabbed her chest with both hands when the pain became unbearable, then jerked back when Sade attempted to sit next to her.

He held up both hands. "I just want to hug you," he said, sounding desperate.

She shook her head and covered her mouth. "Sorry, I can't. Yet."

He moved to the chair and sat. "Don't apologize, take your time."

"Ohhh my God," she gasped. "I can't fucking believe this. I can't believe this." She looked at him and nodded. "And I'm crying over a fucking death I already fucking mourned like I never mourned it before, this is fucking crazy!"

He looked at her with worry. "I'm sorry too, Angel."

She wiped her eyes allowing all her suspicion about Sade to dam the tidal wave of pain. "He was hit by a fucking car, I remember now. Did you know him?"

He slowly shook his head, still looking guarded. "No."

Why did he hesitate? Why was he so guarded? "Can I ask you questions?"

"Please do," he said, seeming glad and yet maybe worried.

She stared at him, trying to figure out what to ask first, trying to stop the tremble in her limbs. Maybe she should match stories. "How did we meet?"

Another fucking hesitation? All this stalling, what was up with him? "What did Bo tell you?"

She wiped her eyes more, focusing and gathering her shit together. "I-I think that's private. Can't you just answer me? Oh my God," she whispered, remembering. "I was trained." She stared at him with wide eyes. "I. Was fucking. Trained!"

"You were, yes," he said carefully.

"By my father, he trained me," she gasped, thinking harder. "But for fucking what? Why?" She eyed him now to see if he knew. "Why are you staring at me like that?

He shook his head slowly. "Just… you're dropping the F-bomb a lot."

She drew back a little. "I'm… is that not normal?"

"Not for you," he said a little emphatically. "Not this much."

God, another problem. She put her fingers to her forehead. "I just…I'm so confused," she whispered. "The word feels like… maybe I used it a lot, like-like- *um*. A thinking word."

He shook his head. "If you did, you didn't do it out loud. I think… maybe you lost some of your training? The mental stuff?"

She thought about that and nodded a little. Then a lot. "That has to be it. I'll get that back then?"

"Or you'll relearn it. Either way," he held his hands up like he was negotiating with a person on the ledge.

She realized in that instant how erratic she was. "Sorry, I'm shaking. I must look like a crazy person to you?"

"You look like I need to hug you. But I won't," he hurried. "And curse all you want baby, it doesn't fucking bother me in the least."

She eyed him, realizing he was fluent with the F-word. "I take it I didn't like using the word if I trained myself not to."

"Maybe. But... if it makes you feel better, I think you're fucking beautiful either way."

Her heart raced as she stared at him. He certainly knew how to use that word well. His F-words were a lot different than hers. They meant *fucking* in the sexual sense, no matter how he used it. At least that's how it felt to her. And she certainly *felt* it. Right between her legs.

He suddenly slid his hips lower in his seat and her gaze locked on the bulge in his jeans. The sight made her body go nuts. "We met in an alley one night." He draped his hand between his legs and her eyes shot to his, finding them burning on her. He held her captive for a few seconds before going on. "I was having my ass kicked and you showed up and saved me. Only I didn't want saving."

The words he said didn't register. She was too busy focused on what his voice seemed to be doing. And his gaze. The deep rough tone literally touched her. All over. And his eyes. They were... hypnotic. Pulling at her. Calling her to gaze into them. Was he some kind of illusionist? Enchanter? This was nuts.

"You okay?" he asked.

Her gaze narrowed and she looked down. "What... what was the last thing you said?"

"That I didn't want to be saved."

Again his voice caused havoc. *Didn't want saving*, she repeated in her mind. "Why?"

"Because I like having my ass kicked."

Staring at him seemed justified as she again asked, "Why?"

He slowly slid his jaw to one side, making her heart hammer in anticipation. "I like pain."

Her breath shot out with his answer. "What else do you like?" she suddenly needed to know but was afraid of his answer.

Again he hesitated, angling his head while staring at her. It appeared like he was just trying to understand her line of questioning, but to her body he was in her face, sliding himself against her. "I like to give pain. I do that by fighting. Did," he corrected softly. "I don't anymore."

She licked her lips, breathless. "Why not?"

"Because I have you."

Oh shit. *Because I have you.* She held tight to the words while needing to not touch them. The possessiveness in his tone sent off a million alarm bells. "How does having me, stop you from fighting?

"It was a job I no longer have, let's say."

*Why* almost came out but she realized she needed to focus her questions better. "So you... no longer like to cause pain?"

He did that gaze burn again until she had the urge to look away, only it wouldn't allow her to. "Never said that, Angel."

If she didn't speed this torture chat up, she'd pass out. "You still like to cause pain?"

"Yes."

"How... do you?"

"I don't."

"Then how..." she shook her head, not following.

"I do what you taught me to do."

This got her attention. "What did I teach you?"

"Many things but in that one, you taught me to change."

"Change?" Okay, finally something that made sense a little. Was she a doctor of some kind?

"You taught me that I can change."

"And you did?"

"The fat lady hasn't sung yet. It's been an interesting challenge, I'll say."

For the first time, her curiosity outweighed her fears with him. She suddenly had a hundred questions regarding this subject. "Am I... like your doctor?"

He busted out in a chuckle that sent waves of new feelings through her, not as bad as the others but nothing that eased her fears either. He lowered his gaze shaking his head a little. "Not my doctor. More like my angel."

## Chapter Nine

He lifted his eyes, gaze back to burning. It devoured all her scattered thoughts in one moment, leaving her breathless and confused again.

"What?" His barely whisper matched the heat in his eyes and didn't help her. She gasped and clenched her eyes shut.

"You remembering anything?"

She shook her head, replaying his statement. *More like my angel.* Was she a missionary? A fucking nun? This was ridiculous! This man was making it hard to know who she was with him! A whore? Glorified prostitute? Call girl? No way, not possible. It just made no sense that she'd be with him.

"Why am I even with you?" The question just blurted out before she could stop it.

He didn't seem the least bothered by it as he slowly shook his head. "I've been trying to figure that out. Still."

"Your theories?" she asked, perplexed.

"Angel is the only thing that works in my mind. You really have no business with me. We're oil and water."

"What… I mean what was my reason?"

He gave her a small grin. "To help me."

To *help* him. "With…"

"My sexual issues."

Oh hell. Hell, hell, hell, back to confusing. "You uh… you have a lot of those?"

"Oh yeah," he nodded, eyeing her with that pensive gaze again. "I'm a sadomasochist."

She swallowed under his expectant gaze.

"We don't have to talk about it."

She sensed he didn't want to and that made her want to. But could she handle the details? Judging by the amount of curiosity that came with this topic, she was leaning in the therapist direction about herself. "I'm fine. If you are."

He shrugged a little, still eyeing her. "You're the doc."

"I am?"

"It's just an expression I use with you."

"Why?"

"Because you're always trying to fix me."

Wow. That felt in line with her feelings about herself. "Do you… I mean when… did you decide to try and be fixed?"

He let out a gasped laugh and lowered his head. "Baby…" he took a while before finally looking at her. "Something tells me you're not ready to hear that answer."

Fire zapped through her body and froze her breath. She was suddenly trapped. The forest around her was burning, and the only way to safety was across the river. Only she had to ride on the big bad wolf's back. She stared at him like a dummy, speechless.

"Yeah," he said, lowering his grin. "That's what I thought. I fucking missed you while you slept." He regarded her as though to see what she thought of that.

Her mind thought nothing of it, but her body continued to sizzle in a constant heat.

"You okay?"

The genuine question was soft and… sexual somehow. She absently grabbed her notebook off her bed and fanned her face. "So you… like to kill people?"

He lowered his head and stroked the bridge of his nose with an index finger. There was something familiar in her mind about it. "I never like killing. I like hurting. Not killing."

"Was it… like accidents? The killing part?"

"No. It was a job."

"You were paid to kill?"

"Basically."

"How did I not turn you into the police is what I'm wondering."

"Fair question." His silver eyes swallowed her whole. "I always fall back on the angel theory when I wonder that."

"Is there… blackmail in any of this?"

"Not on my part."

"On mine?"

"Not that I know of."

"So… we're together because… I happened to save your life and found out you were a sadomasochist… and I fell in love?" She rubbed her temples now. "This is… very stupid, no offense, but it's not making sense."

He gave a light chuckle with a smile. "You're missing a few details and your timeline is a bit off. You'll get it though, I'll help."

He'd help? Help *what,* was the problem. She may have forgotten details, but she was sure she didn't want him to help with her memories. She pinched the bridge of her nose, thinking becoming a literal pain.

"Why are you scared of me?"

The sudden question jerked her insides. "I don't know," she blurted honestly. "I was hoping to figure that out."

"You have any theories? Or maybe Bo?"

She shook her head without thought, wondering if he were prone to fits of jealous rage.

Thick long fingers stroked slowly over his forehead, stirring things in her body. "Sorry. I'm having a hard time with this too."

"With what?"

He leveled his eyes at her. "You not remembering me. You don't remember anything yet? At all?"

"Tell me."

"Tell you what?"

"What you think… I should remember."

He leaned forward, forearms on his knees, regarding her for many seconds. "You should remember… how much you mean to me." He looked down. "And many other things I don't think you're ready to hear."

She bit her lower lip, silently agreeing. She couldn't take hearing him *say* it for sure. "Maybe… you can write it?"

He chuckled a little and shook his lowered head. "Write it. Yeah, ok."

He wanted to show her, she could feel it. He'd mentioned *doing* things to help her memory, but there was just no way she could. The idea of him actually touching her induced panic in odd places. She needed to understand why she felt like she did with him. "I'd… like that. For you to write it. Please."

He leaned back and leveled an angled look at her until she wanted to hide. "I'll do it if…"

Agonizing silence passed as she waited for him to finish. "If…?"

He lowered only his eyes. "Nothing."

"Tell me."

He looked right, rubbing his hands on his jeans, making the muscles in his tattooed arms ripple. But there was something about the nervous act that lessened her fears a little.

"I can only say no," she encouraged.

"Yeah. I don't do good with no, not about this. I just… I just want to sleep with you—not touch you," he corrected quickly, "just be near you."

Alarms exploded all over her mind and body. "I can't," she gasped. "I'm sorry, it's not a no, it's just I can't, not yet."

"Don't apologize, I get it. You don't remember me. It'd be like sleeping with a stranger. I get it."

Everything about his tone said he got it and it was very far from okay. Would never be okay. She wished she could help with that but… "We can talk as often as you like."

He let out a dry chuckle. "Yeah. I'd like that actually."

"It's the best I can do right now."

"I know that," he said, sounding annoyed. I'm not mad about it, I love talking to you. I just love doing many other things to you."

Her breath caught on that panic again.

He stood suddenly. "Fuck, wow. Look I'm sorry, but I can only take so much of seeing you terrified of me before I need air. I'll see you later."

She watched him hurry out on the crutches and wanted to stop him. She wanted to apologize, but the *love to do many other things to you* wouldn't let her speak, it had her locked to what that might mean. And the merry-go-round of conflictions to know and yet never find out had her ready to get off the ride and vomit.

****

Sade hobbled his way to the workout room and looked around. He spotted the punching bag, put Abraham's ugly face on it and beat the fuck out of it for thirty minutes. When the bastard was good and dead, and Sade was covered in his blood, he stopped. It was all a tease for his sadism, like a shadow orgasm that left him moaning for more.

Write it? Fucking *write* it? Nothing like a little letter telling her what he'd done. Where would he start? Ah, yes. Drugging her, tying her up and molesting her. Confirm all the good fucking feelings she wasn't having toward him.

He collapsed onto the weight bench winded and dripping sweat, his feet and fists bleeding. If she'd just let him touch her... he was sure she'd remember him. Remember the good things.

He looked up at hearing a choked huff at the door. "Jesus H. Christ."

"Don't," he warned to a pissed Liberty in the doorway. "I'll clean the mess." He wished he'd bled out more than he had.

"What is up with you?" She strolled to the exercise bike like she dealt with this kind of thing all the time.

"You know what's fucking up."

"You talked to her?" She hung her towel on the handlebars and began stretching.

"Oh yeah. She remembered her father's death while I was in the room. Again. She got to relive him dying, and I got to not be able to do a fucking thing because she's scared to death of me. And then? She asks me what we've done together. And so when I tell her I can't say what, she tells me to *write* it!"

She pressed buttons on the panel before her. "That's actually a good idea."

"It's not a good idea, not when everything I'd write would only confirm that I'm the monster her body remembers me to be. Did you see how she *acts* around me?" he yelled. "And now I'm supposed to just help her make that connection with a dot to dot?" He held a hand out before him, "See... I always knew one day she'd wake up and realize that who she thought she loved was just a dirty spawn of the devil. Took her getting slammed into a fucking wall before the sense got knocked into her, but there you have it. Thank you Karma. I can always count on that cold cunt to end me over and over, only she doesn't ever end shit, she makes it linger and last like a fine wine of sadomasochism. And fuck me, that turns out to be my favorite fucking concoction. Even now I'm turned on by her fear, is that sick? And I'm supposed to *write and convince* her I'm not the monster that I am?"

"Whooooa," she squealed as she peddled up some invisible mountain. "Listen," she said. "Granted she is very suspicious of you, but her wires are all crossed right now. You have to give her time."

"Time for what? What did you not just hear? I am the monster she's afraid of."

"Sade, you were that before this and she loved you then."

"She was confused. And now she's thinking clearly. That's what I think."

"Well…" she huffed, peddling faster, "…I know women love a good erotic book, so, the odds of you… waking her body up is in your favor with the writing thing. Maybe you can just… tell the pretty stuff and once her body wakes up then… she'll let you show her the rest of the story?"

He remembered her wanting to read those silly romance books to him. What other options did he have? Tying her up and making her remember?

Shit, his dick got so hard at that idea. He was not well. He was so not well.

Sade left Liberty and promised to go straight to his room and doctor his feet. That evening, he sat in his bed with a pen and a hundred papers crumpled on the floor next to him. *The fuck to write?* The only thing he had lots of practice with was drawing tattoos, invoices, and police reports. Fuck it, he'd just tell it. No frills, just exact events—minus the part where he drugged her and tied her up that first time. He'd probably tell about the second time because by then, she'd officially earned it. What'd he have to lose? Certainly not her trust.

Before he realized it, Sade was turning page after page as the words poured out of him. He was reliving them and it awakened a ravenous hunger to not stop, never stop. It was the closest thing he'd come to having her, in what felt like forever. Right there on paper, he devoured her until he was burning up. He gasped and clenched his eyes shut when he got to the part in their story where she sucked him. Right after he'd eaten her delicious fucking pussy for the first time.

The pen trembled in his hand as he fought the need taking over him. He gave in to the urge to open his legs. Drawing his knees back, he grabbed the base of his cock tight and pressed his other hand hard against his balls. He held on to that image in his mind—her lips wrapped tight around his cock as it slid so very slowly deep into her pretty mouth. A harsh hiss made its way between his gritted teeth as he rolled his hips hard. He grunted as he relived it. Pushing the head of his cock against her throat. "Mercy," he grit, seeing her gaze locked hard onto his, seeing that fucking adoration in her eyes that he couldn't fathom but had to have. *Suck me. Suck me deep, baby.*

The memory of her nostrils fluttering with her sweet effort to do it perfectly, take all of him deep, so fucking deep, burned through him. Fire bit down on his balls and Sade gave several harsh grunts, bucking his cock through his iron clutch. He stifled a roar, bowing his body off the bed as his furious orgasm took him, turned him inside out, and made him into that writhing, sadistic animal of insatiable hunger.

As he lay in a haze of torment, disgust slowly seeped its way in. Only something demonic could be fed and never satisfied. Except when his angel fed it. She was the only one that had ever been able to command that devil. And now she was gone.

Sade put on jeans and grabbed his crutches, needing to see her. At not finding her in her room, he went to Bo's and found it empty. One wheelchair. One pair of crutches. He looked down the hall and heard laughter. Making his way to the end, he realized it was coming from the workout room.

"I see you didn't forget your strength," he heard Bo say.

Sade put his hand on the doorknob and listened, his heart pounding and his stomach on fire.

"I see you didn't forget your sense of humor."

"Actually I didn't forget anything."

They laughed and Sade's hand tightened on the doorknob, his jaw hardening in fury. Mercy's laughter burned through him. That she was doing it with somebody else made him tremble in jealousy.

"Very funny mister. Don't get smart or I'll make you hitchhike back to your room."

"I have to say, I've never rode double in a wheelchair before. Sade and I used to ride double on our bikes, but this is a step up for me."

The vision of Bo on Mercy's lap or the other way around had him seeing blood. He needed to walk away from that door.

"I can't even imagine Sade riding a bike," Mercy said. "Was he always that big?"

"No, he wasn't! But he always kicked everybody's ass that fucked with me. One of the reasons I love him."

"I bet he got all the girls?"

Sade listened closely, his heart racing at hearing her digging for information about him.

"Actually, I got the girls. But that was fine by him, he never was into girls that much."

"Oh really? Boys?"

Bo laughed loudly. "If it meant kicking their ass, yes. He didn't get close to nobody."

A throat cleared behind him and he glanced back to find Liberty with a quirked brow in a military stance, fists on hips.

Shit. "You eavesdropping on me?"

"What are you doing?" she whispered.

"Just checking on Mercy."

"More like spying."

He turned on his crutches 'til he faced her. "I need to talk to you."

"Let's walk."

## Chapter Ten

He waited 'til he got far enough away from the nauseating laughter before he realized he didn't know how to say it. He fought with the words only coming up with one thing. "I need Mercy."

She put her hands behind her, walking slowly while looking down. "Define need."

Another mind boggling challenge that ran together for him. "I just can't… I'm lost. Before her, I had a sick little routine. When she came into my life, she wrecked it and gave me a new routine. And now that's gone and I'm… I'm stuck with things and urges I don't know how to process anymore."

"Like what things."

"I'll be blunt with you."

"Please do." Like she didn't have the patience for anything but.

"When Mercy met me, I was a full-blown sadomasochist."

"I knew that one."

He paused a little and went on. "Then you know I have ways of dealing."

They made it to the living room and kept going in the direction of the kitchen. "So you don't know what to do with your urges I'm guessing."

He paused in mid-stride, relieved she got it so accurately and quickly. "Exactly."

They made it to the kitchen. "Have a seat, let's do coffee." He sat while she retrieved the items with a confident ease that made you feel maybe all wasn't as lost as it seemed and felt.

"So, what do you have in mind?"

"Besides going insane and killing something, nothing. I just know I need her. The Mercy I knew, the one who gave me other means to deal, she's… just not there." He couldn't bring himself to say gone, that was too fucking permanent, and he wouldn't talk that way out loud.

After getting the coffee on, she turned and leaned against the counter, arms crossed and eyes aimed at him like an armed tank. "There is a lot of PTSD going on here. You, Bo, Mercy—all of you are suffering with it. Speaking of which, I am going to sedate Bo tonight, no arguments. And Mercy? Well, she's got PTSD whether she realizes it or not, remembers it or not. Her body hasn't forgotten the trauma she's just been through. Her instincts aren't matching up to her feelings and vice versa, leaving her in a constant state of anxiety. I've studied her file so I know she's been trained to survive, and she's forgotten a lot of it. Not the physical one, but some of the others may not be present like the day-to-day thought processes when presented with problems. And since most of her training stemmed from childhood sexual trauma, the sexual aspect is her stronghold slash weakness. She can kick ass without thinking but remembering how to process carnal conflict is another animal altogether, and you'd have to be blind not to see she's highly conflicted in that very department with you. Look, I don't know what you had with her, okay? Her body remembers you to some extent—possibly mixing it with childhood sexual trauma? Not sure. Hope not, but not sure. In that case, her instincts at a muscle memory level are at this point—negative."

Sade had been holding his jaw shut and finally forced himself to release it. "How... the fuck do I fix this?"

She shrugged a little. "Nothing to do but wait for her to remember. Give it time, that usually solves it all."

Sade was back to *ready to kill* mode. "There has to be something I can do to help. I can't just wait, I know I can't, I can feel I can't, I won't."

"Try doing things that remind her of the good things. Nonsexual things."

He gave a dry laugh. "No such thing, everything with her was sexual in some way."

She raised her brows and gave a one-sided smile of dry sympathy. "That sucks. I think. Maybe some of the things that weren't too sexual. Had to be something. Familiar smells, feelings, tastes, sounds. Anything that connects her mind to an event in the past to sort of manually connect dots."

Sade thought about that while Liberty poured their coffee. At first he thought there wasn't anything, then things began pouring into his mind. The reading, the soul meshing, the music, the food. He eyed Liberty for a moment. The jealousy. Could he spark that? She was sure sparking the fuck out of his.

"Will you help me?"

"As long as it helps and doesn't hurt, I'll do what I can."

Sade took the cup of coffee and eyed her as she sat. "Well... she used to be very jealous."

"Oh brother," Liberty muttered in disgust, bringing the coffee cup to her lips. "Go on, I'm listening."

****

Sade actually managed an afternoon nap and woke up to the sound of knocking. He twisted on the bed, putting his ear toward the door. Not knocking. Banging. Then yelling. Sade shot to the door without his crutches and yanked it open.

"I don't need *sleep!* If I do, I'll sleep, get away from me with that!"

"Sade!" Liberty and Bo both yelled his name as he hurried across the hall, Mercy following in her wheelchair.

"Bo!" he yelled.

"Tell her man, tell her to get the fuck away from me!"

At seeing Bo's body heaving, his killing instinct hit and he shot his hand between them when he got to the bed. "Wait!" he ordered her. "What do you want to give him?"

"Midazolam. Puts him way under, he won't dream."

"Bullshit!" he yelled.

Sade jerked his face to him, glaring.

"Just saying man."

The vulnerability in his desperate voice urged Sade to hurt something. He jerked his gaze to Liberty. "I'll sit with him and see that he sleeps."

She rolled her eyes, holding the shot up in her right hand. "For Pete fucking sake."

"We can do shifts," Mercy said behind Sade.

What should have made him happy, triggered his rage. "I can handle it," he nearly barked.

"You'll need to sleep at some point."

Sade realized there was no arguing that shit without looking like an outright moron. "Whatever."

"Fine," Liberty said, backing off the bed, "I guess I can take a damn shift too." She pointed her mechanical finger at him, "And you better fucking sleep."

"Oh sure, I'll sleep just fine with you waving that thing around." He looked at Sade. "Make her take last shift and she better not drug me, I'll kick her ass."

Liberty laughed hysterically at that.

"You think I can't?"

"Calm it Bruce Lee," Sade muttered, patting Bo's chest to let him know he wasn't mad and that he was safe now.

"I'm just saying," Bo muttered. "Her claw doesn't scare me."

Liberty actually snickered as she walked out. "I'll be back."

"Take your time," Bo called before muttering, "Mizz Terminator."

"You want me to take first watch?" Mercy asked.

Sade's jaw hardened. "Whatever Bo wants."

"I don't care, just so it's not Iron Maiden. I can't fall asleep with that around me."

Sade pushed off the bed and walked to the door. "Come get me when it's my watch," he said, not looking back.

Wasn't fifteen minutes later when somebody knocked on his door. "Come in!" he yelled from the bed, hoping it was Liberty so he could vent.

The door handle rattled a little then opened. He stared in confusion at Mercy in the wheelchair. The second her gaze dropped to his naked chest, his dick hardened. She wasn't quick to realize she was gawking, making him glad he'd gotten comfy in only briefs. His reflexes warred between the need to protect her sensitivities and provoke her memory. Waking her memory won out and he remained still, watching her.

Her gaze finally made it to his face and a thick fire rolled through him at the look she had. Like she'd just had a fucking orgasm. Jesus Christ, he wanted her so bad. Right in that second. Flashes of her body beneath his, slick with sweat as he fucked her into delirium turned the fire into an inferno.

Knowing her body remembered him, felt like he was one step closer to her, even if the memory was confused. He could definitely talk to her body. So what brought her to his room was the question. "Something wrong?"

She turned the chair and shut the door. "Bo wanted to be alone before he tried to fall asleep."

He eyed her, feeling better that she thought to come see him while waiting. "He should let Liberty bathe him again."

"Again?"

"Yeah. I think that's why he's scared of her."

Mercy snickered with wide eyes. "I bet."

He sat at the edge of the bed, ready to play the tempter. "I can make coffee." He suddenly saw the mountain of paper on the floor preceding the porn story he'd written and jacked off to.

She looked down at it. "You wrote?"

"Uhh," he made his way to his knees and began gathering the mess. "I tried."

"You tried a lot. Did you forget how to write?"

He wadded the papers together and chucked it into the small wastebasket on his right. "Maybe." He caught her staring with wide eyes at his hard cock pushing against his black briefs. The open curiosity made it even harder, and he suddenly wanted to just let her look. While he jacked off. He bet his curious virgin-minded Mercy would benefit from that.

She seemed to remember where she was and what she was doing. "Your room is just like mine," she gasped breathless, looking around.

"You want that coffee?" He made his way to standing.

"Sure. I might need it. Can I have it?" He looked at her, not getting what she meant. "What you wrote for me?"

He chuckled a little and limped carefully to the side of the room that held the kitchenette. "Sure. But it's… rough."

"Too messy to read?"

"Not that kind of rough."

"Well…I promise not to grade you."

"Uh… not that kind of rough either."

A moment of silence stretched before her timid, "Oh."

After he put the coffee on, he walked to the table next to the bed, snatched the notebook from it and handed it to her. "Before I chicken out and burn it."

When she only stared at it, he retracted the offer only to have her reach for it.

"You sure?" He handed it back again.

She grabbed it and put it in her lap like she didn't want to hold it too long. "I think so."

"I wouldn't read it if I were you."

The need to ask why was all over her pretty face, as she once again stroked his cock with that innocent scan of his body.

He held up both hands. "I'm not telling you, you have to read it. But just know it wasn't easy for me to write all that." It had been hell not being able to fuck her, grind his cock deep until she screamed. He sat on the bed and put his palms behind him, watching her gaze drop over his torso then jerk away when reaching his hard dick. Fuck, what a turn on.

"I can put pants on if you make me. It's just… so damn hot. And hard… with my feet I mean. How are yours?" He fought a grin at seeing her fluster over his naughty play on words.

"Oh. Hurt like hell."

He wondered then. "You remember anything about that? I kinda hope you never regain that memory."

"I don't." She peeked up at him, reminding him of that sweet girl he'd accidentally fallen in love with in his condo. "It was that bad?"

He only nodded, holding her gaze, wanting to kiss her.

"I'm sorry."

His heart raced at the brave way she soul meshed with him. Even if it wasn't soul meshing since that's not what she was intending, still. It was close and he was hungry for it. "For what?"

"Just that you have to remember it."

"And Bo."

"Especially Bo," she said.

Especially?

She seemed to regret the confessional slip. "I mean he seems more... unable to take that kind of stuff."

"And I get off to it, so..."

"I didn't mean that, you're just a lot..." He let her struggle for it, almost getting off to her torment except for the topic. "Bigger."

"I'm pretty big, yes."

"Yep," she said with forced ease as she looked down at the notebook, then around as though remembering it contained more indecent things. "Soooo. How long are we going to be here?"

"No clue," he said quietly.

"What are we supposed to do while here?"

"Live, I suppose."

She nodded. "Obviously. And thankfully. Living is good."

"So you have any plans to regain your memory?"

She gave him a confused look. "Plans?"

"Yeah, I mean usually you have a plan."

"I do?"

"Always. Always a plan to overcome shit. It's one of the things I love about you."

"Or loved," she mumbled, lowering her head.

"It's still there."

She pffed and played with her fingers. "Don't see that trait anywhere around."

"It's there," he assured softly, suddenly wanting to fuck her slowly.

She peeked at him. "You sound so confident."

"I am. Cocky too." He grinned at her, trying for playful, but it only earned him a wall of frigidity. "At least you're comfortable with Bo," he added. That was the one thing Sade didn't like. Having Bo anywhere in the middle of him and Mercy.

She shrugged, missing his jealousy. "I ate with him. He was bored."

"Nice," Sade lied outright. "Glad you're not scared of him."

"No, not at all."

"Guess that's not so odd."

She eyed him, looking suspicious of what he meant. Too bad he had nothing but validation for her in the fear department.

"Well, I'm glad you feel safe with somebody," he said. "And with Liberty?"

She shrugged. "I can't say for sure. Are you two related?"

"No, why?"

Her lips briefly turned down with her shrug. "You act alike is all."

"I think we're both cut from the same cloth."

"Which is what?"

"The *'life's a bitch and then you die'* one."

"At least you have somebody you can relate to."

Sade cocked his jaw with the sudden need for vengeance. "And she's a great doctor. She reminds me a lot of you."

She pffed. "I see no resemblance whatsoever."

"I do."

"Well, I'm glad you're in such good hands."

"Good hand," he corrected, winking at her when she looked at him. The tables had turned enough that he was having fun even if he wasn't gaining good ground. Any ground was good to him at this point. "Helps when she's handling heavy loads." He waited for her to take the bait.

"She needs a strong hand to handle you, I'm sure."

"Not a good thing when wet and slippery." Her gaze narrowed in open suspicion. "During baths," he finished, hating himself suddenly for the lie. But he hungered for her affection, even if it was borne out of jealousy. It was proof that it was there, proof that his Mercy still lived in that body.

Her brows slowly went up. "Because you wouldn't want to fall and not be able to get up."

He grinned, kind of glad she didn't bite too hard. Reminded him of the old her. Always ready for a challenge. "Right."

"Well, nobody will be bathing me, that's for damn sure, I'm not an invalid."

Ohhh ouch. "I try to be a good patient."

"Hmm," she said. "I feel sorry for Bo."

"Yeah, he's scared of her claw."

"I talked to Bo about starting a workout routine tomorrow."

That fiery jealousy returned. She'd done more than just talked to him about that. "That's fantastic," he lied again. "Liberty's a great spotter if you guys need one."

"Wow, she's quite 'handy' isn't she?" She laughed loudly at her joke. "Bet she gives a scary hand job."

Sade's breath gushed with the sudden jerk of his cock at the bold little sexual joke. "Scary can be fun."

"Not for me, thank you."

"You don't like scary hand jobs?"

"Very funny," she muttered.

"You gave me a hand job once."

"Ooookay," she gasped, looking down.

"Sorry, I forgot you're sensitive to sex."

She eyed him, appearing insulted. "It's not that I'm sensitive to it, it's just weird talking about it like this."

Sade's heart hammered, looking for a safe angle to proceed through that wall. "I was just saying you were good at it, I didn't mean anything else. Much better than any other woman that…" Shit, wrong direction.

"Must be quite a history of women you have, I bet."

"Why would you think that?" he said, trying to sound offended.

"Well, with the…" she flopped her hand at him, "…condition you have."

"Sadomasochism?" The déjà vu was making him giddy.

"Right."

"That automatically means I do it with a lot of women?"

She looked at him, buying his feigned offense. The confusion on her face was priceless, sweet and arousing as fuck.

"It's okay, I'm used to people assuming I'm a whore." He lowered his gaze. "Truth is, I was rarely with women. Or men," he added at seeing her confusion still.

"Then how… how did you…"

"Quality over quantity, baby." He eyed her. "When I finally did it, I made it count." He watched her reaction, liking that he could stare at her.

"So this was like... a once a week thing?"

"More like twice a year."

She gave a sound that could have meant disbelief or shock, maybe both. "Wow. I thought..."

"That I fucked women all day and all night, I know."

"No, just... more than twice a year."

"Right."

"Right," she said firmer, annoyed that he might not believe her. She scratched at her cheek then played with the corner of the notebook and Sade's heart beat in his cock while he waited patiently for her to voice what was on her mind. "Wish I remembered something about you." She paused, shaking her head a little before muttering, "Us even."

"You saved my life," he said.

She jerked her head up. "In that alley?"

He smiled at her. "No, in general."

"Oh."

"I didn't need saving in that alley, didn't want it, not until..."

She eyed him as he struggled for the right words, not wanting to scare her off. "Not until you made me want it."

"Want... what?"

"You. Life. Hope."

He watched as each word sank in and made a seemingly positive mark. "Sounds right, I mean it feels… true. Not that I think you'd lie, it's just my body seems to have a journal of its own and I guess I'm comparing notes." She said all that while staring at the notebook in her lap.

"I get it, Angel."

"I better go check on Bo," she said, wheeling the chair in reverse.

He was suddenly sorry he'd gone the stupid emotional route. Should have stuck with the sex talk.

"I'll knock when it's your watch," she said at the door.

He let her go, sighing in frustration. "I'll bring your coffee when it's done," he said to himself. Sade sat in the silence, feeling like he'd just got some kind of fix. He was happier than he'd ever been since this whole ordeal started. Having Mercy, then not having her, made getting any part of her back some kind of amazing.

His dick throbbed in the wake of her absence with ideas for project *Never Forget Me*.

It would help if he could get her to agree that she needed his help. And if that meant seducing her to get her to admit that, he was more than happy to try.

## Chapter Eleven

Mercy looked in on Bo and saw him drawing. "I'm using the bathroom and headed your way," she called. He looked at her and smiled with a salute while Mercy quickly wheeled herself to the privacy of her room to hold her head and catch her breath. Dear. God.

She looked down at the notebook in her lap and quickly wheeled to the bed and threw it on top. Maneuvering her way to the bathroom, she managed to get herself onto the toilet and sat. Closing her eyes, flashes of that man bombarded her mind. His body. Who the hell needed a memory to know he was ridiculously sexy? Not her. It was a distraction to her memory. Maybe.

She had to admit she wasn't *as* scared of him as she initially was. Maybe it was because of watching him with Bo. Caring for him the way he did. She didn't miss the fierce protection in his eyes with Liberty. Or the way he valiantly saved Bo from sedation by offering to stay up with him. That was just… totally anti-sadomasochistic. She'd been reminding herself that's what he was when she wanted to feel too comfy with him. Which was quickly increasing.

The direction she was headed in with Sade seemed good, but her body screamed bad. And yet she couldn't help it, he was a huge magnet of sexual stuff that pulled her constantly. Which brought her back to the idea that she had been some kind of whore or slut.

She finished her business, hissing at the agony in her feet. She needed to elevate them. Back in her room, the notebook on the bed caught her attention. She rolled to it and looked back at the door before grabbing it and stuffing it under the mattress. She headed to Bo's room when voices and laughter made her pause. Leaning her head, she listened then peeked into Bo's room.

He waved at her, and she waved back. "I'm going to the kitchen for a drink what do you want me to bring you back?"

"Oh!" he snapped. "Can you get me some more ice cream?" He lowered his voice with a smirk on his face, "Liberty gave me like two spoons!"

Mercy laughed and headed toward the kitchen, slowing when the voices came into hearing range.

"Yes, I think so," Sade said. "Thank you so much, I appreciate it."

"You owe me."

"I definitely do. Mmm. You made this? Fucking delicious. Your talents are endless I see."

"Bribery will get you everywhere."

Sade laughed and the sound sent a burning in her stomach. Mercy strolled in, not wanting to hear anymore. "Kitchen's open?" she called.

"Oh yeah," Liberty said. "I was just leaving."

"Yeah, I'll be right there," Sade said. "Don't start without me."

"Ohhh, right. Be kinda hard to," Liberty sang as she went.

Mercy stared at him, biting her tongue on *start what, what are we starting?*

"Can I get you anything, baby?"

The term annoyed her in that second, especially the way it still had power over her body. "Um no." She realized she'd have a hard time getting Bo's ice cream. "Well, yes. I need to get Bo some ice cream."

"I can help with that." He got a bowl out of the cabinet, and she watched as he opened the freezer, her eyes taking notes. Always taking notes of his body, what the hell was up with that? "What flavor?"

She jerked her gaze up to his. "Uh, vanilla I guess."

"That what he said?"

He sounded sure it wasn't. "He didn't specify, I'm guessing."

"And you guess he'd want vanilla?"

She shrugged. "I didn't really think of it."

"You like that flavor?" he got the vanilla out.

"I…I think I do, yes."

He opened the drawer and pulled out a spoon grinning as he scooped ice cream into the bowl.

"What's so funny?"

"Nothing," he said. "Vanilla is a good choice for you."

Funny she'd remember that could mean sexual inadequacy. "I like chocolate too."

"And strawberry?" He glanced at her with that grin, like there was some secret joke on her about it.

"Not so much," she lied. Well, it wasn't her favorite.

"I love strawberry." He winked at her and returned the ice cream to the freezer.

"Really," she said, feeling like sarcasm was needed, but of course she couldn't think or remember how to be that.

He handed her the bowl of ice cream. "You sound surprised."

She stared at the bowl and took it from him. "You don't seem like a strawberry kind of guy."

"Strawberries remind me of..."

She looked up and he shook his head. "Never mind."

"No, tell me," she said, regretting it the second she did.

"I really can't."

She dove in again. "You won't you mean. You better go, I'm sure Liberty is wondering what happened to you."

"Yeah, and Bo's ice cream is melting. You'll probably need to spoon feed him now." He leaned against the counter, crossing his legs and making things bulge.

"Fine," she said, irate while staring at him. "I don't like the way you always tease me."

A look of surprise lit his face that was annoyingly handsome in that moment. "Tease you? That's not teasing. But I am good at teasing if you want me to show you."

Heat flooded her body as she fought to stay focused. "Everything you say has some kind of hidden meaning. And then you have this grin like the joke is on me."

He stared hard at her for a few seconds, making her heart race even more. "My apologies, Angel."

"Stop calling me that, please."

Anger flashed in those gray eyes. "Why?" And yet the word was a mere caress, making her hate how quickly he turned the tables.

"You're doing it again."

He chuckled and shook his head, pushing off the counter and grabbing the crutches before heading out. "See you when it's my turn, baby."

His turn? "What turn?" She rolled after him.

He kept crutching his way along, not looking back. "When I take your post with Bo."

Her cheeks burned at remembering the obvious. But her brain had gone blank on the term for some reason. She'd thought something else altogether, something… sexual. Taking turns. Why would that word mean something sexual to her and negative at that? Was it a memory returning? Had there been turn taking between them?

She suddenly wanted to go back to her room and get that notebook to find out, rage making her tremble. She was not the type to share, she was so fucking sure of that! Was that why flirting with Liberty came so easy with him?

Later. She'd definitely read it later.

\*\*\*\*

Sade went to the workout room and entered, shutting the door.

"You are so bad," Liberty huffed from the treadmill.

"Oh my God, she is soooo jealous." He leaned his back against the door with his eyes closed in utter joy.

"You love that I see."

"You have no idea."

"Does that mean I can quit being so nice to you?"

He pulled his head forward. "You're being nice?" Sade had to laugh then eyed her in her workout clothes—baggy shirt, baggy jogging pants.

"What!? Don't look at me dude."

"I'm not."

"You clearly are."

"I mean not like that, I'm just…" He angled his head then straightened it. "You got any other clothes that actually fit you?"

"Fit me! My uniforms fit!"

"Yeah, I mean something different than your special agent… anti-feminine look."

She got off the treadmill, glaring at him. "Cute, asshole." She wiped her sweaty face on her shoulder and sat at the Bowflex machine, gaze forward.

"I just think if you had something else that would show your sex—"

"Oh fuck you! You can damn well tell I'm a woman! Ask Bo!"

"No, not Bo."

She squinted an eye at him. Pulling the cables forward. "Little shit say something about me? What's wrong, he's mad I'm not into his pretty face? Scrawny little shit, I'd break him in two."

Sade laughed, not doubting it for a second.

"Fine, you want slutty, I'll give you slutty," she huffed, back to gritting her teeth and glaring forward.

"I never said slutty, just a little more telling."

"Fine, fine." She picked up her pace, pulling faster. "I'll be more telling, you'll see. It'll be loud and clear."

"You can't go too extreme, she'll know."

"Well, that's too bad Mr. Macho, if I like you, I just can't help myself?" Her arms pumped now as she owned that fucking machine. Impressive.

"Well, I'm going to get a shower. I just wanted to let you know how it was going."

"Go get off your goddamn feet before I get my KG and shoot them off your fucking legs. It's like I'm the only adult here," she muttered breathlessly.

Her KG? Sade laughed not even wanting to know. He left the Marshall, as he came to think of her, and slowed next to Bo's room as he passed. Why did they need the door shut? The fire in his gut returned and popped all his celebration balloons instantly. The idea of her giggling and laughing in there... God he hated that.

Once in his room, he made his way to the bed and collapsed face down before rolling onto his back. What exactly did he plan to do with Mercy? He needed a real plan.

He considered various scenarios that all led to one thing. Having her closer to him. That's all he wanted. To touch her. Smell her. Taste her again.

****

"We have a little problem," Liberty said, staring at Sade from across the small kitchen table next to the island. "I received word from Kane that when we get the word to move, we are to take the secure tunnel to a garage at the back of this facility. There's a Batmobile apparently, and from here, we go to a city with a PO Box that will have a key to another safe house. The problem?" She lowered her voice and leaned in. "The tunnel leading out opens with Kane's fingerprints *or* Mercy's voice."

Sade waited to get the issue, still not following.

"Sooo, her voice isn't the problem. It's what she has to speak into it. A code that only she knows. He made her use a favorite rhyme and not tell anybody when she was younger. The only thing he has is the hint. No more nightmares." She quirked a brow and leaned back. "That's the hint. We having fun yet?"

"Fuck," Sade whispered, looking right.

"So here's the deal," Liberty continued. "Operation Memory Lane needs to be stepped the fuck up. So, we're having a party."

"A party?"

"Well, if we're going to play your little jealousy angle, I need a good reason to dress differently. Suspicion and anxiety are common symptoms of amnesia, and we don't need to provoke the wrong shit in that head of hers."

"Like what kind of shit?"

"Like we're up to something," she hissed. "This needs to not look staged!"

"Okay, so, a party, what kind?"

"Fuck, I don't know, a birthday?"

"And whose birthday?"

She gave a shrug. "Mine, I guess!"

"Wow. What happens if she doesn't remember?"

"Well, we can't fucking teleport, so I foresee hitchhiking in the wide ass open."

"Jesus." Despite the sucky ass news, a yawn took him. "What time's this party?"

"Tonight. Go to bed. I'll take over watching Bo until he wakes up. We'll have the party at seven?"

"Sounds good. And you'll announce it at?"

"Breakfast? Be pleasantly surprised. And you'll need to talk to Bo. I'll get your little Mercy ready for a competition. You're sleeping sitting up. Go rest."

Sade nodded, not missing the rare softer tone. "Going." He got up and stopped a few feet out. "We got music?"

"We got that media get up and satellite. But leave your dancing shoes behind please, there will be no dancing for you, only sitting your ass down and staying off those feet." She paused before a firm, "I mean it," as though knowing his rebellion.

Sade made his way back to his room and collapsed onto his bed falling asleep nearly immediately while remembering that night he danced for Mercy. And Mercy had danced for him. This would be his first major act to trigger something. Besides his triple X diary that she may not read.

## Chapter Twelve

Mercy's stomach was in knots as she looked through the clothes before her. She'd been wheeled to Liberty's room and ordered to pick from the mountain because they were suddenly having a party out of the blue. For Liberty's birthday, no less. Mercy really wanted a reason to be suspicious but at the same time, she was sick of feeling like she should be. She was tired of being confused.

She went through item after item. They were close to the same size and Mercy finally chose something that would cover her well. Despite the urge to look pretty, she denied it. Was ridiculous to feel the need to dress up. She wasn't sixteen at her first prom.

Did she even have a prom? She didn't remember it if she did. What would Sade wear? She eyed Liberty's body for the first time, sizing it up. As she measured and discerned perfect curves, disgust hit her. Just great. She considered her own body next. Not a voluptuous curve in sight.

"You want me to make you a birthday cake?" Mercy asked, forcing herself to be nice.

"Aww honey, no thank you," She dumped shoes before her next. "I plan on getting shit faced."

Visions of her stripping down on a table hit her. She dreaded how this would all end. Sade better not drink. She didn't want two drunks on their hands, not while her and Bo were incapacitated. What if there was an emergency, or a fire? Would be very selfish and stupid of them to do that, fucking idiots.

"I can cook something maybe," Mercy offered as Liberty brought a jewelry box to her next. How long had this woman lived here? Did she always go to safe houses with so much stuff?

"That kitchen is just as much yours as it is mine. You do whatever you want to."

"Can I borrow this one?" Mercy held up the long black dress, and Liberty walked over and snatched it from her, holding it up.

"Oh dear God, no!" she shrilled. "You'd look like a *nun* in that. No, no, you want to look pretty. Let me help you."

Mercy bit her tongue with the nonsense in her head while Liberty gasped and held up another black dress. "Now thisssss is what I'm talking about!"

Mercy tried to decipher what the hell the thing was. Looked like a dress that had gotten blown to shit. You couldn't make out one gaping hole from another. And yet, she couldn't find a reason to say no to Liberty's stupid helpfulness. Did she never possess any manipulative skills? Backbone?

Then there was that little part of her that got a little thrill at dressing… inappropriately. She felt like somehow in all of this, Sade was provoking her and the urge and need to kick back was there.

"And this…" Liberty put the black dress down and snatched up a red one, plastering it to her body with gyrations. "…is what I'm wearing. You like?"

"Wow, hot," Mercy said, biting her tongue on, *who is your date?*

"Right? Whoever this shit belongs to has amazing taste."

"This… isn't your stuff?"

She shot a look at Mercy. "Hell no."

It wouldn't be the first time the woman gave an answer that demanded more of an explanation she wouldn't be giving. She looked down and around, feeling like she was trespassing all of a sudden. "Who is this stuff for?"

"Not sure," she said, sounding honest.

"You have theories?"

"This entire place is ridiculously stocked, honey. I'm not surprised at all. I even found a room with male selections! Can't wait to see what our guys look like all dressed up too. Oh!" she squealed, holding up a pair of red spiked heels. "I might break my neck in these, but it'll be worth it!"

Boy, it surely fucking would. Mercy had visions of tripping her as she stared longingly at the pile of shoes, seeing a pretty pair that she'd love to wear. Too bad she'd gotten crucified. You could kinda say she'd even died and was buried. Just waiting to be raised from the dead now.

*Our guys?* The sharathon thing poked hot holes in her stomach.

"People think I can't be a woman because of this," she yanked her glove off her hand and wagged her mechanical fingers. "Oh but I can."

The burning sensation went up a thousand degrees at her sultry tone. "Of course you can!" Mercy said in rooting excitement for her. "You'll knock them dead in that." Or him. "I'll go check on Bo to see if he's found something to wear."

"Oh no you don't!" she gasped. "I have to get you ready, fix your hair and do your makeup."

"That's not—"

"Oh pleeeease," she begged, "I never get to do stuff like this," she whispered. "Just this once?" She came at Mercy then. "Let me help you out of those clothes."

"No! I can do it. In the bathroom."

"You sure, I don't want you hurting your feet."

"I'm positive." Jesus, this bitch was nuts if she thought she was touching her or looking at her. Her skin crawled as the ménage ideas crowded in on her.

"Fine, take it to your room and I'll come by later."

"I'm fine, I can do it. I need to go see if Bo needs any help."

The woman finally gave in and sighed. "Okay, yes. Go take care of your Bo, I'll have a peek in on our Sade." She winked and hurried out of her room, leaving Mercy staring after her in silent disgust with the urge to ram her head against the wall.

And *our* Sade? It was so time to back the hell up. Sade was supposed to be *hers,* God help her if it turned out she was part of some triangle bullshit. She'd sure be telling him that was a hell-fucking-no-go.

Another idea suddenly hit her. Him being tired of not being remembered. She resisted tears of frustration as she wheeled herself to her room and slammed the door. Then she speed rolled to the bed and pulled out that notebook that would give her answers she needed, to help her remember.

Anger zapped her tears away at remembering Bo's words *I know he loves you. A lot.* Really? Sure didn't feel like it with the way he acted with Liberty. He'd say it was just friendly of course, nothing more. He'd say that with words fraught with grins and double innuendos. *Loved me my ass.*

He was playing her. She could feel it. He was playing something. Just how the hell did she end up with him? It must've started off one way and evolved into some kind of... victim relationship. She gasped, realizing. *I met him right after Dad died! At a nightclub!* Dear God! She'd likely been depressed and not thinking straight—vulnerable. And the sadomasochist took it and ran with it, took advantage of her need to help people too!

She opened the notebook, ready to unravel the mystery of Mr. Sadomasochist. She'd know what direction to go in once she did.

****

"A party?" Bo wondered. "How's that going to help her memory?"

Sade sat in the chair by his bed, hating to think it wouldn't help. He scrubbed his head with both hands, not sure if he could stand another day with her not remembering.

"What's up man?" Bo asked.

The concern in his voice slammed him with bullshit out of left field. He opened his mouth to answer, afraid to use his voice. "I don't know how to exist anymore, Bo," he said. "I know that sounds so fucking stupid."

"Nah, man," Bo said extra softly. "I get it, she's your rock. Your anchor in the storm."

Sade sniffed a little, eyeing him. "You writing poetry now, or what?"

"Fuck no!" he said. "I'll shit flowers before I pull that out of my head." Bo stared at Sade for a few seconds and shook his head. "Tell me what you got in that head of yours to help her remember. You gotta go easy, though."

Sade eyed him. "Why?" Bo suddenly looked uncomfortable, and Sade leaned forward with a pointed look. "Tell me Bo, I need to know everything so I know how to help her."

"She's just… paranoid man."

"But not of you."

"Nooo, not me. Just you. And Liberty too."

"Why Liberty? And why not you?"

Bo's face crimped with exasperation. "She's *jealous man!* Even though she doesn't remember you. But I think maybe it's more an 'isn't he supposed to be all into me' kind of thing and if so, 'why is he all up in her grill,' you know?"

"Yeah, I know. But why you say it like that? Like you're not sure she's got nothing to worry about?"

"I'm not, I just…" He shrugged his shoulders and held them up while staring into the air before him. "I guess I wonder what you're thinking. I know you're thinking something, and I just can't figure out what on this one. Usually I can name why you do what you do, but this one…" he shook his head, that clueless look on his face, "I get nothing but what the fucks."

"Well that's what the fuck's going on. I need her to remember who she is and get through this wall between us. I don't know how long we're going to be here before the next mountain of shit hits the fan, Liberty already got word that we need to be ready to move."

"She did?" Bo sounded worried.

"Yeah, and guess where we're going? Nowhere, unless Mercy remembers the code to the tunnel leading out to our transportation." Sade raised his brows, nodding at Bo's sudden understanding. "Shit's far from over and so she needs to remember for more reasons than me needing her. Although I swear to fucking God I don't think I can live one more day with her not remembering, I'm not lying to you."

"Right, right, man but… what shit is left you think?"

He looked at Bo dumbfounded. "What shit? Kane is out there moving on plan Z!"

"What's plan Z?" He screwed up his face, more worried.

Sade realized how in the dark Bo was on the details and felt suddenly guilty. "I'm not real sure, but the fact that he's at the end of the alphabet on ideas means it's either going to go half-ass good or way bad. If it goes bad then whatever shit happens, that's the shit."

"With your dad, you think?"

"With whoever! But I do imagine that bastard is at the head of the avalanche." Sade scrubbed his head. "I just don't know what is coming. Can you see us on the run with no vehicle and no place to go? Three cripples?"

"And a terminator," Bo said. "Sorry, I'm just… I'm freaking out. What about her dad, does he know about Mercy not remembering?"

"I assume, yes."

"So we'll just help Mercy regain her memory. We got a plan?"

"Yes. The birthday party for Liberty. I'm going to put on music that will hopefully help her remember."

"Oh, good one."

"Yeah and if that doesn't work, I'm going balls to the wall with trying to use her jealousy."

Bo's brows shot up with that. "Uh-oh. Don't like that sound of that."

"Me either, but I'm desperate. I need you to play along."

"How?" Slight disgust quirked his lip.

"Nothing trashy, just look oblivious, like you're not seeing it."

He stared at Sade then his brows slowly narrowed. "Oh my God, no! No, no, no, that is a *very* bad idea."

"What—why?"

His jaw dropped in a huge gawk. "Dude! I need you to know that she is *already* suspicious of you, I told you that, she's *looking* for confirmation that you're a piece of shit and *that* right there…" He nodded vigorously with wide eyes, "That would do it!" He scooted up higher in bed and leaned toward him. "For some reason, whatever bad vibes she's got with you, crossed wires," he swirled his fingers at his head, "has her convinced there's something negative about you. Do that stunt and you prove it, you connect the wrong wires."

Sade growled, knowing he was right and sank back in his chair. "I was thinking it would spark her possessive side. I know she has it, I already see she's jealous, she's just not sure how to pursue it or what to do with it. I was hoping to get her in a position that makes her remember why."

"Ohhh-ho-ho," he said with wide eyes, "she'll choose alright, but you may not like what. Sure you'll spark her, and in comes Mercy Armageddon. No, dude, don't chance it."

Sade flopped his hands and let his head fall back. "The fuck do I do?"

"What if…" He looked at Sade full on now. "What if you used me and Liberty?"

"How?"

"I mean let me and Liberty you know, get kinky? But only not really!" he hurried with scared eyes.

"But… what would that do?"

"Well… it would make Mercy less worried about the two of you, allow her to let her guard down man, maybe you can use it as an opportunity to get some quiet time with her? I'm thinking you need to spend time with her without it looking like you're trying too hard."

"So just 'hey, while Bo and Liberty are busy, how about we' what?"

Bo shrugged. "Talk. Talk about helping her regain her memory, she's not opposed to that."

"She told you that? She won't let me get near her hardly."

"Yes, she told me, who wants to live without their memory? But if she's busy playing detective with you and Liberty, she won't be in a position to just relax with you, let it flow, let it come on its own. I think this may be like a touchy orgasm, you gotta," he flicked his tongue, "draw it out."

"Oh I'd love nothing more than to draw it out that way."

"I can imagine." He shot up both hands, "But I don't! You know what I mean. Foreplay man. Drag it out. Prime it."

"So you'll keep Liberty busy and that'll leave us…"

"Aloooone."

"I definitely like that part, I'm sick of her always wanting to be with your ass."

"Trust me, I *feel* that one!"

Sade eyed him with a grin. "Thanks man."

He shrugged. "Eh."

"I need to make sure Liberty will go for this, you aren't currently her favorite person."

"Pffffft. She can fuck herself with her middle robotic finger." He shot a wide stare at him. "She probably does." He sobered then and whispered, "All she has to do is agree not to drug me, or bitch will meet Curly and Mo." He alternated his fists, making Sade bust out laughing.

"Curly and Mo, huh?"

"Damn right."

## Chapter Thirteen

Mercy sat in her bed with her jaw dropped, the notebook shut tight, her heart racing and her privates on fire. She'd read their first meeting. At his tattoo shop. Oh. Dear. God. He was… so… She didn't know the word for that, she only knew her body felt like she'd just exited a roller coaster ride that had sexual attachments on the seat!

She'd never get the image out of her head of his face hovered over her butt, *smelling* her sex and being turned on by it. How he'd wanted to *hurt* her while he was aroused did… odd things to her. It wasn't serious pain, it was a tattoo, maybe that's what prevented her from being too disturbed. And he *was* a sadomasochist, but she'd not known that at the time. Had she? Surely not, why would she let him touch her if she'd known that? Odds were unlikely.

He'd said she'd wanted to help him with his sexual issues, but surely it didn't start out that way? Then again, she would've known about his condition if she'd wanted to help him. Was he telling the truth about that part? She really didn't know enough yet.

And had she been aroused when that had happened? She couldn't imagine not being. A Sex God with his hand on her butt. She must've been a wreck, how would she not be. Given her condition now she was sure she had been a mess. A very hot one. You may forget things, but you didn't remember things that didn't exist. Right? *Lord, I hate this. Please help my memory come back.*

She fanned her face and jumped when a knock sounded on the door."

"Come in," she yelled.

The door opened to her six-foot sex god dilemma. He made his way toward the bed on his crutches, and she was a fly in a web as she remembered the notebook! She needed to hide it! She needed to fix her face. She needed to check if she was hanging out of her clothes. She needed to not stare at him.

He stopped at the bed, concern on his handsome face. "You okay?"

"I… uh, yeah. I'm on…fine. I'm fine." Her voice broke on a squeak.

His gaze narrowed and then lowered to the bed. To the notebook. "Oh." Like that explained everything.

Heat burned her cheeks, and she looked down, clearing her throat.

"I was going to attempt cooking something for the party but… I'm not that great at it. Was wondering if you could give me some pointers."

"Oh," she said, relieved for the out. "Sure. Now?"

"We can get started, if you want. Not sure what I'm doing, maybe you can help with that part too. Just direct me, I can do it all."

"I'd be happy to. Let me get dressed and I'll meet you in the kitchen?"

"Works for me." He turned and headed toward the door like he was ready to leave as much as she was ready for him to go. Was he embarrassed? That would be helpful. "See you in a few."

And there he went, without turning back. She flopped back on the bed, gasping, heart still racing. Her hand touched the notebook and she lifted it again. She'd stopped at the part where Bo showed up at the shop. She was now dying to know how that ended. Screw it. She flipped to the page and quickly read.

"I almost forgot."

"Shit!" Mercy yelped, slamming the notebook to the bed, glancing at Sade's head in the door.

"Sorry, I should've knocked. Was going to ask if you needed me to get you anything."

"No, I'm fine. Thank you though." Now leave!

"See you." He shut the door, and again Mercy flopped back on the bed with a moan of shame.

What must he think? Why did he write all that? Did he mean to be so... X-rated about it? Something about him said that was all he knew, and it wasn't necessarily intentional. And if it was, why would he do that, seeing she was skittish in that area? God, who exactly was she before this? What did she let him do?

The need to find that out burned her fingers. Tonight. She'd finish reading all of it if it killed her.

She wondered then. Just how experienced was she in sex anyway? Her body said *zero,* but she was sure the things he wrote said otherwise.

She hurried to get dressed only to discover there was nothing quick about that puzzle. By the time she settled on the only possible way to wear the contraption, she was positive it couldn't be right and yet if it wasn't, then her chest down to her pubic hair would be uncovered. So it was backless. Which meant braless. That wasn't so much a problem as the halter being for a woman with actual fucking tits. She undid the hook behind her neck and tied the bitch so it actually fit. She'd have a fucking crick in her neck with the size bow she'd made.

All that was left was her hair. She grabbed the small clear makeup bag Liberty had dropped off and dug through it. She found bobby pins and fought them into her hair only to pull them all back out again. What if…

She yanked open the drawers and pulled out a pair of scissors and proceeded to cut the hair over her eyes. Interesting. Not too shabby. She added plenty of makeup now that you could see her eyes. When she was done, she was pleasantly pleased. Hello Cleopatra. She blew a kiss at herself in the mirror and turned sideways to see what she looked like. Oh my. Foxy Lady. She stuck her butt out a little farther, but it got lost in the folds of material. The only part that showed her body was where it hugged her waist and curved over her upper ass. Just enough mystery to make one curious.

When she got to the point of shoes, she stared at the ugly black Crocs she'd been wearing. It was the only thing Miss Liberty allowed the three little handicaps to wear. Except Mercy was in a dress, the guys weren't. She found black socks at least to blend her feet to the shoes.

Plus the dress covered her feet. She'd just have to keep it that way. Mercy remembered Liberty's spiked *everybody look at me, like me, fuck me* heels and wanted to spit.

God, what was she doing? She was going to a damn party, not a competition. And she wanted to look pretty. Nothing wrong with that fucking crap, my *God!*

****

Liberty had agreed gladly to the change of plans—not liking the idea of pissing Mercy off. As Sade inspected the freezer supplies, he wondered if Mercy decided to stay and read his journal. The look on her face when he'd walked back in and caught her reading said she was extremely affected. And not in an entirely negative way. Her arousal screamed to him, begging him to answer it. And what did she think of him now that she was reading? He suddenly wished he'd not written so crassly and direct. He'd written with everything he was, his heart and mind, and a hard cock. And the former was expressed with the latter.

"I was thinking I'd sit in the kitchen and let you take the wheelchair to Bo so he can get around."

Sade turned and froze at finding Mercy there. His eyes locked on the halter top and the milky skin between the strips of material. Holy. Fuck. His dick grew rock hard as he searched the material for her nipples the second his mind told him *no bra.* He finally looked at her face. She'd... done something.

"I cut my hair," she helped, pointing to her eyes.

"Wow," he gasped. "Fucking beautiful."

She pffed and looked down, the silver earrings dangling. He was suddenly so elated that they had changed their plans to letting them be together. The idea of being anywhere but glued to her side made him unstable.

She eyed him and his nipples and cock tingled with the memory of his own body piercings that he'd quit wearing years ago but now... he suddenly wanted to impress her. "You look nice," she muttered.

He refused to wear a suit like Bo and settled for black slacks and matching dress shirt untucked. But seeing her pretty smile and pink cheeks made him glad he'd crammed himself into the stuffy outfit.

"You're staring," she muttered, looking down.

"Sorry. You're just..."

"It was a bit big. I don't have enough at the top… lord, shut up Mercy," she muttered.

He made his way over to her on the crutches, and she looked up, that fear in her gaze knotting his stomach and making him unsure. "Can I help you into the chair?"

"I can… kinda walk, I'm not entirely cripple." She raised her feet, showing her black Crocs. "You like my dress shoes? I'm all matching."

He smiled. "I do actually. I need to get me some like that."

She giggled, looking at his, glad he had the ugly crocs on too.

"Just let me help you." She looked up at him, maybe hearing the need saturating his tone. "Please. Keep the doc happy."

"I doubt she'd be happy with you carrying…" She rolled her eyes then. "Okay."

Sade thought about how to do that now, setting the crutches against the island. "I'm going to put one hand behind your knees and the other behind your back. Put your arm around my neck."

"Okay," she mumbled, wrapping his neck tight as he got into position.

Sade stifled the orgasmic moan at finally *feeling her.* "Fuck you smell edible," he gasped, barely biting his tongue on *I want to eat you right here, right now, on the table.* He made the transference, not wanting it to end.

He grabbed his crutches and backed away before he put his lips on her. He'd devour her if he did. "I'll bring Bo the chair and be right back."

She nodded, not meeting his gaze, telling him the little non-incident shook her. This was going to be slow fucking going. But a very big part of him loved slow and tormenting.

He made his way into the wheelchair and placed the crutches along his shoulder and between his feet.

"You got it?" she asked.

Her concern made him smile. "Yeah, we're quite a party. Three cripples, one wheelchair and a pair of crutches."

"I could walk the crutches behind you."

"And you could ride me on the way back?"

He glanced back, happy to see her smiling.

"Piggyback," she muttered.

He was thinking more of her riding his cock but yeah. "See you in a bit."

"Take your time."

He was glad she was unable to go anywhere. Once he returned, he stood the crutches next to the snack bar and sat across from her. "So, I was thinking we could do hamburgers and french fries?"

She smiled at that, making his heart speed up. "What, is that too American? Too simple?" She was so fucking beautiful when she smiled and the brief warmth of it suddenly drove him to have more.

"You're staring again."

"I am. Maybe I'm waiting for your answer."

She blushed and looked down, making him feel guilty. "Yeah, that sounds good."

"What will I need?"

"Two more hands to start. How do you plan to do this on crutches?"

He cocked his jaw and squinted at her. "Good point. I wasn't thinking of that."

"We have pizza? That's easy."

"Tons. Boxes and boxes of it in the walk in freezer."

"There's a walk-in freezer?"

He pointed at a silver door next to the fridge.

"I thought that was the pantry!"

"Nope."

"Wow, this place is like…"

"The Batcave?"

She giggled a little with a twinkle in her eyes, making his heart skip a beat.

"Why do you do that," she whined.

"What?"

She looked around. "Keep staring at me. I feel weird, like you see something out of place."

"That's not it."

"I don't even want to know."

"You don't? Good, I didn't want to tell you."

She raised brows at him, a slight smile on her lips. "I think I might be rebellious."

"You are." More excitement made him grin before it slowly faded. "So… how far did you get into my little journal?"

Her eyes widened briefly before she looked right. "Not too far. The tattoo shop."

"Hm. Now I'm embarrassed."

"You should be. You should be ashamed in fact."

"I should, yes. I mean I am."

Her gaze slowly meandered back to him. "And you're a terrible liar."

"I am, yes," he laughed. "It's hard for me to feel bad about one of the best memories I have."

"Oh my God, stop," she muttered, stroking a hand across her brow.

"It's true."

"No doubt, I'm not saying it isn't, it's just pathetic that you would enjoy something like that so much."

"Pathetic!" He put a hand on his chest. "Seriously, where did you stop? Exactly?"

"Bo shows up. It's like reading a soap opera."

"And you can't wait to keep reading?"

"I dread what's coming."

He bit his tongue on so many things, feeling like he needed to choose his words carefully. This was it. He was positioning. "You like music?"

She widened her eyes and pursed her pretty lips a little. "I think? Do I?"

"Yes, you do. I have some planned that I know you like. To hopefully help with your…" He pointed to his head.

"Right. Good." She nodded before narrowing her gaze. "Is that what you're wearing? To the party?"

He looked down. "I was, why?"

"Oh, nothing, you look fine."

He grinned. "I do?"

"I mean it's not a ball or anything."

"Well, you look so fucking hot in that."

She lowered her head and it made his dick hard. "Um. Ok. Don't know why thank you is so hard. Was I always bad at accepting compliments?"

He gave a slow smile, loving talking about her. "Maybe."

"So what do we have to drink in this place?"

"Would you like a cocktail?"

"Uh." Her brows furrowed and she shook her head. "I'm drawing a blank. What is that?"

"A mixed drink." He gave a small grin with the grimace she gave.

"Am I a drinker? I mean I don't want to if I can't handle it."

"Are you still taking any meds?"

"Just Ibuprofen when I need it."

His licked his lower lip as the sudden idea hit him. "You should be fine." She could stand a little help loosening her mental straps. He'd just make sure she didn't go too far.

"You sure?"

He gave her a small smile and wink. "You can trust me, Angel."

She regarded him with a pointed glare. "You realize you look and sound like the big bad wolf right now?"

He busted out laughing in light shock. "What? Not me, never."

"We'll see."

"We will?"

"If you were honest in your journal, I'll find out."

"I was…extremely honest."

"Hmm." She raised her brows, staring at her laced fingers on the snack bar.

"Too bad you can't use your feet, or you could dance with me."

She eyed him. "You can dance?"

He nodded, watching her struggle to remember. "I don't remember," she mumbled.

"It'll come."

"I don't remember even if I can dance." She eyed him, her eyes reminding him of emerald jewels. "Can I?"

He nodded again. "Very well."

"Really! Like... how?"

"Oh my God." He held his chest. "Some of the sexiest pop ballet I've ever seen."

Her jaw dropped with narrowed gaze. "How can I not remember something so major?"

"You only danced once for me. And you had been out of practice for years." He licked his lips, watching her dancing in his mind. "Best performance I've ever seen done in panties and a t-shirt."

She covered her face with both hands and the vulnerable gesture tempted things in him he'd not tasted in a while. "Jeez." She flopped her hands on her lap and looked around. "Five forty-five. We should probably put the pizza on around six I think."

"I should probably say fuck it and give in."

"To what?" she asked, looking worried.

"To walking up to you and kissing the fuck out of you." His dick got so fucking hard at seeing it for the first time—desire with that fear. And the concoction was staggering.

She fanned her face, not realizing she demonstrated he'd just made her *hot*. Dear God.

"You're hot baby?"

"Oh my God, stop," she whispered. "I'm not…used to that."

"Practice makes perfect."

"I bet Bo can use some help," she said.

He gave a deep sigh at seeing his fun was over. For now. "I think Liberty can handle him. But I'll go double check," he added at seeing she needed a moment. "You want to get comfortable on the couch and wait? Maybe read a good book?"

Her pretty green eyes flashed with knowing and lit him up all over again.

"No," he said, "you definitely can't read my book since it affects you so much."

She gave a light gasp. "Affects me," she muttered, back to twisting her fingers on the counter before her. "Of course it does, it's full of some weird man doing weird things."

"Yes, to you."

"Well I don't even remember it, how do I know you're not just making all that up?"

He threw his head back and laughed then finally met her annoyed gaze. "I'm not that creative."

"Says you."

He nodded at her. "Okay, okay. I could be making it all up, being very creative. But why would I? What in the world would making all that up, do for you? Or me for that matter. I'm trying to help bring back your memory."

"Or maybe you're making new ones? Maybe the old ones weren't that great?"

His smile slowly faded as he stared at her. "Don't say that. They were beyond great, they were fucking phenomenal."

She raised her brows. "Wow. I must've been awesome."

"You were. And are."

She straightened up and looked toward the living room. "Think I'm ready to get comfortable now." She made moves to get off the stool.

"What are you doing, you can't walk."

"Oh come on," she whispered, already hobbling slowly. "It's not that bad," she said, her words breathless with pain.

Sade hurried as fast as he could to her with the crutches. "That's far enough for you."

"Yes," she gasped, hands trembling as she worked the crutches under her arms. "How come your feet are so much better than mine?"

He shook his head, hobbling carefully to the couch after her, staring at her fucking bare back and ass. "I wouldn't say *so much* better. Fuck, you look amazing in that."

"Oh, let me get to the couch, stop where you are and I'll slide you the crutches!"

"I'm halfway there."

She plopped down on the couch. "Here, here." She slid the crutches along the glassy floor and Sade jumped to avoid the collision with his feet. A half roar of agony came with his palms hitting the cement floor, barely missing a face plant, all while Mercy squealed *oh my God oh my God.*

"I'm sooooo sorry, the floor is slippery!"

"Don't worry about it," he grunted, sitting for a moment.

"You're bleeding," she gasped. "I'm so sorry."

"Mercy, just stay on the couch," he said as she crawled in her black dress toward him.

"I'm not even using my feet," she huffed, sitting next to him and reaching toward his foot.

He slapped her hand away. "I don't think so."

"What?" she cried softly. "I'm just seeing."

"You use your eyes for that."

"I mean I wanted to see how bad, silly."

"Oh it's fine, it's perfect."

She sat with her legs straight out, hand over her mouth. "I am so sorry."

"Yeah, you said that already."

"Well I am, what else do you want me to say, how was I supposed to know the stupid thing would go flying?"

"Thank you for listening to me."

She choked with light offense. "I was just trying to help."

"I know. Thank you. Really, I owe you."

She eyed him with worry now. "We're good, no need." She crawled and retrieved the runaway crutch and sat back down, handing it to him. "You need the wheelchair for a while. Bo and I can share the crutches."

"I just fucking brought it to him."

"Well you just earned it back."

"Good. Then I can offer you the same taxi service you gave him."

She went quiet and he eyed her before using the crutches to get up. Yeah, that's right. Busted, baby.

"I'll be right back," he said. "Stay put."

She crawled her way back to the couch and climbed up, mumbling, "I'll try not to fly off."

He grinned as he left, glad she still had her sense of humor.

## Chapter Fourteen

At Bo's door, Sade knocked softly.

"Come in," Bo yelled.

"Stop moving before I slice you open," Liberty ordered as Sade opened the door. "You're not an ADD six-year-old."

"No, I'm an ADD twenty-four-year-old who can shave himself. Sade!" Bo cried, "Tell Scissor Hand she's being ridiculous, I don't even need to shave!"

"You need to shave, you're starting to look like a drunk," Liberty said.

"No, that's them stupid Crocs you have us all wearing, we all look like mental patients."

She aimed the razor at Bo. "And call me a name again, you get your jugular cut." Now she aimed it at Sade. "I'm not risking him opening his cuts. Sorry, padre."

"But you'll cut my jugular?"

"Damn right I will."

"Don't mind me," Sade said. "I was just coming to leave the crutches. Decided to use the wheels."

Liberty's hawk eyes flew to his feet, and he was glad he was standing on the evidence oozing in his socks. "Good. Finally acting like you have a lick of sense. We'll be there as soon as Mr. Pretty Boy lets me finish."

"You just like touching me," Bo mumbled while Liberty went back to work. "Look at her, see what I'm saying," Bo angled only his eyes at Sade while she held the top of his head in her claw. "This is abuse."

She only smiled and suddenly Bo began to ow-ow-ow. "Now that's abuse," she muttered. "I can crush your skull if you get too pissy with me."

"See what I mean?" Bo gasped.

"Crutches will be right here. You're in good hands."

"Good hand!" Bo corrected. "There ain't nothing good about her claw. Ow-ow, I'm sorry!"

"Better be," she said, smiling while carefully navigating his face.

Sade shook his head with a grin and got himself into the chair. "We'll see you two love birds at seven?"

"Or sooner if he cooperates," Liberty said. "Get the music ready. Guess I'll be the only one dancing. Unless you know how to dance on your asses." She laughed as he shut the door.

Sade thought about that. He did know how to dance off his feet. He used to perform a lot of his dance moves on his knees, stomach and back, come to think of it. He might need to wait 'til Liberty was too wasted to notice or care, he wasn't going to do that in front of her. His public performance days were way the fuck over.

Back in the living room, he found Mercy in the same place. "You want to help me put the pizza on? I'll be your ride." His cock jerked hard at imagining her in his lap.

She gave a snort as he rounded the couch and eyed her. "Oh, you're serious."

"We do need to get it on and you did say you'd help." He loved how everything he said was pure sexual innuendo.

"You want me to sit on you?" she said, hoping he heard how crazy that was.

"I do. Yes. Very, very much." He ignored her suggestion that the idea was preposterous. "You ride with Bo and not me?" He couldn't bring himself to say sit on Bo, the idea made him crazy.

"That's different." Like that were obvious.

"How fucking so?"

Her jaw dropped. "Because we're… you know."

"More reason for you to sit on me."

"Stop saying it like that."

"You started it."

"But I didn't mean it like you clearly do."

He shrugged a shoulder. "Are you going to ride me or not?"

She looked straight ahead and gave a sigh.

"I won't bite you."

That earned him a glare. "Really."

"Unless you want." He had to laugh at her look. "Trust me when I say you're not a coy little virgin."

"Something tells me that's all thanks to you."

He put a hand on his chest. "I merely directed what was there, and begging."

"I think you had better just roll yourself over and do the job."

"Can I have a kiss instead?"

She leveled an incredulous look at him.

"What? Just a small one. On the cheek." He rolled near the couch and leaned, giving her easy access. "Please," he mumbled.

"For what?" she shrilled quietly.

"For busting my foot, if you must have a reason."

She gave a light huff and leaned in. Sade turned and intercepted her lips with his, grabbing her face and holding her while he tasted her sexy fucking lips briefly and let go. He rolled off while she was still in the shock and awe phase.

"That was wrong," she called behind him.

"No baby, that was right," he called back, not the least sorry. "My foot agrees," he added as he made his way to the kitchen. As silly as it may have been, he still wasn't happy that she rode in a wheelchair with another man and not him. Bo was his brother, but who was he to her? Just a stranger.

After he managed to get the pizza in the oven from a wheelchair, he made his way to the media center along the stone wall.

He finally located the control for the large TV that he hoped held the music collection since there was nothing but that. He studied the control and saw fireplace. Hmm. He hit the button and that huge space that appeared to be an empty slab of black granite lit up with a low roar.

"Ohhhhh neat," Mercy said. "Who would guess that was a fireplace!"

"Who would guess you'd need it?" He aimed the control at the TV and pressed power.

"It's romantic."

He glanced back at her, remembering the word he'd heard her use before. It was still considered foreign to his brain, but not his body. It meant something to her, and he considered it a doorway in. "I forgot you like romance."

"Well if it makes you feel any better, I don't remember liking it."

He turned his chair and faced her. "You don't?"

She shrugged. "Not really. I know the concept, but I don't have the feeling of the memory of it. Should I assume we never did romantic things?"

"No, you shouldn't."

"What did we do?"

He raised his brows and saw the remote allowed you to search songs right on it. "Stuff."

She snorted. "Like what?"

"You'll have to read."

"Oh Lord. If you can't tell me then it's likely not romantic."

"Depends on how you define romantic."

"How do you define it?"

He scrolled through the classic selection and found her song that she danced to. "You. Dancing for me. In your panties and t-shirt."

She gave a roll of her eyes. "Figures." But he didn't miss the flush in her cheeks or the way she fiddled with her fingers in her lap.

He watched her closely as the song came on loud enough to *feel* it. She soon began bobbing her head, and when the words came, she began to mutter them, making his heart want to leap from his chest.

"I know this," she suddenly gasped, looking at him.

He gave her a smile, so happy with that. "You should."

"I should?" She moved more now, letting the music take her. "Only looooove," she sang softly, "can make it rain…."

"This is the one you danced to for me."

Her jaw dropped. "In panties and a t-shirt?"

He made his way to the couch to get closer. "God, yes."

Her mouth remained gaping and her brows narrowed as she fought to remember, all while her body moved to the tune. She finally gave a sharp exhale of "I don't remember!" She nailed him with perplexity in her pretty green gaze. "This song?"

"Yes, that song," he said, his hopes slipping a little.

She continued singing then shook her head without stopping. "I don't remember dancing to that! Amazing that I can't remember! And you said I did some kind of contemporary ballet? Oh, I like this part! Looooooooooove," she wailed out of key. "Rain ooooover meeeee."

Sade found himself torn with being disappointed and enraptured with her here and now. There was plenty more memories to jar. Maybe a little alcohol to help with the process.

"Where you going?" she called over the music.

"Get us a drink."

"I'll take a coke."

"A coke," he mumbled.

He wheeled himself to the bar at the back of the room and inspected the supplies. Finding all the ingredients he could want, he mixed with practiced ease and returned to the couch and handed Mercy hers.

She took the small glass. "Orange juice?"

"Yep."

She raised her brows and sniffed then jerked her head back. "Oh my God!"

"And alcohol. It's called a Slow Screw. Come on, try it. A sip."

"It smells awful."

"Then don't smell it."

She took a sample taste and her face tightened with a grimace. "Oh shit, that's nasty! Tell me I wasn't a drinker!"

"You weren't a drinker."

"You're lying?"

"No, I'm not lying," he said, finding the remote and turning the music down enough that they could talk. "You weren't. I'll never forget the first time you drank in fact."

She eyed him and took another sip. "What happened?"

"You'll have to read it."

"Oh come on!"

Sade downed his drink and set it on the table while she eyed him. "What was your drink?"

He glanced at the empty glass then back at her. "Something I really love." She waited with raised brows and he grinned at her. "A Screaming Orgasm."

She gave a huge eye roll. "Figures." She took another sip and looked at it. "Not so bad after the first few sips. Is everything about sex with you?" she asked, seeming genuinely curious.

"With you, yes. Otherwise, it's mostly about pain in some form. But you taught me new tricks."

"I did?" She raised her brows and stirred her drink with the straw, making the ice clink. "Like what? Or do I have to read? And do I even want to know?"

He shrugged, putting his feet on the coffee table. "You taught me how to soul mesh."

"Soul mesh?" Her brows furrowed with her squeak of disbelief. "I taught you how to soul mesh? Excuse my Latin but what the fuck is that?"

Sade busted out laughing and shook his head. "I think it's French, but it's something you were very good at."

"Is that a sexual maneuver or something?" Her face screwed up, making him want to kiss her.

"No, it wasn't sexual, but I did use it during sexual things."

She bit her lip and nodded then stared into her drink before taking another sip. "I almost remember that," she muttered.

"Really?" His heart sped up.

"Yeah, no. Not really. I'm just…" She wagged her hand. "Was joking. It's not ringing a bell, my mind literally drew a picture of this blob next to a fish net of some kind." She eyed him. "What?"

"It was so much more special than that."

She looked at him around her glass as she sipped, nodding. "Sounds… kinda corny. Even creepy, don't you think?"

It was Sade's turn to roll his eyes.

"It does, admit it."

"It did at first until you did it."

"Are you sure you're not mixing me up with somebody?" Sade glared at her, and she cried, "I'm kidding! Jeez, you're all sensitive about the mesh memory!"

"They're us."

"Well, I'm sure I'll get them all back any minute, you said that." Again she eyed him as she drank more and he realized she was asking.

"Yes. I'm sure."

She downed all her drink, making Sade wonder what was going through her head. He could see her wheels turning and hoped he didn't have to drag it out. "What if I don't get them back? Then what?"

His heart hammered fiercely at the idea. "I prefer to think positive."

"I mean how great are these memories, it was only a month, if that."

"If that?"

"Well, maybe you miscalculated." She stared at her empty drink, stirring still. "I don't see you as the type of guy to mark off days on the calendar."

He stared at her for a long while, trying to figure out how to put his anger into words without saying something he'd regret. "The memories are very fucking great. I never want to forget. Ever. I'd rather die than not have these memories. Is that great enough for you?"

"Wow," she said, looking amazed. "Yeah, so for sure I'll remember them, they sound impossible to forget, really."

"Yes, they are."

"Can I get another one like this? It was delicious," she said with a tipsy exuberance.

"Absolutely."

Sade made his way to the bar and made her another one, a little stronger this time. That would be enough for her. She'd be at her limit with that. And then what? Perform sexual acts to jog her memory?

Finally, Bo and Liberty made it to the party—Bo on crutches, Liberty behind him. The strained smile he wore said he was biting his tongue hard. What a show.

Sade wasn't surprised that both of them took all of thirty minutes to get shit faced. After Sade burned the pizza, he decided to pop popcorn to go with the show Liberty was soon putting on.

By the time he got back with it, he realized that their little plan was in full swing with Bo playing the pimp and Liberty playing his whore. Quite well, he might add. It had Mercy in a very foul mood when he returned. "Mind if I sit by you?"

"Oh, by all means, this is a free country. Couch is plenty big enough for two." He handed her the popcorn bowl before moving from the wheelchair to couch. "Popcorn to enjoy the show. Nice."

He sat next to her, and she moved over, putting twelve inches between them. Wow. Sade couldn't help be amazed at how the insignificant act could cause such a dense ache inside him. He mentally threw a *fuck it* card down and made the next move, reaching for her hand. She didn't fight him but she didn't reciprocate either.

Liberty danced to the media center and changed the music and then gyrated her way back to Bo. If he wasn't mistaken, she seemed to be already shitfaced. He glanced at Bo's goofy grin and realized so was he.

Sade angled his head toward Mercy. "I use to dance."

"Did you," she said loudly. "What kind?"

"The dirty kind. At my dad's nightclub. Not something I'm proud of."

"Did I know this before?" she asked, leaning in too far, like her depth perception was off.

"Not that part, no."

"Ohhhh nice," she said, with raised brows. "Now I know something I didn't before. I'm starting to feel like a new person." She nodded and Sade felt bad that everything he said and did pointed to some reality she didn't like.

She moved to the music in her seat like maybe her body remembered how. He angled his head and watched her.

She leaned over without looking at him. "You're staring," she informed.

He smiled. "Yes, I can't help it."

"It's not nice to stare." She shook her head, dancing back into her spot. "You like being stared at?" She looked at him now.

"By you, yes."

She rolled her eyes, her cheeks turning pink. She gestured in front of her. "Go ahead then."

"Go ahead?"

"Dance for me. Give me that memory back."

He stared at her, trying to figure out if she was serious while his cock grew harder by the second. She had no idea what kind of dancing he meant. It would be worth it just seeing the look on her face.

"You promise not to laugh?"

She nodded real big and yelled, "Promise! What about your feet, I forgot," she said suddenly worried.

He shrugged and stood. "I'll live." Would be worth the sacrifice if it helped her remember.

Sade pushed the coffee table back, giving himself room. Walking back up to her, he stopped at the couch when she was staring up at him, curiosity mixed with that ever-present heat in her green gaze. He gave his body over to the music and began his filthy dance right before her, keeping his eyes locked to hers while he invited her to fuck with erotic rolls of his hips and body, before grabbing his cock and flicking hard to let her know he wouldn't be taking no for a fucking answer.

Her jaw slowly dropped wider as she pressed herself further into the couch, her eyes following his hands as they slowly removed his shirt then threw it in her face. Her audible gasp came with a darted gaze toward Bo and Liberty. Before she could get too worried about the audience, he fell forward, bracing his palms on either side of her before straddling her legs and bringing the nasty to her pretty, shocked face.

Unlike the women he'd danced for before, she sat frozen beneath him as he kissed her and fucked her without touching. He was close enough to hear and feel her gasps on his skin as she stared at the show before her.

He leaned his face to hers, not breaking his sexual assault dance, gasping in her ear. "No touching," he teased.

"Ohhhh," Bo cried.

Sade noticed Liberty out of the corner of his eye climb onto Bo's lap. He looked long enough to see if Bo was okay or if he needed rescuing now that Liberty was clearly drunk. But the way he held her hips tight, and the heat in his gaze at a thousand degrees as he watched her, said he was all too fine. Thank God for that. He was actually hoping that might happen.

He turned to Mercy to find her glaring at him. "No, don't stop looking." She shoved him off of her and grabbed the bowl on the coffee table. "Have some popcorn," she hissed, dumping it on him before hobbling out of the room with no crutches.

"Fuck," he muttered, getting in the wheelchair and racing after her.

"Let me give you a ride," he said behind her.

"Get away from me," she muttered.

"What's wrong? It isn't whatever you're thinking, I can assure you."

"You're a pig, go fuck yourself. Maybe you and Bo can do Liberty in fact, she looks like she's open for that."

"Mercy, stop!"

"Fuck you and don't call me Mercy!" He stopped at her door where she fought to open it. "I don't like Mercy," she grit, looking at him with hate burning in her green gaze. "She sounds like a pathetic little stupid girl with cotton balls for brains. Soul mesh? That is the *stupidest* thing I've ever heard. And you're stupid for liking it." By then she was in the door and slammed it in his face, leaving Sade confused and dumbfounded. And pissed. How dare she fucking talk that way? About the woman he loved? Her!

He hurried to his room and slammed the door as hard as he could, hoping she would *feel* it in her bones the way he felt the pain her ugly words caused him. Everything was fucked up, and the Mercy he knew was gone. Just fucking gone. And this person she was now barely fucking liked him.

## Chapter Fifteen

Mercy limped her way to her bed and threw herself on it. She wanted to be sad, guilty, something, anything. But all she was, was… pissed. The way he'd stared at Liberty… how dare he? And what the hell kind of person had Mercy been that he thought it was okay to do that with her sitting right there? At *all* if he's supposed to be *in love.* Ha!

She may not remember who she was, but she'd be *damned* if she was going to stand around and put up with that. The old her obviously had some hang-ups and thank God, she didn't remember those. And Mr. *you'll have to read it.* Fuck him. Fine, she'd read it.

She grabbed the notebook from the table and began where she'd left off. It didn't take but five minutes for her to forgot her anger and become fascinated with the man Sade, and how he perceived her. As she devoured the words, she struggled to remember them. Flashes, sparks, anything. But it was like reading a story of him and another woman. She had to keep reminding herself that it wasn't another woman, it was her, just to keep from getting pissed.

She shut the book with a gasp as she realized. She was *jealous!* Jealous and couldn't remember shit! Wait a minute, no. No, she wasn't jealous. Not literally or actually. No, this was more like… conceptual jealousy. Her brain knew she was supposed to be the love of his life and so she expected him to behave like it, and when he didn't, yes, conceptual jealousy switch got flipped.

But God, reading him and this person she once was, it was like reading a stranger. And it was becoming sadly clear that either A: He had no idea what love actually was, or B: she had been a complete, blind, moron.

She continued reading and again, everything faded away. Soon she was at the part where she first went to his house. He had her there to interrogate her, only he'd lied and said he needed help cleaning his condo. And she fell for that? Maybe he'd been a great *player*. Maybe he'd hit his head and lost the memory of how to be that, because he sucked at it now. Or maybe hitting her head knocked sense into her!

Her lip quirked as she read on.

*Then I gave you that naughty drink to loosen you up. That was the first time I encountered your fiery side.*

Naughty drink? What did that mean?

*When you woke up, we had a nice chat.*

Woke up?

*And although I never found out what you wanted, I decided the strange anomaly that you were was worth going to prison over, and so we signed a contract.*

Signed a contract! What! The actual! Fuck!

Mercy read on, mouth stuck open as she tried to follow the events. It was like they'd been given by a rambling drunk. They'd signed a contract, and she had no real clue why.

She skimmed on and got to something interesting. Only to read, *"And then I did that thing that made you tie me up."*

She slammed the notebook shut and scrambled out of bed only to realize she had no transportation. Making her way onto her hands and knees, she crawled to the door and opened it. Looking left and right, she then crawled to Sade's door and knocked.

"What!"

She opened the door and saw his bandaged feet at the end of the bed. "What thing did you do that made me tie you up?"

He bolted up in bed, looking at her.

"Sorry if you were expecting other company."

"I wasn't," he barked. "And I'm not telling." He laid back down and Mercy slammed his door shut and crawled to his bed. Climbing up, she gasped and lowered back to the floor.

"You're naked!"

"And?"

"Cover yourself!"

"Why? This is my room."

"Because I asked you to."

"That's not asking, try again."

"Please cover yourself for crying out loud."

She heard him sigh, and the bed moved around. "There."

She got back up and gasped, dropping to the floor again. "Sade!"

"You didn't say cover *what!*"

"Oh my *God.* You are such a player, aren't you? Playing on words, playing on lives? Playing in your little stories, guess what I meant, guess what I did. How am I supposed to remember anything with your sloppy recollection?"

He sat up and stared at her. "You want to remember?"

"Of course I do! Do you want to help me? And what the hell contract did we sign and *why?* So much of what you wrote baffles my mind, why are you leaving so many parts out?"

"I'm not a writer. You suggested I write it. Are you ready for me to show you?"

She sat with her jaw dropped. "I'm ready for you to *tell* me."

"I'm not telling you that."

"Why not?"

"Not necessary."

"This must paint you in a bad light, I'm guessing? I don't even get to know how I managed to tie you up. Was this some sexcapade or-or sadomasochistic thing?"

"No."

"Then what?"

He crossed his legs and looked right then shook his head. "I can't tell you."

"Why not?"

His hot gaze pinned hers suddenly. "Because I'm not proud of it, okay?"

That wasn't what she'd expected to hear and suddenly felt... bad. The guilty kind. "So what, we've all done things we're not proud of." She climbed on the bed, keeping her gaze averted. "Look... I would like for you to help me remember. But... you have to trust me too."

"You don't even like me."

"I never said that."

"Angel," he muttered. She saw his head shaking out the corner of her eye.

"Can you please cover?" He jerked a pillow over his groin and she let out a sigh of relief, looking at him. "Okay, fine. I'll try harder."

"I don't want your charity," he muttered, still looking away.

"Then help me remember."

"I'd have to touch you for that."

"Fine."

He looked at her and she nearly exploded from what she saw in those desperate depths. "You're fucking not ready," he said, looking down.

"Of course I'm not, I don't remember crap, but I mean that's the whole point. Helping me remember."

He covered his face with both hands and scrubbed it a few seconds. "I don't know."

"Well how else am I supposed to remember?"

"Time. Time, that's all."

"And you're okay with that?"

"I don't have a fucking choice," he yelled at her.

The burst of anger lit her own. "And how is that my fault?"

"I never said it was," he yelled again.

"You blame me!"

"I don't fucking blame you. I blame *me!* I'm the reason this happened, all of it!"

"Then help me fix it!"

"I can't play that game with you."

"What game?"

"You putting yourself in my reach then denying me. I can't handle it!"

"Fine then I won't."

"You can't help it!"

"Then… make it so I can."

Silence stretched between them. "You don't know what you're asking."

"Maybe I don't, but… I want to remember," she gasped, fighting her frustration. "I need to. I'm sick of… knowing things and not knowing them, feeling and not understanding what I'm feeling. Please," she begged.

"I can't start something if you won't let me finish it."

"I give you my word."

He shook his head. "Your word," he whispered.

"What?"

He looked at her for many seconds. "You once told me that. And I believed you."

"Did I disappoint?"

"No, Angel," he said quietly. "But… you don't even remember me or even who you are."

She swallowed down a wave of emotion. "Why did we do a contract then?"

"Because *I* didn't trust you. I didn't *know* you. I suggested it and you agreed. At the time, I did it just to have you, to play with you. To *use* you. I didn't think you really wanted to help me, but I was ready to have fun letting you try."

She stared at him, swallowing, appreciating his honesty. "Well then, maybe that's a good idea, we'll do a contract. I don't trust you, you don't trust me, so it works perfectly. We'll have Bo and Liberty witness it if you want."

The way he stared at her made her almost wish she'd never come to his room. Almost. "Angel, you got a fucking deal."

"Good," she said, ready to vomit right there. "You draw up your conditions, I'll draw up mine. We'll exchange them."

"When?"

"Thirty…" She realized she wanted to finish that journal first. "An hour. And a half." His brows raised. "Before we chicken out."

"Not a problem," he challenged.

"Fine then." She climbed her way to the floor.

"Take the wheelchair."

"No, I got it. You need it more than me," she said lightly, feeling stupid, knowing he was probably staring at her ass.

"See you soon, Angel," he said as she shut his door and made her way to hers. "Shit, shit, shit," she whispered, crawling her way back to her bed. She'd done it, hadn't she? She was in the shit now. She'd felt sorry for him, that's what she'd done! No, no, it wasn't just that, she'd also secured a means to learn about who he really was. And who she was in the process. Wow. Maybe some of her old moronic self was coming back.

She quickly got on the bed, pulled his journal out and read the rest. During the final pages, it all crashed in on her, line after line of sadomasochistic nightmare. But the nightmare was all his, not hers. She sucked in his pain and agony until she couldn't breathe with it. His torment, his sadistic drive, loving the pain while loathing it. His tug of war was so vicious in his mind and body. Did he realize what he'd written? What he'd shown her? He likely didn't see it as clearly as she did, and judging by the self-condemnation, he was still blinded to it and by it.

So this was it? What she'd wanted to help him with? Freeing him from that torment? She very much could believe she'd tried. Especially after reading that. But what had hooked her and brought her to that point in his life, was still the big question. Something had to have happened to make her want to help him to begin with.

Her mind replayed the things he'd done. The things she let him do. The things she'd done to him. She gasped and fanned her face. No wonder she was a wreck around him. Her body remembered all that. If only her mind would, so there wasn't only terror to go with that. If only she could remember the other things that went with those acts. And *those acts.* It was like reading... bad porn gone wrong, some kind of... triple X-rated, horror story. Dear. Freaking. God. He was right, she shouldn't have read it.

But she had. She closed her eyes and the images of his sweaty body between her legs, behind her, pressing into her stole her breath. She gasped several times for air suddenly wondering... *what did that feel like?*

*You tasted better than anything I'd ever put my mouth on. I had every part of you. There was nothing that got my cock harder than licking your clit till you shuddered in orgasm and screamed my name, except when I buried it as deep as I could go. That... that was fucking heaven. And seeing that look in your eyes...that love...*

Her mind flew to the final words he'd written in his journal, the ones that hit her the hardest.

*Baby, I miss you.*

She clutched her chest at remembering that part. Why did that hurt? Steal her breath? He missed her and... she... was sure she was angry about it. She didn't like him missing this other woman she couldn't remember how to be. Worse, she felt like the evil impersonating twin sister. Yes, she got the amazing guy but what did it matter when you knew deep down it wasn't you they loved, but somebody else?

Oh God, if she just remembered then it would fix that mess in her head. She wanted to remember. She wanted to remember, yes, that's what she wanted. She wanted to *feel* that memory, she wanted to taste what he painted, feel it, not just... try to or imagine. She could never imagine that. She needed to remember, and he needed to help her.

She bolted up in bed realizing. No! No, no, no, she didn't need to remember it. She needed to live it for the first time. Now.

## Chapter Sixteen

Sade sat on his bed, dumbfounded. But only for a moment. Desire kicked in and he hobbled to the kitchenette, looking for that pen he'd seen. Grabbing it off the microwave, he limped to his bed and sat, snatching the tiny notepad from the table that he'd found in a drawer.

Contract. What would he put in this contract? Fifteen minutes later, he was on the last paper with *nothing* worthy of a contract. Everything he tried to write bound him in ways he didn't like or limited him in a way he might need.

He finally settled on the only thing he could agree to. And if she couldn't agree to that, then it was pointless.

Putting the paper between his lips, he grabbed the crutches, headed to her room, and knocked on her door.

"Come in."

He opened the door and made his way to the bed and gave her the paper. She promptly opened it up, read, and then aimed furrowed brows at him. "You want me to agree to let you do whatever you need to? No specifics? I'm just supposed to sign that? Do you know what that would require of me?"

"Trust?"

She choked with wide eyes. "No, not trust! Would require me to be a brainless *moron*!"

"So that's no."

She stared at him, mouth still ajar then looked down, shaking her head at the paper. "This is preposterous." She looked right and grabbed her pen on the bed. "You had better not make me regret trusting you, Sade, I mean it."

His heart hammered as she signed her name on that crooked line below the sloppy one sentence. "Date it."

She glared up at him then looked back down. "Maybe you can do that."

"No, you."

"Well I don't know what date it is."

He gave her the date and she grumbled and mumbled as she wrote it then handed him the paper. "Do I get a copy of this?"

"Do you want one?"

"Well yes, I need to file it at the clerk of courts—jeez, no, I don't really want a copy. Did I not have *any* sense of humor before?"

Sade's grin found its way to his lips. "You did."

She handed him her contract and he took it.

"You mind if I sit?"

She shrugged, hugging the pillow tighter to her body. He knew why she did that. To hide her fear from him.

He opened the paper and read. "Tell you everything." He glanced at her and she nodded while he read on. His brows raised and he looked at her fully. "You want one hour sessions and you get thirty minutes of that? For what?"

She shrugged with wide eyes. "For whatever."

"I thought this was about me helping you remember?"

"It is, but it's also about me learning."

"Learning what?"

"About you."

He looked down, a strange fear and déjà vu hitting him. He'd been in this same moment before. With her. "Fine. Will the contract be floating?"

"Floating where?"

"Meaning we can both agree to change it if we so choose."

"Both?"

"Yes."

"Sounds... fair."

He could hardly believe he was sitting there negotiating a contract with her for anything. "I get the first half hour."

She studied him now. "Ladies first."

Hmm. He was pretty sure that wasn't a great idea. But... "Okay."

"What happens during these sessions?"

"Whatever we feel needs to."

"That's very vague and *broad*."

"It is."

"When will we know what will happen in a session, I mean shouldn't we be able to prepare?"

"I think that would adversely affect what we're doing."

She tapped the pen on her knee. "So shock factor, you're going with shock the memory back in?"

"I just think you knowing before might set up blocks we don't want."

"Ah, but not knowing sets up fears."

"I'm weighing that into the equation."

She laid back on her bed. "You've given this a lot of thought."

"Enough, I think."

"Okay so, one hour a day?"

"Unless we feel more is needed."

She looked off to the right, biting at the inside of her cheek. "When do we start?"

"Tomorrow night?" He was sure he saw her flinch with that. "You get the first thirty," he reminded. "I hope you're merciful."

"I can't make any promises," she said.

He smiled and leaned, taking the pen from her and signing her contract. He handed both back to her and she inspected it, handing it back.

"Date."

"Ah, sorry." He dated it and gave it to her then held his hand out. "Shake?"

She eyed his hand like a poisonous viper before shooting her hand out and putting it in his for a quick, barely shake then jerking it back.

But the brief electrical contact was all he needed. "'Til tomorrow then."

"What time?" she asked, sounding breathless.

"Nine o'clock?"

"Where?"

"You tell me," he said. "Ladies first."

The offer seemed to throw her and she flustered for a few seconds. "The sauna room."

His dick jerked hard. "Nice."

"Fully clothed, of course. It's just private."

"Of course."

She pushed hair behind her ear, eyes flitting now. "I'm tired."

He nodded. "I'll let you rest. See you then."

"Sure," she muttered, looking a little ill as he got up to go.

He wanted to soothe her, but that would defeat the purpose. He also wanted to kiss her on the cheek but couldn't allow himself to. Not now. He was too close to breaking. It would already take everything in him to pull off thirty minutes of God only knew without becoming the monster clawing just beneath the surface of his skin.

All that was left was spending all night and all day on what he'd do for their first thirty minutes. Along with what she'd do.

As usual, his sadism was front and center with potential ideas while yet another element slowly circled the circumference of his mind—an unfamiliar predator. It was almost as if it knew to hang back far enough from the alarms. He'd have to be careful. The last thing he needed was some hidden freak-addiction ruining his chances with helping Mercy.

****

Sade bolted up in bed, breathing hard. He blinked the darkness away, listening. Had something woken him? His heart hammering, he limped his way to the door and opened it, listening. He finally heard a grrr…grrr noise on and off then an occasional clonk. He quickly peeked in Bo's room and found the bed empty. Then he spied the large plant turned over on the floor. Heart racing, he looked in on Mercy and relief flooded him at seeing her in bed.

Sade carefully crept back to his room and got his crutches, then made his way toward the living room where the sound was coming from. Finding the large space empty, he headed toward the kitchen where the grr grring became sporadic. The hell was that? Sounded like something rolling on the floor.

He finally got to the corner of the wall where he could peek into the kitchen unseen. The fridge was open. He looked below the door and saw something that looked like the bottom of an office chair. Sounded like Bo maybe, grunting. The hell was going on?

Sade slowly made his way behind the island so he could sneak up in case there was trouble. When he finally got a visual, he stopped and stared, confused. "The fuck are you doing?"

Bo screeched like a little girl. "Jesus fucking Christ, man! You don't sneak up on people! I'm getting dessert is what I'm doing, I'm starving, and I wasn't waking the drunk Iron Horse."

"What the fuck are you wearing? And riding on?"

He looked down. "Man, I found this under that big planter in the room, makes for a great wheelchair when you're desperate. Can you grab the fucking ice cream sandwiches? I got the munchies bad."

"I thought you had the wheelchair?" Sade realized what he was wearing. "Dude, please tell me why the fuck you're wearing a dress."

He let out a deep goofy laugh. "It's Liberty's. She made me her bitch, man." He grinned up from the floor while Sade reached in and got his *snack*.

"I was about to ask how it went with you and Lady Liberty."

"Oh my God, dude," he whispered, leaning to look at the living room a moment then back up, his face crimped. "She puked all *over* me while…"

Sade's brows raised. "While what? I'm not going to guess man."

He moved his finger in and out of his mouth then made a gagging sound, causing Sade to wince in disgust. "Yeah, man. Was fucking *nasssstyyyy*. Then she like passes out." Bo smacked one hand onto the other in demonstration before scooted himself away from the fridge and shutting it. Sade watched him propel himself toward the island with his hands like a mental patient on a skateboard. In a red dress.

Bo made his way off the little board onto his knees then pulled himself up the barstool. "Fuck," he gasped when he was sitting finally. "Everything… *exhausts* me!" he said flabbergasted.

Sade sat next to him and slid the box of ice cream sandwiches next to him. "You're still healing."

He tore into the box and opened one, moaning in ecstasy with his mouth full, taking another huge bite before he finished the first. Sade watched him devour it in three chomps.

"You're gonna get a brain freeze, dude."

"Mmm," he said, chewing slowly with his eyes closed. "Don't care," he mumbled, opening another one. "Duuuude," he whispered, turning to Sade. "I think she put something in my drink, I'm sooooo fucking hiiiiigh." He took a huge bite again, grunting and smacking loudly. "She's so fine bro," he whispered.

Sade grinned. "Liberty?"

He nodded real big and slowly, making Sade laugh. "I thought you didn't like her?"

"I soooo liiiiied," he shrilled. "Did you not *see* her in that red dress?" He lifted the material. "This one?" He put his hand on Sade's chest, stuffing the rest of his ice cream in his mouth. "Dude," he mumbled his cheeks full as he shook his head, "no words." He kept shaking with long sweeps. "No. Words!"

Sade moved the box out of his reach and Bo looked at him with narrowed gaze, ice cream sandwich caked on the edge of his mouth. "Come on man," he whined.

"You're gonna be sick."

He plopped his head on the counter and moaned. "What am I going to do now?"

"About what?"

"Her man! How am I going to face her after she vomited all over my dick!?" He squinted his eyes at Sade. "She's not going to want to look at me now, she's probly all embaaarassssed and shit." He propped his head on one hand, his eyes closed. "She's soooooo amazing man. So hot. I was really, really, really, ready to have a fucking orgasm too. It's been so *hard*." The final words came with a hiccup and belch.

"Time for you to get back to bed."

"Wait man, wait, wait. What about you and Mercy? Did you even *get* anywhere with her?"

"We signed a contract."

He stared at him, blinking rapidly as he tried to focus. "A *contract*?" he whispered all amazed. "Woooooow man that's..." his gaze narrowed. "What...what the fuck for again?"

Sade shook his head. "I'll tell you tomorrow when you can think straight."

He tried to snap to attention which amounted to swift sways and leanings. "I'm up man," he said with his eyes half closed. He patted Sade on the chest. "I'm here for you. You know that right? You're my bro, my hero."

"Okay, that's all for you."

"Waaaaait, I just wanna tell you somethin', hold on." He grabbed a fist full of Sade's shirt and looked up, his eyes blinking into focus. "Listen. Listen to me, okay? Listen."

"I'm listening."

He nodded then. "You're like… a father to me. Only…fucking two years older." He snickered lowly, putting his forehead on Sade's chest before jerking it slowly back up. "But I can still kick your ass!" He tried to grab Sade's face between his hands, his fingers nearly gouging his eyes. "I love you man," he gasped. "You know that right?"

"I know that." Sade removed his hands, not knowing where the fuck they'd been.

"You gotta know that. S'important you know."

"Let's get you to bed."

He suddenly looked around like he was lost. "Shit…"

"What?"

He looked at Sade confused. "How'd I get in here?"

"On your planter."

His face screwed up for a second then he busted out laughing. "Ohhhh my fucking God!" he squealed. "Don't tell Liberty I knocked that plant over. I didn't mean it."

"I'll tell her a rat did it."

"Yesssss." Sade limped his way to the other side of him when he turned to get off the stool. "A fucking *rat*." His silent laughter snorted out. "That would be a big ass rat, right?"

"Yes indeed," Sade said. "How about you get on my back and let me walk you back to your room."

"Awwwwwwww maaaaan, that would be so much *faster*. The plant-mobile is *deceptively* impoooosible to steer!" He busted out in silent snickers again. "Took for-eeeeever to get to the kitchen, I was like a pinball bouncing off everything I touched and I fucking touched eeeeverything."

"Jump up man, can you?"

"Yeah man, I can jump. Maybe I should get back on the stool. Fuck I need to piiiiissss!" he squealed.

"You'll have to wait now hurry."

"K man, I'm on the stool, now what."

Sade backed up. "Grab hold of my shoulders and wrap your legs around me."

"Roger that!" He worked his way onto Sade's back finally.

"Hold the fuck on now."

"Dude, don't make me laugh or I'm going down."

Sade got the crutches under his arms and made his way carefully with his embarrassing load.

"These are the days man, these right here, you know?"

"Yep," Sade said, out of breath in ten feet.

"So you signed a contract with Mercy," he whispered loudly in his ear.

"Shh, private man."

"Ohhhhh right, shhhhh. Got you."

Sade opened Bo's door and navigated around the mess, turning carefully and sitting on the bed with him.

"Thanks man," he whispered, flopping onto his back. "You're the best. I love you man," he said in a tiny voice that tugged at Sade even though he was drunk. He knew he meant it.

Sade stood and helped move his legs onto the bed, amazed that he was already out and snoring lightly.

He checked on Mercy again, unable to resist going to her bed to make sure she was okay. He stared down at her in the dark, wanting so much to stroke his fingers along her skin.

He turned to go.

"Hey," she said, disoriented. "What's wrong?"

He turned back around. "I was up helping Bo get snacks and just wanted to make sure you were okay."

She was quiet a bit. "I'm fine. Thank you."

"You're welcome. Do you need anything?" Part of him silently begged for her to need him to lay with her.

"I'm okay. Thanks for asking. You?"

His breath froze in his chest at the surprising question. "Nah, I'm good." He was sure that was the biggest lie he'd ever told in his entire life.

"Okay. Night."

"Night."

The soft sound of her voice, without the fear, wow. He didn't realize how fucking bad he needed to hear it. Missed it. Craved it.

He finally found his way back to sleep after tossing and turning, contemplating tomorrow night when he'd have thirty minutes to do whatever he wanted with her.

Just the idea soothed him. Soothed him right to sleep.

****

Sade stared at the box before him on the table and eyed Liberty. "I found it in one of the closets."

"What is it?"

She pulled out items until his heart began to hammer. "This is Mercy's stuff?"

"Looks like it. Memories," she whispered. "Thought you could use the ammunition."

He gasped and wiped a hand over his mouth. "Yeah. Definitely." He touched the ballet slippers, his heart hammering. "She lived here you think?"

"Not sure. Maybe came once or twice but she certainly doesn't remember if she has. This stuff could've just been stored here."

"Right." He pulled out a small teddy bear. "Wow," he whispered, stroking it. He pulled out a book and realized it was a scrap journal of all her milestones. "Holy shit," he breathed, gliding his fingers over the precious memories, feeling like they were the key.

He looked up at Liberty. "I got her to agree to let me help with her memories."

Liberty quirked her brow.

"We signed a contract." Hope brought a smile to his lips that he couldn't resist.

"A contract, huh? You might need it. Just don't get too kinky on me," she eyed him. "I'll bring that to your room. Don't want her seeing it before it's time. Better get your game on."

He nodded, closing his eyes in relief. "I got my game on." But this changed things. Gave him so much more. Even gave him ideas to follow with. Keep the memories coming.

## Chapter Seventeen

Mercy made her way to the rendezvous at 8:58. Not too eager, not too careless, not too exact. That was what she was going for. She knocked on the door and looked around. She'd dressed in layers of clothes in case he planned to get physical. He'd have to work at it. She'd resorted to *praying* about what to do in her first thirty minutes. Lo and behold she still had no fucking clue!

"Come in," a voice said.

Shit, he was there already. She glanced around once more and opened the door.

"Lock it please." It was pitch black inside.

"Can I turn on the light?"

"Sure."

She felt along the wall and hit the switch then jerked her head a little right, at finding him in a towel.

"I just worked out and showered."

"Okay." She sat on the nearest edge of the long bench opposite from where he was. "So…" she began. "Me first."

"Yes." He looked at the clock on the right wall. "Thirty minutes and counting down."

She took a deep breath and jumped right in. "So… I'd like to know what you did that made me tie you up."

He stared hard at her, his back against the wall, one leg hanging off the bench the other stretched out. He locked his hands behind his head and closed his eyes. "Tried to kill myself."

Her breath froze in her chest as she sat there stunned. That was not the answer he was supposed to give, it was supposed to be something bad. She realized in that second that she'd planned on using anger for her resolve to… be able to even do this without getting too caught up in the wrong emotions. And now this. This non-anger producing answer. This heart-wrenching answer. "But… why would I tie you up for that?"

"I threatened to do it again and succeed."

Shit. She swallowed, trying to think. "Why?"

He shrugged, leaning his head back with closed eyes. "Don't really know."

"Any theories?"

"Nope."

She chewed her lip, staring at him. "If you're not going to be forthcoming with me in this…"

"Why do people try to kill themselves, Angel? They want to die."

"Why would you want to if I was… I mean I thought you…"

"Not at that time. Not yet."

"How long did you stay tied?"

"Until I convinced you to untie me. Maybe three days."

She thought about what else she needed to know, eyeing the clock. Twenty-five minutes left. "So I untied you and you were... okay?"

He let his head flop toward her. "Then I tied you up."

Her heart hammered with that news. "That wasn't... "

"In the journal, I know. I didn't put that."

She gasped now. "So all that stuff you did... I was..."

"Tied up, yes."

"Oh my God," she whispered.

"Yep."

"That's like raping. No wonder I'm scared around you. What about that last thing you wrote, was I..."

"No. You were free. And you begged for that one, remember?"

She did remember reading that, but she wasn't sure. She needed to understand why he'd want to die though. "Tell me why you blame yourself for your mother's death?"

Head down, his gaze slowly rolled up to hers. "Who told you that?"

Oh crap.

"Bo's got a big mouth, little shit."

"Don't blame him, he was just trying to help me understand."

"Understand what?"

"It was when I first woke up and asked how we met. He told me about the alley and the beating. He added his theory as to why you did that when I asked him."

"I like pain," he said, his words firm. He looked up at the clock then back at her. "I like giving it and receiving it."

"Do you know why?"

"That I like it?"

"Yes."

"I learned to like it."

"From what?"

"From being forced to have orgasms, being beat when I didn't cooperate."

Oh Jesus. "And… what was I trying to undo? How was I doing it?"

"You were trying to make me get off to sex without pain."

"Did I… manage?"

"Yes. Until I fell in love with you. Then it all stopped."

Her heart thundered at his love confession. So bold and firm. "What stopped?"

"My dick stopped. Refused to work."

"Because you loved me?"

"Your theory was my body didn't know how to be aroused without pain and the love element derailed my ability to get it hard. No pain in love. I could get it hard but then when I'd think of how much I loved you..." he shook his head slowly. "Dead."

"And I tried to help with that?"

"Yes."

"Like what did I do?"

"You taught me how to feel." He rubbed his chest. "All in here. You were trying to help make a connection to my dick."

Wow. That actually made perfect sense. She couldn't help but feel a sense of pride with that.

"Fifteen minutes."

She rubbed the sweat from her palms along her legs. "And did you... did you learn? At all?"

"A little. I was the little engine that could. Only mostly I couldn't. But you didn't seem to mind."

"I'm sure I didn't."

"How are you sure?"

"I... I just don't see that as something I would be bothered about."

"You weren't."

She nodded. "Good to know."

"Yet."

Yet? "What do you mean?"

"Eventually, I'm sure you would be bothered."

"No," she said, pretty sure she wouldn't.

His gaze slowly moved up to the clock then back to her, heat simmering in the depths. Waiting for his turn. She knew she only had around twelve minutes. "Are you scared?" he asked.

"Are you?" The question came without thought.

"Maybe."

She gripped the edge of the wooden seat. "Of what?"

"Of you."

"Of me?" The words came on a breathless exhale.

"Of what you will do to me."

"I'm... not doing anything."

"You will."

She swallowed, unable to think as her eyes flitted to the clock. Seven minutes. "So... you said... you loved me?"

He cocked his head at her. "More than my own life."

Her heart hammered again. "Did you... ever... hurt me?"

He lowered his gaze for a long while. "Not on purpose."

"Shit," she barely gasped. "Like..."

"Like the sexorcism," he helped.

"You said... you said I started that. Wanted it. Begged for it."

"You did."

"So…"

"So it doesn't make it right. Nothing will ever make it right to hurt you. Not you."

She stared at him, holding her breath as the seconds ticked. She was drawing a blank now. She eyed the clock. Four minutes. "I'm done. You can go."

He turned on the bench so that both legs draped over the edge, palms next to him. He stared at her what felt like five minutes. Long enough to make her want to scream *what are you looking at what are you thinking—planning!* "Do you remember anything at all about us?"

She stared at him then shook her head.

He turned his gaze down, making her feel like a failure.

"I'm trying. Though." She cleared her throat. "I uh… have been practicing a kind of meditation I remember. Thinking it may help."

He looked at her again, a look of desperation in the depths of his silver eyes. "That's good," he said softly. "I know you're trying. Don't worry."

But she did worry.

Again he stared at her silently.

"Are you… practicing telepathy? Cause… I'm not getting anything."

He gave a light laugh. "Just like looking at you."

Her heart hammered and she nodded. "Okay."

"I'm not sure if I've ever told you…" he lowered his head.

"What?"

He leveled those bright eyes on her again. "That you're the most beautiful woman I've ever known."

Mercy's stomach flipped around and she couldn't stop the smile on her lips as she rolled her eyes.

"It's so true," he assured.

"You're not so bad looking yourself."

"Really?" he acted shocked and she snorted.

"Please, surely you know you're gorgeous."

He grinned at her. "You once said something like that."

She nodded, not liking to talk about the part of her she didn't remember. They sat in silence, but it was anything but quiet to her. He stared at her and she decided if that's all he wanted to do, then she'd give him that. She was a little fascinated with his fascination of her and maybe even a little flattered. She couldn't deny the good feeling it gave to know he liked her to such a degree that he'd forsake himself for her. She angled her gaze at him and bit her lower lip, letting herself look at him. He was breathtaking. She wanted to stare boldly like him, but she didn't have the same grit as he did in that department.

She suddenly needed more air than the little box had to spare.

"You okay?" he whispered.

"Just…" she fanned her face, "…kind of stuffy in here."

"You're hot," he said, like it was the answer to a riddle.

"Yeah. That's another word for it."

"I like that you're still arouse by me," he said.

Oh God. She cleared her throat, not sure how to even answer that, so she didn't.

"Want to know the first thing you ever cooked for me?"

She looked at him. "I cooked for you?"

He smiled. "You did. Spaghetti."

She laughed a little and rolled her eyes. "That's easy."

"I had come back from fighting and you were… so pissed at me."

Her heart raced, watching him recall with his head lowered.

"I fought for the old man on some weekends and it was your first time seeing what that entailed. You offered me money so I'd quit. At which point I found out you were not working for money like you'd said. At which point…" He shook his head and stroked his cheek. "I realized… you were for real, I guess." He angled a look at her. "Naïve as all fuck, but real. And good. And sitting next to me. In my life. Caring about me."

Mercy's breath got stuck in her chest at the sadness his words evoked. That such a small thing would be earth moving to him said he must've really had a sucky ass life.

"Same time tomorrow?" he asked, looking at the clock.

She jerked her gaze up and realized it was over. Sadly. "Sure. Yes. You can even go first if you want."

He smiled at her, "There's my Angel."

## Chapter Eighteen

The next session, Mercy got there early enough to be the one waiting for him. *There's my Angel.* Why had those words felt so good? The whole session had gone very different from what she'd expected. He'd been sweet. Normal. No doubt that's what she saw the first time around. Sadomasochist-smashochist. He was just a damaged human who needed a little hope. And she'd given him that.

She took a breath as she reached the sauna room. Looking around, then down briefly at her jeans and perfectly fitted red t-shirt, she opened the door to the sauna.

"You're early," he said.

"Oh shit!" she gasped, turning away. He was naked! And that pissed her off. "Aren't you worried just anybody might walk in?"

"I let Liberty know I was coming in. You don't want her seeing me naked?"

She flustered and choked on gasps. "I don't care personally but I'd think you should."

"You don't?" He sounded disappointed.

"You're supposed to like me," she said emphatically, "so you should guard your...nakedness, I'd think."

"Wow," he muttered.

"Wow, what? You sound amazed."

"I am."

"Why? I mean I may not remember a lot of things but it seems wrong to just let other woman see your body if you say you like another person, love even," she reminded, annoyed that she was having this conversation. "Are you decent yet?"

"I think so."

"I mean are you covered?"

"I have a towel."

She sat down and looked at him. "Oh my God! Sade!" she cried, jerking her head away at finding him with his palms on the bench behind him and leaning back with his privates all big and forward.

"You want me to put the towel on, I take it."

"Very funny, Sade," she said.

"You sound breathless again. Maybe we should hold these sessions in bigger spaces. Towel's on."

"Maybe you should just keep your clothes on and we'll be fine."

"So my nakedness makes you breathless?"

"Your balls—oh God not your balls, you're audacity— oh shut it," she said at his laughter.

"I'm sorry, baby, I'm picking at you. I love picking at you. Remember?"

The sudden test caught her off guard. "I-I… I'm not sure, I'd have to think about it."

"It's okay," he said.

But there was sadness in his tone that bothered her. She wanted to assure him but at the same time didn't feel like she should. It wasn't her fault she couldn't remember shit.

"So, I get to go first you said?"

"Well, it's early."

"Right." He looked at the clock. "Five more minutes."

She realized how stupid that was. "We could start now and finish five minutes early."

He angled a smile at her. "If you want."

She shrugged. "Fine with me."

He stretched his legs out, and the towel did little to hide the size of his manhood. "I love when you check me out."

She jerked her head away with a sound of disgust. "It's like a train wreck."

His deep laughter rang out and she couldn't resist the good feelings it gave her. She fought to appear indignant, or at least not so damn happy or turned on.

"I don't think I ever thanked you," he said.

"For what?" She was half afraid to know.

"For saving my life that night. I was pissed for days about it but… I just wanted you to know what that meant to me."

She suddenly wished she remembered it. "Was it bad?"

He presented the scar and she leaned and looked at it closer, wincing. She regarded him. "And then I tied you up?"

He nodded. "You sure did."

"And... did odd things like soul meshing."

He shook his head with a smile. "Maybe that's why I thought it was the most adorable thing ever. So odd. So different. But..." He pulled his feet in and leaned with his forearms on his legs. "Now that I look back... pretty sure it was while staring into those beautiful green eyes that I fell."

Confusion hit her. "Fell?"

He looked at her with raised brows. "You need me to spell it out for you?"

She was suddenly intimidated by the question that was clearly simple to understand. Her mind raced to connect what he'd meant. "No, I know what you mean."

"Do you?"

Her heart raced hard as she shot out the risky answer that could be the wrong presumptuous one, "You fell for me, I get it."

He stared at her for a moment then lowered his gaze. "Yeah. That."

Okay, why was he mad? What did he want her to say? Did he want some reciprocation about that? "I'm sure I... knew that." Fuck, great, stupid answer.

"I'm sure you did," he said, keeping his head lowered, then looking at her. "How'd you sleep last night?"

She looked at him, wondering his angle. "Fine, why?"

"Just wondering," he said softly.

"You? How'd you sleep?"

"Not a wink."

"Are you in pain?"

"Something like that. Good thing I get off to it, right?" He gave a little laugh that made her feel guilty for not being more for him than she was.

"I'm sorry."

"Nothing for you to be sorry about, baby."

A deafening silence stretched between them, making Mercy feel like these sessions were the worst idea ever. "Did I tell you I started practicing meditation? Liberty gave me a book. To help with training the mind."

"Really? Well, you were a nurse, you should pick that right up."

"Yeah, that's what I was thinking too." She smoothed her hands over her jeans and eyed the clock.

"You can go now, if you want," Sade said.

Great. Put it all on her. "You can keep going."

"Alright," he said, clasping his hands together before him. "I was thinking," he began. "That… we could change the contract."

Ah, there it was. She'd felt that one coming from the very beginning, since they'd first discussed sessions. "How?"

"Do you trust me?"

He was good at these curveballs, always throwing things at her she wasn't ready for or didn't know what to do with. She thought about what he said, wanting to answer honestly. "I think so."

He finally looked at her until she felt uncomfortable. "I want to try something tomorrow. Will you meet me in my room? At the same time?"

Light panic hit her. "For what?"

"I just have an idea I want to try. To help you remember."

"Like what?"

"Thinking that knowing would spoil the effect. It's nothing to worry about, nothing sexual."

She relaxed only a little. "Okay. Sure." She should've taken the time to think about that one. But her mouth seemed to like being open and saying things on its own.

"Perfect," he said, looking at the clock. "Would you like me to walk you back?"

Time's up? She cleared her throat. "It's okay."

"It happens to be on my way," he said with a grin as he stood. "I just need to dress." He removed his towel, and before she could jerk her head away, her eyes locked onto his huge erection. Her heart hammered in her chest and privates as she fought to tear her gaze from it.

He turned to get his clothes, saving her the impossible task but now she had his gorgeous ass to stare at. And stare she did. All the tattoos on his back, side, and neck—he was breathtaking. He turned to sit on the bench, and she snapped her gaze to the door.

Once dressed, he walked with her back to her room and before she could open the door, he put his hand on it. She looked up at him and he slid his fingers along her face. Before she could react, his lips were on hers, pressing softly. Then they were gone. "I'm gonna go to the kitchen to grab a bite before bed. You want anything?"

She gasped and shook her head.

"Night, Angel."

She stood there, awestruck, breathless, and quaking in her skin. He glanced back as he went, and she quickly opened her door. Making her way in, she shut and locked it. Shit. What an amazing kiss. His lips were... so full. He'd made them so soft for that kiss.

What in the world did he want her in his room for? What did he have planned? She suddenly opened her door and looked down the hall. When the coast was clear, she hurried into his room for a quick look around. Anything that would indicate his plans in there. She hobbled to the bed and looked under it. Then hurried to the bathroom for a look around. She thought she'd spied a suspicious something hanging on the tub and figured out it was just a back scrubber. She hurried out and made her way to the door then remembered the closet. Shit, she needed to get out of there. Hurrying, she went to the bi-fold doors and opened them. Looking she peered around for anything remotely suspicious.

"I'll come in a minute," Sade said at the door.

Oh shit! She looked around then hurried into the closet, falling into the back wall as she managed to shut one side of the closet. Oh God, were they both shut? She was so busted. What was she doing in there? She was... looking for... shoes? Extra pair of Crocs? And then panicked when he came in because... well she realized she should have asked.

She held her breath at seeing him sit on the bed, his back facing her. He laid down and she jerked more into the closet when his head was in her line of vision. If he looked, he'd see her. She clenched her eyes shut, hoping the sudden movement hadn't made a noise.

Letting out a slow breath, she listened as he got up again. Oh God, he was in the bathroom! This was her chance, she could leave. The bathroom door opened and she glued herself back to the wall, one of her crutches clonking lightly on something. Oh God. The main light turned off, leaving only the bathroom one to shine into the room. She peeked through the slats as he sat on the bed again. She let out a careful breath wishing he'd go see Bo.

Oh shit. What if he tried to go see her?

He laid down, and her breath caught at seeing his naked chest. She let her breath go when he put a hand behind his head and draped his other across his midsection. She watched the rise and fall of his chest, her eyes catching the glow of white skin between the dark ink of his tattoos. Shit. How long would he take to fall asleep? She looked around in the closet, careful only to move her head. It was too dark to see anything even if there was something.

She jerked back to watching him at hearing him sigh. He seemed to be looking down at something. She lowered her body and angled her head to see. *Oh my God.* He was naked. His hand was on his cock, stroking slowly. Her heart slammed her ribs as she gradually leaned so she could look out the bi-fold door that was partially open. *Oh. My. God.*

The muscles in his stomach and pecs rippled with his strained grunts and gasps. He pulled his knees up and Mercy's breath hitched when he let them fall open. Holy…. His enormous size sent heat biting her lower stomach and between her legs. She watched through a fiery haze, her eyes desperately trying to catch every ripple and flex of muscle—his arms, legs, stomach. She fought to breathe quietly as he gripped himself and moved his hips in and out of his tight fist. His perfect ass came off the bed with his lusty grunts and long heated hisses that nearly made her orgasm.

His head went back with a groan and her eyes locked on his open mouth and neck muscles standing out. *Oh God, oh God.* Her privates throbbed as she watched him in silent ecstasy.

"Fuck, yes," he gasped, looking down at himself again. His hand moved quickly over himself, making the bed shake. Again his mouth opened wide with a harsh hiss. She froze as his head turned toward her, then away in ecstasy. "Mercy," he whispered, shooting panic through her. "Suck my cock," he croaked. "Suck it, baby." Her own mouth watered as it hung open in shock. He was talking to himself. Mercy's privates were on fire as the bed shook more with his vigorous strokes. He looked down again, rolling his hips slowly then bucking fast. His head shot back, this time with teeth bared before his mouth flew open in a half roar.

*Oh my God, oh my God.* The sound and sight of his orgasm rocked her unlike anything she'd ever felt. She was officially addicted to it.

Her heart pounded so furiously in her body, she was sure he'd hear it as he gasped for air in the aftermath.

He slowly sat up, his body still heaving, back facing her. He stood and went to the bathroom. She watched his gorgeous body as he walked with a sleek grace, aching to touch him. What would he feel like under her fingers? Was he soft? Hard? Both? What would he feel like on her lips? She closed her eyes, never wanting something so much. She wanted to know. She had to know. Not remember, know.

She pressed her body into the wall when he came out with jeans on. She listened and heard his door open. He was leaving? Shit. Where was he going?

She waited for a few seconds then grabbed the crutches. She could say she came in looking for him at this point if he returned. She got to the door and opened it slowly. Listening, she heard mumbling in Bo's room and hurried across the hall then quickly slipped into hers. She locked her door and leaned against it, gasping for air. *Oh. My. God.*

## Chapter Nineteen

Sade hid in the closet, just as Mercy had done. God, jacking off knowing she was watching had been a fucking rush. It's the only reason he was able to finish. He wanted so bad to bust her and then he had the idea to pay her back. He couldn't wait to see her face when he told her he knew she'd watched. He wanted to ask her what she thought, how she'd felt. Had it made her pussy hot? Jesus fuck. His cock was hard just thinking about the conversation.

He'd do it when he tied her up tomorrow. He'd let her get settled in bed before announcing his presence. Then it hit him. What if she freaked? In a bad way.

He put his hand on the closet door, ready to come out but not so sure he'd already waited too long. He'd better just let her fall asleep and sneak out after.

Sade settled for watching her. His heart picked up speed when she began to undress. Oh fuck. That was a bonus he wouldn't feel bad for. She climbed under the covers, making his breath come faster. She was sleeping naked? Fuck double bonus. His dick jerked hard at seeing her tits, fucking God he missed them. His entire body tensed with the need to feel them on his tongue and lips again while he owned her body with his hands.

She picked up his notebook and opened it, flipping pages. Fuck, reading that while naked? *Baby, are you going to be naughty for me?* He prayed yes. *God please, yes, be naughty for me.*

She glanced at the door then began reading. He gripped his cock when her hand slipped under the covers. My. Fucking. God. He quickly opened his pants and unzipped them, working his impossibly hard cock out. She slid down in the bed a little and drew her legs up, then let them fall open. Fucking God, yes.

It created a tent, fuck baby, come on, move the covers. Oh Jesus Christ, what was she doing with her fingers? She licked her lips and parted them as her gaze locked on the notebook. He strained to hear and picked up light gasps finally. Her legs opened a little wider and her eyes closed. Full blown fantasy now. What did she see in that pretty mind? Oh, he'd find out. He stroked his cock slowly in one hand while sliding his fingers all over the slick head until he couldn't breathe from the fire it created. He worked his balls out of his underwear, needing to put them in a vice. At the rate she was going, his sweet angel was erupting in orgasm in less than one minute.

And he wanted to come with her when she did.

She pulled her legs back farther and arched her back now. Her head lolled side to side with her mouth open in ecstasy, pretty brows drawn in desperate focus. Jesus Christ! Move baby, move the fucking covers, please. They slid off on one side like a miracle. Oh God, yes, like that yes. The entire side of her body was visible now, and fuck she was beautiful. His favorite tit was begging for his teeth and tongue, nipple erect with the sharp arch of her back and tilt of her head. The column of her neck stretched long, whispering *suck me, Sade. Please. Bite me, kiss me.*

"Oh God," she gasped, straining. Worry edged her tone like she wasn't sure what to expect. Fuck, was this like her first orgasm in a way?

He stroked his cock faster as her hips pumped and squirmed. The cover slid more off as her other hand went between her legs. *Oh my God!* Her finger was *in her pussy,* she was fucking fingering it. It was the winning touchdown for him.

Sade fought to be quiet as she wiggled her middle finger inside her pussy and finally came apart. Her back arched hard with the spasms, toes pointing, mouth open with that delicious shock. But it was those stifled cries and gasps that did it to him. Sade clenched his own eyes as his orgasm raged forward. Gripping his balls hard, he grit his teeth as he mentally shoved his cock in her pretty open mouth and rammed the head against her throat. Hot come shot hard and long into his hand while his body made him swear on his grave to fuck her mouth first chance he got. Yes, yes, he would, he promised.

He leaned against the wall in the closet, gasping quietly as her moans slowed and softened. His cock jerked with the sound like she kissed the head of his dick and licked along his balls with each breath.

And no pain. There had been no pain, just all fucking pleasure, all her, all his sweet angel. Oh *God* he needed her.

Took her an hour to go to sleep and Sade finally slipped out of her room, his feet promising he'd pay dearly for that one. It was worth a fucking bullet to the head as far as he was concerned. Just so he lived to do it again and again and again, another day.

****

Mercy stared at her body in the bathroom mirror, her head angled in curiosity. She stepped closer and then looked down at her breasts. Her heart raced at seeing her nipple deformed looking. Her gaze shot back to the mirror. What had happened, and how did she not see that before? Was she born like that?

Iron butterflies chewed at her intestines. She leaned a little, glancing at the clock on the small table by the bed. Thirty minutes 'til their next session. Felt like a countdown to Armageddon. Flashes of Sade on his bed touching himself heated her body to boiling. How would she face him now and not look like she'd seen that? She felt like it was written all over her. God.

And what did he have in mind with her? Something told her *sexual,* even though he'd said it wasn't. She closed her eyes, her heart hammering as flashes of his face in ecstasy burned her. The bed shaking, the sounds, the way he'd called her name. *Her name.* Mercy.

Too bad she didn't really *know* who she was. It was like miming her own identity. She felt like an imposter in somebody's body. Taking a man that didn't belong to her but did. But this man wanted Mercy and only Mercy. Or so he thought.

How did it come to this? She was at a one-eighty with him. Was she this weak before with him? She didn't doubt it one bit. Her heart tried to beat out of her chest, and she took a deep breath. There was so much suddenly *there* with him. She knew he was the one putting it all *there* in order to help bring her memories but all he had to show for it was a flood of estrogen. Without that initial fear she'd had with him, all those crazy symptoms in her body seemed to turn on her in a good bad way.

Maybe she should just take the plunge and give it a shot. It had to be hard on him, having her go from loving him passionately to not even knowing him. She could at least fix the being afraid of him part. And she could let things… just happen if they should.

The idea he might see her naked suddenly terrified her. *He's seen you naked, dummy.* But she couldn't get over the sensation that this was his first time with her too. It was goddamn strange and she hated this not remembering shit! An avalanche of emotions hit her until she trembled with uncertainty. *Please, please, let me remember so we can be done with this and go back to whatever amazing thing we shared.*

She turned around to examine her backside, and more dread hit her at seeing the white lines along her legs and butt. Those weren't birth defects. Did Sade know what they were from? How would he not? She turned forward again and looked at the ugly nipple. He surely wasn't attracted to that. Had to be a defect he made himself blind to or just ignored.

She wrapped the towel around her, feeling more than just naked. She felt... open and stupid. Maybe even dirty. God, she was tired of analyzing everything—why she felt this, why she thought that. She pulled the pouch of makeup toward her. She didn't allow herself to wonder again who it was for. Time to save her brainpower for remembering more important things.

Finally, dressed in a black miniskirt with a little flare, and fitted black tank top that showed her shoulders, she made her way on Liberty's makeshift crutches that fit Mercy better than the guys.

Stomach nearly sick, she knocked softly on Sade's door and looked down at herself. Was the skirt too short? Too slutty. Or childish? Had she been slutty before? How had she dressed? Did he like slutty? Or innocent? Should she ask or was it stupid to?

The door opened and her courage crumbled just at the sight of him. And smell. Dear God, it had to be the most erotic smell she'd ever encountered. Or remembered encountering. He towered before her in only jeans. The light at his back made his muscles stand out in the shadows and sent her heart to pound furiously between her trembling legs.

He looked her over without a word, no greeting, his face unreadable as he stepped aside to let her in.

She made her way into the room and looked around for a hint of his plan and immediately spied items on the table that might be unusual.

"Have a seat on the bed."

His firm tone made her legs tremble more. Was he angry? Her brain flew through their last session, trying to remember a point where she'd done or said anything to upset him. Oh God, had he somehow found out she'd been in his room? Had she left some kind of evidence?

She sat on the bed and leaned the crutches next to her, following his slow steps in her peripheral vision. He walked without crutches now, though carefully, and sat in the chair at the small table.

He finally looked at her, slight strain on his face as his eyes lowered over her. She smoothed her skirt as he took his time in his silent perusal until she felt like a stupid little girl pretending to be a woman. A clown with makeup, trying to impress the wrong audience.

That silver gaze slowly raised back to hers. "I want to do something that you may not like."

Her heart hammered now, mouth suddenly dry. "Like... what?"

He glanced at the items on the table next to him. "Like... tie you up."

More adrenaline flooded her. "And?"

"I've tied you up before and I think it might help." His eyes raised to hers. "That's all."

That wasn't all. She was sure of it. But this was it. As she stared at him, she finally knew something. And knowing something—anything—was goddamn awesome. No, she didn't just know it, she was sure of it. She wasn't worried about remembering, she was more concerned about having him. Now. Remembering could come later. "Alright."

He locked a solid gaze on her, like maybe he wasn't expecting the cooperation and waiting for the *but.*

"Where would you like me?"

"On the bed."

Controlled hunger in his deep voice sent fire licking through her body. "On my back?"

"Yes."

"Now?"

"Yes."

The urgency in his tone should have scared her. But the fear of pain or dying wasn't what made her tremble like a leaf. It was what she wanted him to do that stole her breath, longed for him to do. Touch. She wanted it, was ready. His touch. Somehow, someway. Anyway, every- way. She wanted to be at his mercy. With her body, her mind. Her heart. She wanted to feel him the way she once had and couldn't remember. The sloppy, passionate words in his journal had lit a fire in her. They were saturated with everything she wanted and craved. They burned in her, hotter and hotter until the fire roared in her veins and stained everything with a ruthless power. And now, she was burning, starving, dying. Drowning. She didn't want to understand why or who or when. She just wanted him to feed what her body craved—had to have.

Him.

That's all that mattered, all she'd let matter.

On her back in the center of the bed, she stared at the ceiling in a sudden calm, putting her arms out at her sides.

In silence, he took her left arm and began restraining it. His fingers glided over her skin in a reverent anticipation and awe.

Her breaths became erratic as that hunger burned in her. He moved to her right leg next. Very slowly, he slid it open and she gasped, heat throbbing between her legs. She'd removed the ugly Crocs and black socks, too ashamed to leave them on. But now she worried he'd see the round band-aids covering the holes on the top and bottom of her feet and for some reason, stop the program.

Panic hit when she couldn't remember which panties she put on.

He stroked his fingers along her ankle and calf as he restrained her with some soft white material, then moved to the next. Again he slid her leg open, grazing her skin with a near trembling touch that sent heat straight up her leg.

Black panties. Satin. That's what she had on. *Thank God.*

She finally let her eyes dart toward him, desperate to know what he was thinking. Her gasp shot out at finding his head angled and staring between her legs. The vicious lines in his face fanned the fire in her blood until it slithered in her muscles like a slow seduction.

At her other arm, she looked at him as he repeated all the same steps, not changing a thing. Finally done, he stared into her eyes, spearing her through and through.

Their gazes remained locked as he sat next to her on the bed, his face seeming more tormented than ever. He slowly leaned toward her, his gaze on her mouth. She didn't close her eyes, didn't breathe, wanting to see him, never stop seeing him. Near her. Touching her. She wanted to brand every bit of him in her brain.

He paused and hovered near her mouth and Mercy parted her lips, tasting the cinnamon on his hot breath while remaining perfectly still.

His eyes roamed her face before locking on hers. She couldn't resist the whimper from the violent connection. A firestorm swirled in the dark silvery depths as the tip of his nose touched hers. "Did you have fun?"

She swallowed and gasped. "W-what…"

"Last night?" His nose moved down to her ear. "Hiding in my closet?"

"Oh God," she whispered.

"Yes." He licked at her lobe, making her gasp. "I have to know. Did you like it?"

Shame and desire warred in her as she pulled on the restraints with so many needs.

"No closing your eyes, Angel."

She could hardly catch her breath as she opened them, immediately sucked into his hot gaze.

"I'm so glad you watched me." He stood next to the bed, and her gaze lowered to his hands undoing his pants. In one move, he pushed them down to expose the strain of his huge cock in tight black briefs. He slid his hand over the outline of his thick length angling up in his underwear. "Did it make your pussy hot? Watching me?"

Jesus. Took all she had to answer with barely a nod.

He finished kicking his legs free of his pants with a gasp. "I fucking know it did." Eyeing her body, he climbed on the bed and knelt between her legs. The veins in his hand stood out as he stroked his length again then lowered the front of his underwear.

*Oh my God, oh my God.* He was impossibly huge up close.

He held his cock with his legs open while staring between her legs now. "I know I said nothing sexual but…" he bit his lower lip and slid his finger over the very center of her panties, making her cry out. "I so fucking lied," he whispered, his eyes slowly rolling up to hers.

She was nearly grunting with need, her stomach clenched impossibly hard.

"Truth is, I can't wait another day to feel you." His finger navigated inside the edge of her panties and her mouth flew open. "Right here." He dipped inside her and she bucked her hips in response. He bit his lip hard, his brows drawn in concentration. "Fucking wet, Angel," he whispered. "Just like my cock." He continued teasing her opening with slow nudging that had her body reaching, demanding more. "Watch me, Mercy," he whispered. "Watch me stroke my big cock while I play with your *gorgeous fucking pussy*."

She did watch. Her eyes burned with desire as his fingers swirled over the thick head, making it shine until she squirmed in the restraints for more, anything.

"Where do you think I went after I made my cock come last night, Mercy?"

Her heart pounded furiously at his tone. She locked her gaze on his secretive one, not missing the bad boy look there.

"I went to your room. And hid in the closet."

Her mind and body connected the dots immediately and she gasped in shame. His finger pushed with more aggression before she could care about anything but him going deeper, and touching that spot he'd called her clit.

"I watched you, Angel. So fucking beautiful touching your pretty pussy. Pulling your legs so far back while you rubbed your clit and fingered yourself."

"Oh God, yes," she gasped at the slow stroking of his finger on the upper wall inside her. So good, so good. Her finger hadn't felt anything like that, he was making everything impossibly hot.

"Look at me, baby," he whispered, his voice strained with hunger. "While you squirm like that in my bed. Do you know how long I've fantasized about this? For a fucking nightmare eternity."

His finger sank deep suddenly and hit bottom for an electric flicking that drew all her breath from her in one instant. She bucked her hips, wanting it again, more, faster, harder. God, please.

"Is your clit on fire, baby?"

"Yes! Please, touch it."

She gasped when he jerked her panties roughly to the side. She looked down to see him kneeling closer to her, his finger back to stroking at the shallow spot near her entrance. She stared at the large head of his cock moving toward her body. She reached for it with desperate thrusts and grunts.

"That fucking look of ecstasy on your face, right there. That's what my body aches for." His cock finally made contact on her clit, a brief touch. "Work for it," he ordered. "Move your pretty pussy for me."

She pulled on the restraints, flicking hungrily against the barely there touch of his cock. "Please, fuck."

"Please, fuck," he repeated hotly, his breath shaking as he slid his finger deep inside her again. "I know how bad you want my cock, I do. You want it right here." He flicked rapidly against that deep spot, drawing high-pitched cries from her. "Ramming hard and fast, no stopping. That's what you want." He pressed the head on her clit again and she gave a sharp cry, quickly wiggling on it, only to have him pull back, seconds after. Her nails bit into her palms, her teeth into her lip.

"Please, Sade." She was ready to say whatever he wanted. "Fuck me, please, do it, I need you."

He clenched his eyes shut like the words alone hurt him. But he shook his head and slowly looked at her. "I like giving you this pain, Angel. I'm so hungry to give pain. To get pain," he whispered, torment in his face. "You have no idea how much I want to do to you, what I want to do."

"Do it," she gasped. "Please. Do whatever you want."

"You don't know what you're asking."

"I've read," she strained through breaths. "I'm not scared."

His hand splayed over her stomach. She felt the tremor in it as his nails dug then dragged down to her privates, his eyes closed. "I learned something, Angel. Something new. About you. About me."

"Tell me," she cried, writhing for more. "Tell me what you like. I want to do whatever you like. I want you to use my body, please."

His hands grabbed her waist and bit extremely hard with whatever urges he was fighting.

"Don't fight it, let it come," she whispered. "Let me feel it."

His body heaved, lips parted with labored breaths. His gaze slid up to hers and there was something in it that struck sudden fear in her. The instability, the ledge he teetered on was there in his tormented eyes. That thing he feared in himself, suddenly stared back at her. "I'm going to make you come now," he whispered, his voice warning. "Then… maybe I'll play just a little."

## Chapter Twenty

His words alone nearly gave her an orgasm, the promise in them, the mystery of what he'd learned about himself. Her. She needed to know what that was. If it was new, did that mean the other her didn't know about it? The excitement of having something they both remembered together, while he touched her like that, stole her breath and mind.

He removed his finger from her pussy and put it deep in his mouth while staring at her. Pulling it slowly out, his eyes rolled shut as he focused on the taste. Lord, she'd never seen anything so... incredibly sexy.

He moved on his knees closer and wrapped his hands around her hips with a fierce grip that shot a thrill down her spine. He worked her up and down over the head of his cock, letting it barely tease along all her aching parts. Finally he sat, letting her ass rest on his upper legs. He moved the head of his cock to her entrance and she nearly flew apart at the promising pressure he put there.

"You're going to come quickly for me, Angel. Do you understand?"

Oh God. She nodded, not knowing if she was supposed to.

He pushed only the thick head inside her, and her mouth flew open with a cry as she pulled on every restraint, head back in ecstasy. Her body clamped down on him, trying to suck him deeper. Jesus. She looked at him now and his torso heaved as he throbbed in her entrance while staring between her legs. He reached down and stroked softly over her open folds, feeling every part of her above, below, around him until her cries were incessant from the torment.

His fingers made their way to her clit where he stroked alongside it, holding a promise of something devastating to come any second. She panted loudly, her moans nonstop as she braced for it.

His drunk gaze meandered up her body and finally locked onto hers. While staring at her, he began to slowly squeeze her clit between two fingers. Mercy gasped and thrashed her head as he gradually increased the pressure.

She thrust her hips, fighting for more of his cock inside her, cries louder, worried maybe, as his squeezing got harder. The torment of jerking herself on the pulsing tip of his cock was the most delicious thing ever.

"Sade!" She looked down in shock at his fingers scissoring urgently on her clit. "Oh God! Oh God!" She erupted with an explosion, shrieking long as she bowed and thrashed with the intense orgasm gripping her. He suddenly gave a violent buck of his hips and Mercy screamed with the shove of his huge cock deep inside her.

He remained exactly still once he was buried and she lost track of space and time as she lay there, shocked at what she'd just felt. So fucking glorious, dear God.

He disconnected from her completely and Mercy's body gave an errant cry at the total and instant absence. It was as painful as it was alarming.

She watched breathlessly as he went to the bathroom and turned on the water. Her heart raced as she waited to see his intentions. He came out, and the sight of his cock standing erect made her heart stutter all over the place.

He walked over, his face firm as he untied her. She sat up, rubbing feeling into her wrists as he walked to the table and sat in the chair, his legs open and hips forward. "Undress for me." He grabbed hold of his cock and made it stand tall while his other hand hung casually between his legs, watching her.

She wasn't sure where to start. She stood up.

"Don't stand on your feet," he muttered, rolling his hips and making his cock push through his fist.

She felt a little safer with his concern, but that didn't keep the tremble out of every limb as she sat back down. She'd do her top last.

"Your top first."

She jerked her gaze to his harsh one.

"Top. First," he reiterated, letting her know it wasn't negotiable.

Heat spiked between her legs at his strict tone. She parted her lips for more air, very close to positive that she loved him that way. Commanding. Commanding her. Owning her. Using her even.

She looked down at her top, reminding herself that technically he'd seen her already. *Just... act like you've done this before.*

She removed her straps first then slowly pushed the top down to her waist, keeping her head lowered.

"You're fucking killing me, Angel."

His hoarse whisper sent her heart between her legs to pound with a fury. God, she needed to answer the deep hunger she heard and felt in him.

His eyes were locked on her breasts as he sat there, stroking himself so very slowly, his full lips open wide, black brows drawn in agony.

To think she had that power over him gave her courage. She hooked her thumbs in the top now bunched at her waist and began working it down with her skirt and panties. She finally managed them to her ankles and kicked them off, back to scared out of her mind as she sat completely naked before his stormy gaze.

He propped his heels on the chair legs, rolling his hips extra slowly now as his gaze burned just as slowly over her. "Stand."

Her breath caught at his command, and she slowly stood, swallowing down her fear.

"Turn, Angel. Do it slowly, and God, don't you *fucking* hurry."

She gasped and did as he said, clenching her eyes tight when her back was facing him. She yelped when he was suddenly pulling her arms behind her.

"Hold them together. Just like that." He slid his finger along the crack of her butt, sending a shiver through her as he got one of the ties from before and secured her wrists behind her, tight. "Sit."

She sat on the bed, looking up, her gaze not making it past his enormous cock.

"Open your knees, Angel." He stroked his finger under her chin, drawing her gaze higher. "Keep your ankles together."

She stifled a moan as she spread her legs and held her feet together.

Grabbing another tie, he knelt before her and tied her ankles tight together. She couldn't stop her cry when he leaned in and licked the deformed nipple, before sucking it into his mouth with an explosive hunger. She arched her back, trying to give him more, spreading her knees.

He climbed on the bed behind her, and she gasped when he put one of the ties over her eyes then secured it tight. Careful hands stroked her face, then slowly over her shoulders and arms. His cock moved against her back and she moaned with the need to have it in any way possible.

He suddenly took hold of her head in both hands, his fingers firm as he tilted it to the right. With one hand, he slid the hair away from her neck, his fingers stroking along her shoulder blade, then sliding up to her hairline and back down as though tracing her. His breath shuddered on her skin as he suddenly gripped her hair on the right and clamped his hand on her left shoulder.

She closed her eyes with nonstop gasps as he held her neck stretched before him. Her moans followed when the tip of his tongue licked from shoulder to hairline, a low, eager growl in his chest that promised lethal things.

"Do you trust me?" he whispered in her ear?"

"Yes," she nodded.

His mouth turned into a storm on her neck as his lips, teeth, and tongue sucked, scraped, and bit her. "Oh God!" she cried, her breaths loud and harsh.

His fingers pulled harder in her hair, dug even harder on her shoulder as he devoured faster and faster until her mind spun in senseless oblivion—a mess of nonstop moans and begs.

He turned her face to his mouth and kissed her with such a force, she could scarcely breathe from it.

She was abruptly fighting to steady herself when he unexpectedly lifted off the bed. She looked around, the blindness making her confused and disoriented. "Sade," she whispered when he didn't seem to be there anymore.

She heard him in the bathroom and angled her head, listening for signals as to what he had in mind next.

Her heart beat a furious pace as she waited. He was suddenly there, she heard his breathing. His hands slid under her legs and he lifted her in his arms.

"Sade," she whispered, unable to keep the fear back now.

He didn't answer as he carried her. He seemed to sit and her foot rested on what felt like the cool tub.

"Talk to me," she whispered, needing to know at least what he was doing, planning. He leaned with her and she screamed when her body touched cold—cold water. "Sade," she gasped. "W-what… what are you doing, talk to me."

While she sat in the tub, he placed a hand on her back and chest and slowly pushed 'til she lay back.

"Oh God, oh God," she whispered as the water reached her chin. She fought to push herself higher with the bottoms of her bound feet, angling her tied hands on the tub beneath her to keep from slipping. "Sade, I'm scared, please," she barely managed through the rising panic..

She felt his legs on either side of her in the tub now and she tried to figure out where he was, what position he was in.

"Sade, please, wait."

He was kneeling over her she realized. His harsh breaths came faster as he slowly sat on her stomach, pushing her down into the tub and holding her there.

Panic raced through her muscles, and she fought not to give into it. "I'm scared, I'm scared, Sade, please," she said, tears stinging her eyes. Her breaths shot out as she fought to calm down, fought for some memory of some kind of training. She reminded herself she had training in things. She could fight him if it got crazy. She desperately sought to remember anything to help her. Fighting was all she remembered, and it seemed available to her when she wasn't *trying* to bring it. *God help me.*

Her body shook violently and his weight suddenly left her stomach and cold fingers gripped the top of her neck beneath her jaw, tilting her face up. Hovered right above her mouth, their harsh breaths mingled, hers panicked and his something else she couldn't see and really needed to.

His mouth ravaged hers with a brutal hunger, growling and sucking the breath from her. She felt his cock stroking over her nipple and despite the cold and fear, it sent tiny heat strobes to her clit.

He pulled up with a painful sounding groan and the sudden release on her neck sent her too far into the water. She pushed with her feet to get back up, turning her face, trying to think through the panic. "Sade!" she gasped. Her feet slipped, and she went under. Hysteria hit her, and she pushed frantically with her feet and hands, surfacing finally. "Sade!" she screamed and gasped, "Help me!"

## Chapter Twenty-One

Sade knew he'd fallen.

He'd been on a slippery slope with this from jump. Just bring her to the brink, that was his idea, his plan. Reach her limit, breach that fucking wall in her head keeping her from him. But the second he set her in the water and her panic hit, he knew it. He'd brought himself to his own ledge.

Dark desire drove an agony through him he couldn't escape. Like those nails in his feet, he was held to its immovable and inescapable torture. Lusting for it and loathing it all at the same time. It was like the sexorcism high, only it had a target. Mercy. Fucking his Mercy while she was terrified.

Sade had tried not to show his arousal in that basement. Abraham had threatened Mercy and he'd gotten so fucking hard. He'd finally allowed himself to poke at that new and strange animal in his mind, find out enough about it to understand, and now... now he sat and chatted casually with it, discussing the logistics of fucking her pussy, her mouth, her untouched virgin ass—especially that—all while she was terrified.

The part of him that loathed his dark desires stood just behind this new animal, hiding in a corner. Hiding while it took care of business.

He gripped her throat in his hand, lifting her out of the water a little more. Her racing pulse in his palm and fingers said it was exactly right to fuck her mouth. Make her take him in that terror.

He knelt before her and rubbed the throbbing head along her lips and like a new baby bird she blindly licked and tasted, gasping her hot breath on him, fighting to be a good girl.

"Just lick it," he gasped with that sadistic hunger. "Just like that. Don't suck. Just lick it, make me burn with it."

He slid his fingers into her hair at her forehead then made a tight fist, pulling hard until she winced. He tilted her head back, and she continued to lick as commanded, her brows furrowed in worry and fear. But it was the sight of his pre-cum shining on her pretty lips that sent hunger storming through him. He lowered his mouth to hers and licked it up with lusty growls.

"Such a good girl," he shuddered on her mouth. "So trusting, aren't you?"

There was something to be said for that, even in the throes of this thing that gripped him. Her ability to trust when she had no real reason to, no memory of who he was. The stupidity disappointed him as much as it aroused him. Mercy wouldn't have done it.

He went back to letting her lick him, letting her feed his new addiction. "Fuck," he hissed, "you're setting my cock on fire. Take the head now, only the head and suck it." He reached behind him. "Open your knees for me. Wide, until they touch the tub."

When he felt her slipping more into the water, he tightened his grip in her hair, making his cock throb. He realized in that moment that he liked that part. Saving her. "I got you," he whispered, stroking his fingers between her pussy lips. He found her ass with his middle finger and pressed against that perfect opening. "That's it," he whispered, watching her gasp on his cock and moan frantically. "Suck it while I fuck you here for the first time."

With every moan and pant, her ass contracted. His heart thundered with what he was about to do. Shock her. When his finger barely penetrated, he shoved in fast and deep with a growl, bringing her panicked cry and thrust of his cock deep into her mouth. "Take it fucking all," he ordered, fucking her ass with long, deep strokes.

"Your ass is so tight on my finger, your body is so tight. And your fear boils my fucking blood, Angel, makes me *fucking* hungry, do you know that?"

Her nostrils fluttered rapidly with his cock deep in her mouth. He slowly pulled out, still fucking her ass with vigorous thrusts, rubbing the head over her lips and face as she gasped incessantly, thrashing her head and body under his biting hold.

The dark desire pumped his cock and body until he grunted and groaned to its demands. He closed his eyes at feeling the animal wanting more. More power, more control.

Panic hit Sade for an instant, and his sadistic fury answered. He shoved her beneath the water for several seconds then yanked her out by the throat and pinning her to the tub. He roared in desperation, and she screamed and choked while he kissed her wet mouth. "Fight me!" he yelled.

He yanked the blindfold off, needing to see it. His cock jerked hard at finding the stark terror in her wide eyes. Heaving with the hunger, he kissed her again, still holding her while she fought to thrash out of his grip. She managed to knee him in his balls, and the pain shoved any sanity back, and he sat on her, forcing her body down into the tub again. He turned and yanked the lever, letting the water out. The look of abject fear in her wide eyes fueled that animal and he reached behind him and slid his finger inside her. "Yes," he whispered as she squirmed and fought him, her body thrashing, sliding under the water. He grabbed her by the throat and lifted her back in place, holding her still.

Gasps began filtering in with her screams as he rammed his finger faster in her.

The water lowered to a few inches and Sade flipped the lever and shut the drain.

"On your stomach, Angel," he rasped.

"Stop this, please," she begged.

He flipped her onto her stomach. "Don't hide, don't fight it, let it come, is that what you want me to stop, Angel?"

"I'm sorry," she gasped frantically, the top of her forehead against the tub to keep her face out of the water. "Please, I didn't know, I didn't know!"

Sade lifted her hips to put her on her knees and she refused to bend them.

"Kneel." He wouldn't call her Mercy, she was nothing like her. She was the absence of Mercy, the sick addiction he loathed but craved. The one Mercy had fought against.

"No, please no."

He yanked her hips up and spanked her ass hard. "The water!" She turned her face to the side, sputtering. "Take it…take it out," she screamed, raising her head back and grunting.

Sade flipped the lever and opened the drain for a few seconds then shut it back. An inch less was all he'd go. "Now kneel."

"The water," she cried desperately.

"There's less." He pulled her hips up, and she knelt this time.

"Sade, please. My arms hurt. M-my face."

Fury stormed through him at those words and the urge to hurt something gripped his body in a vice of power until he heaved and seethed with it.

She grunted and panted, still fighting to keep her face out of the water. She began crying and then screamed, "Do it! Do it, you motherfucker! What are you waiting for!"

Sade's emotions did a one-eighty at the *Mercy* in her tone. He wanted several things at once now. Her fear, her anger, her submission, her fight. He decided to make her choose for him.

Biting his fingers into her hips, he slammed his cock inside her impossibly tight pussy. The shriek she gave him said she chose fear. Sade growled and snarled, staring at his cock buried to the hilt in her.

Still no fucking Mercy.

She put her forehead to the tub again as Sade clenched his eyes tight on that other dark fire kindling inside him. The hot bite of her pussy tickled that need to fuck her senseless for hours and hours.

"I fucking hate you!" she screamed at him. "I hate you! I hate you!"

Those words... They were a holy water bomb right in his face, and it drew forth all the demons, all of them ready to kill.

That panic slammed him again, allowing his sanity to surface again. He pulled out of her, stumbling out of the tub and falling into the vanity, grabbing hold of that life-line *I fucking hate you.* He trembled and looked around, growling and panting. Oh God. What the fuck had he done?

He crawled to the tub and fought with Mercy's ties. "Jesus, be still!" he gasped, letting out the water. "Fuck, fuck," he whispered, shame cutting his breath.

Mercy let out a sob as he untied her. As soon as she was free, she lunged at him, wrapping her arms around his neck and crying, "I'm sorry, I was scared! I do trust you, I do!"

Confusion slammed him as he held on to her. Why was she doing this? What was she doing? Who was she? Why was she?

Who the fuck was he?

That answer grew increasingly difficult to figure out with every second he spent with her, every second she tore him more apart.

"I'll do it, I'll try again. This time I'll do good, I promise."

His heart ached at hearing the absence of the woman he knew. Would he ever get her back?

The box.

Desperate, Sade pulled her by the hand to the bedroom, stopping to carry her when he realized she was limping. He laid her on the bed and she stared at him, sobbing like she was so sorry. How did she get so confused? He was the guilty one. It was like she was more confused than before. Had he fucking broke her worse than she was?

If she remembered, it would fix everything. He spun and went to the closet and grabbed the box down and hurried back to the bed with it. "Get dressed," he said, feeling like the devil while she was naked. She hesitated like she'd argue. "Do it, Mercy, please," he gasped, finding his own underwear and getting them back on.

She slowly got dressed, crying quietly now, making him cringe with self-loathing. When she was done, she whispered, "Tie me, please."

He stared at her, rocked with confusion at the odd request.

"Tie me, please, just tie me. I'll show you," she whispered heatedly.

He shook his head a little, stuck in confusion.

"Tie me, goddammit!" she screamed, laying on the bed, all four limbs spread. "Please," she added in a bitter beg.

Sade didn't know why or what, but doing what she asked suddenly seemed like a good idea. Something told him that before things got any better… they'd get worse.

\*\*\*\*

He was tying her, thank you, God. She would show him, she would show him she was his, she trusted him. After he tied the last arm, he suddenly clenched his eyes tight and pulled away from the bed.

Mercy watched as he walked away, leaving her panting with the need to make it right. She'd been scared, she didn't remember her training, she was sure she'd trained for that kind of thing. Relearn, that's what she'd do, that's all. Problem solved.

Sade stood next to the table, his head down. His body heaved in the silence, making her own quake for him. The memory of his cock shoving inside her made her gasp. It had hurt and felt good all at once. Then she'd said that mean stuff to him. She was pissed, that's all, just pissed. She had a temper, everybody had a little temper.

God, what was he doing? He paced with his hands on his head and finally turned and came to the bed. Grabbing that box, he sat next to her with it.

"I uh… have some things I need to show you." He swiped a hand over his mouth and his head. Had he always had short cropped hair? She liked it, but she wondered what he'd look like with longer hair. Would it be wavy and thick?

His tone said he was trying hard to put things right too. She'd messed everything up, he was a wreck. She could see it.

"Tell me if you remember any of these things or anything about them." He finally looked at her, and the confusion in the depth of his eyes stole her breath.

"Okay," she said. "Is this the plan? You said you had a plan to help me remember?" She hoped to get him back on track, remind him what the goal was. She'd helped him before, she could do it again, even without remembering. She could feel that much, she could do that.

He nodded and then held up a little teddy bear. She'd honestly not expected anything in his box of tricks to help but… something seemed familiar about the stuffed animal. It made her sad. When no "why's" came, she narrowed her gaze before shaking her head. "Kind of, maybe. But nothing specific is coming, just feels… familiar."

"It's okay," he said softly, setting it down. Her heart ached at hearing the hopelessness in his tone. Like he didn't expect this to help either.

He pulled out a small wooden box next, and her jaw dropped. "That's my jewelry box!"

He stared at her. "Are you shitting me? You fucking remember?"

She nodded and gasped several more times. "Yes. Right off. My dad gave me that when I was ten!"

Sade grabbed his head with both hands and held it. "Thank fuck!" He looked up at the ceiling. "Thank you," he mumbled then hurried and pulled out the next item. Ballerina slippers.

"Those are mine!"

"Oh fuck, Mercy!" he gushed. "You're remembering, baby!"

She hid her sob with a little laugh as tears sprung to her eyes. He quickly took out the next item and she stared at the handkerchief, waiting for recollection then shook her head. "Sorry."

"It's okay, Angel." He pulled out a book next. "I'm going to show you each page." He got closer and turned the pages for her.

She shook her head and apologized through several pages then on the fourth, she cried, "Stop! That, I remember that. I know how to play the piano! I used to play it for my dad!"

Sade's mouth was suddenly on hers and Mercy's hunger erupted immediately. She kissed him but then he pulled away abruptly. "Fuck, let's keep going."

Her heart pounded with a million emotions, need and frustration leading. He turned the next few pages and slowly her heart began to sink as she shook her head. "Sorry."

"You're doing amazing, don't be sorry."

But as he turned and turned it was item after item of strange stuff. "I... I recognize a few items in some of these pictures but don't know why or how."

Sade looked in the box and pulled out papers and held them up. "Remember this?"

She studied the hand drawings carefully and slowly shook her head. Sade presented the next one. Again, nothing. He went through three more. Nothing.

"It's okay," he assured her.

But it wasn't okay, she heard it in his tone. His hope was slipping.

Mercy gasped at the paper plate with the glitter hands. "I remember!" she nearly yelled. "I made that when I was thirteen. It was... it was for..." she fought to connect the missing pieces.

"Don't try too hard. It'll come."

"It was for something, I can feel it," she muttered as he went through the remaining items. A potholder, crocheted items. Both completely unfamiliar. He angled his head and reached into the box and pulled out a couple of pictures. It was while she was looking at the strange people that shit crashed down on her mind, only they weren't memories.

## Chapter Twenty-Two

"Sade? Why are my things at this place?"

Sade regarded Mercy, dread slowly hitting him at realizing what he'd just done. How had he not even considered that? Sade continued to stare at her, fear tying him in sudden knots. *Tell her. Just tell her everything, it's time. Nothing to lose, only gain. Worst case scenario, it might jar her memory. Kane would just have to forgive me. And not die.*

"What aren't you telling me?" she asked, suspicious now.

"I'm going to come out and say this. Just right out." He rubbed one hand on his forehead, staring at her.

She stared back at him, appearing worried now.

"This place... belongs to your father."

She continued staring at him, a mixture of disbelief and anger crimping her face. "My... dad...w-what...why..." She closed her eyes a second. "I don't remember that." She slowly opened them, another realization dawning. "And... how would you know that?"

"Because I know your dad."

She turned her head a little, her eyes not leaving him. "But... you said you didn't."

"I didn't know the dad you were referring to."

She stared at him fully. Fully confused, fully fucking scared. "Just... come out and tell me," her voice quivered. "I-I've got too many missing pieces already, you're not helping."

Sade sat next to her and took a deep breath. "Mercy. Your dad... isn't..."

"Isn't what, isn't what, don't stop," she said, agitated.

He lowered his head feeling like shit. "Isn't dead. He's alive."

After many silent seconds, he chanced a look at her. She stared at him like he were a joke, a very bad fucking joke.

"That's not... not something you should do or say. Why would you do this? To get memories? Is that what you're doing?"

"No, no!" he hurried emphatically. "Your father led two lives, he-he rescued you when you were nine from a very bad life." Sade realized he was not prepared to tell the whole story, and stuttering it out like he was making it up as he went, was the last fucking thing he needed to do. "Look," he said. "He made me swear not to tell until he came back. Your dad is Kane Cross, the most lethal man—vigilante—in Los Angeles. He hunts killers and he takes them out. But he's a good guy."

"Vigilante?" her face screwed up while she shook her head. "My dad is no vigilante!" She let out one laugh.

Sade got up and hurried to the door and opened it. "Liberty! Liberty!" he yelled.

A few moments later, she came out of her room. "Coming! Jesus, you'll wake the fucking dead," she muttered, hurrying down the hall in a black silk robe.

He opened the door and hurried to the bed and covered Mercy's legs. "Tell her about Kane."

Liberty regarded Mercy tied to the bed then eyed him. "Ummm, Sade?"

"It's too late, she already knows."

"Tell her what?"

"Show her pictures, something. Prove he's Kane Cross. Prove to her that her father led two lives, she doesn't believe me."

"He's telling the truth," Liberty said.

Mercy choked out a huff. "And I'm just supposed to believe you? I don't even know you," Mercy said, her voice edged with growing anger. "Untie me while you're parading around in your underwear," she snapped at Sade.

"I'll leave you two now," Liberty said, quickly turning to go.

"Don't leave, make him untie me," Mercy yelled. "Bo! Bo, help me!" She erupted in screaming now.

Sade ushered a muttering Liberty out of the room assuring her he'd take care of her then locked the door. He faced Mercy who kept screaming at the top of her lungs for Bo.

"He's not going to come," he yelled. "He knows too."

She gasped and glared at him. "You're saying my dad is alive! Do you realize how cruel that would be to say if it weren't true?"

"Of course I fucking know that," Sade said making his way to the bed. "Do you realize how cruel it is for you to think I'd ever do something like that?"

"Cruel? You? Why would I ever guess Mr. Sadomasochist would be cruel, sooooo sorry to insult you!"

"It's not what you think. Yes, I want your memories but now we need them."

She stared at him, her eyes wide and narrowed with another round of confusion that had her chest heaving. "Well, do tell."

He paced now, not liking how this all felt. "We're supposed to be ready to evacuate any day and there's a tunnel leading to our transportation that only you know the code to. So, it's actually more than just me wanting your fucking memories, it's me needing to make sure you're alive when shit hits the fan."

Sade watched her reaction, trying to follow what was going on in her head. Judging by the sick look on her face, nothing helpful. He paced, waiting for something, anything from her. "Talk to me, goddammit!" he yelled.

"You... you need my memories," she gasped. "Just not the way I thought you did."

"Don't fucking even," he said, pissed. God, he needed to take a minute and get his shit together, not fight with Mercy.

"You are one selfish bastard," she muttered. "You tie me up and make emergencies just to get your memories. You want memories? I'll give you memories. I remember Bo. I remember opening the door and meeting him for the first time. I remember how sweet he was, how cute too."

Sade stared at her, fighting back his sudden rage. "You're lying."

"Oh, I'm not. I can tell you what he wore. Light blue shirt? Dark blue denim jeans and those goofy tan bowling looking shoes?"

*That's fucking great!* is what he should be thinking and saying. But she was rubbing it in his face that she remembered Bo and not him. She was just trying to hurt him. But why? Because she thought he'd lie about her dad? Lie about wanting her memories? So fucking stupid.

"That's good, Mercy."

"Is it? Don't try to pretend you're not jealous out of your mind."

"I'm not pretending, I am fucking jealous out of my mind."

"Good!"

He sat at the table, staring at her, his body trembling. "What else do you remember?"

"Not a damn thing."

"Would you lie about that?"

"Maybe."

"Why the fuck would you?"

"Because maybe I'm sick of you and your need for memories." She jerked on the restraints. "Why don't you get out of memory lane before life passes you by?"

"There is no fucking life without Mercy!" He slammed his fist on the table. "Don't you see that?"

"Well too fucking bad!" she screamed, furious. "You're a pathetic pussy, that's what you are! Need a woman to hold your fucking hand? I don't know what I ever saw in you!"

Sade toyed with the pain inside him, trying to decide what to do with it. He clenched his eyes tight as too many things train wrecked in his head.

"I wonder why I remember Bo and not you?" she said. "Strange, isn't it?"

Sade covered his face.

"I even feel safer with him. Guess that's not so odd, given your background. Maybe I don't remember you because I'm trying to block it out? Ever thought of that? I mean think about the shit in that journal of yours. Think about the shit you just *did!* I was clearly a delusional fucking idiot to be with you!"

Sade paced now. "Stop," he whispered.

"Maybe you couldn't get your dick hard because your brain knew something wasn't right."

"Stop," he yelled.

"Or what," she yelled back. "Who are you to tell me what the fuck to do? You tie me up to jar my memories, terrorize me to jar my fucking memories!? All for you to get your precious *Mercy* back? Well *fuck you and fuck your precious Mercy!*"

Sade stormed to the bed and got an inch from her face. "Stop!"

She slammed her forehead into his, making him stagger back and blink around inky dots. "Fuck," he gasped, his adrenaline spiking as he shook his head clear.

If there had been remorse on her face when he looked at her, it would have made all the difference in her world. Maybe. But it wasn't. It was pure hatred. Hatred for him.

And all he could think in that moment was needing Mercy. Having Mercy back. One way or another.

His sadism shoved its way into his skin and filled his cock as he stared at her. "Change of plans, Angel."

"Don't call me your angel, your angel is a stupid fucking bitch!"

Her screaming fury made Sade's hunger burn hotter. And the animal was out. Walking slowly around the bed, eyes on what he was about to break down and own. But before he did, he'd have her fucking weeping and *begging* for him. He'd make her eat every fucking hateful word until she confessed it. Liar. Filthy. Fucking. Liar.

****

Mercy's heart pounded as she watched Sade turn into another person right before her eyes. She held her jaw firmly together, determined to not bow down, holding on to her anger. Reminding herself why she'd said those mean things. *She* was just something in the way of what he wanted. And it wasn't her.

"You don't scare me," she muttered, snapping her jaw shut when it wanted to tremble.

He crawled slowly onto the bed, his gaze locked between her legs. Mercy's chest heaved as he made his intentions clear. In one swift dive, his mouth covered her panties in a growl, bowing Mercy off the bed as she pulled the restraints in shock. He kissed her, his mouth pressing and moving like a vicious storm all over her privates.

She couldn't keep from fighting the brutal force, his mouth was hot electricity shooting into her right at that spot. She shuddered, gasped, and jerked with it. His hands slammed down on her upper thighs, pressing her hard into the bed, making her take it like he commanded. There was no escaping the assault. He forced his mouth tight to her body and sucked, pulling at that boiling spot. His hungry growl vibrated into her, and Mercy gave several shrieks as her body exploded in spasms. His growls strained, and his fingers shot under her ass, pulling her impossibly tight to his mouth. Mercy's shrieks continued as she jerked and convulsed with the pleasure.

Before she could recover, his mouth was on hers, pushing her lips open with that same hunger, tongue plunging, fingers biting at her neck and jaw. Her cries flowed into his mouth as he devoured her mind with his kiss, sending her world spinning.

The storm strayed from her mouth, a hot path along her jaw 'til it reached her ear where he rasped the heated promise. "You *will* remember." He bit her earlobe, making her shriek and turn her mouth, need and hunger burning through her.

"Make me," she gasped. "Make me remember."

He suddenly shot off the bed and walked to the small fridge. Pulling out a bottle of beer, he opened it and tilted it up. Her eyes feasted on the thick muscles moving in his neck then to the heaving of his chest and abs. Her stomach clenched at seeing the bulge pushing hard in his underwear.

He growled when done and threw the bottle. Mercy jumped at the shatter of glass while Sade sauntered back to the fridge and got another one. Again he guzzled while walking to the table. He set it down and sat heavily on the chair and leaned forward with his forearms on his knees. What was he thinking? God, she needed to know.

He finally sat back, one leg cocked out and grabbed the beer and drank, his other hand hanging between his thighs. He had such beautiful hands. She raised her eyes and found his gaze locked hard on her, making her insides jump. The fierce premeditation there made her tremble inside. He put the bottle to his lips and tilted his head back, not breaking the stare, not blinking.

Mercy's heart raced when he stood. Again he threw the bottle and this time she couldn't stop the small scream.

Fear pumped through her as he walked to the small media center and turned it on. He flipped through the search then stood there with his head lowered while a choppy violin sound blasted through the room.

Her heart hammered to the tune as he slowly turned and made his way toward her. His eyes locked on hers just as a deep drag of bass tickled her ears and skin.

He came closer until he towered next to her, a wall of muscle in black briefs. Whatever was going through his mind had him extremely aroused, which had Mercy breathless. He climbed on the bed, hands on either side of her head with knees straddling her chest. She gasped up at the heaving abs and chest right before her. A spike of heat tingled between her legs as he grabbed the bulge in his briefs with both hands and thrust his hips to the music.

The sight of him touching himself made everything sizzle inside her. He lowered the front of his underwear, and she gave a whimpered gasp when his cock was free. The sight of it so close up, shocked her. In a way, he was her first. He'd given her first orgasm. She wanted him to be her first everything. God, what was he going to make her do?

Her breaths came faster as their tub episode flashed through her mind. She didn't like doing that in water. She'd been blind and scared. Now, there was nothing to fear, so why was she so scared? Doing it wrong? Not satisfying him?

His stroked along his length slowly and she finally looked past his beautiful manhood to the brutal face staring down at her, his perfect teeth bared as he moved his hips. She pulled at the restraints wanting so badly to touch him now.

He suddenly latched iron fingers in her hair, and she gasped as he held her head firmly to the bed with one hand. He opened his knees more and lowered himself, stroking her face with the entire length of his cock. She parted her lips, never hungrier to taste anything in her life.

He moved to the rhythm of the song, rubbing the hot muscle over every inch of her face, across her nose. Mercy breathed in, devouring him with all her senses. He finally rubbed the thick tip over her lips, teasing, making her reach for it with her tongue. She lashed and licked and even though it wasn't her first time, it felt new. He wrote about her sucking him, how much he loved it.

A dense jealousy suddenly filled her that she couldn't remember what he had loved. She wanted to do it again, better than before. She wanted to make him forget the past and remember this, right now. Her. Him.

He hissed and slid his cock into her eager mouth, moving in and out to that song, pushing the thick head against the back of her throat and holding it there when the bass dragged. She watched him, taking all of him, loving all of it. She wanted to make him come, to give him the same insane pleasure he'd given her. But more than anything, she wanted to feel him between her legs, his cock thrusting deep inside her while he kissed her senseless.

"Remember my cock, baby," he gasped.

She nodded with a moan and his fingers pulled harder at her hair until pain shot through her scalp.

"I know you fucking do," he gritted. "Your mouth remembers. Your pussy remembers. And you will fucking remember before this night is over with." She grunted with his firm thrusts. "You're going to swallow every fucking drop. You want that?"

She nodded, her jaw burning and aching.

He growled and held her head in both hands now, his fingers biting still as he pumped his cock in and out, shallow then deep. He hissed and looked down, watching her mouth.

Mercy waited for him to look at her like he had before. Look at her while he did this to her. His lips pulled back in a growl. "Ffffucking teeth feel good on my cock."

She'd been fighting not to hurt him, forgetting he liked pain. She allowed her teeth to rub along him more and he gasped, looking down at what she was doing. His brows drew together hard and his mouth remained opened as she created more friction with her teeth. "Oh fuck," he grit.

Delicious heat spiked through Mercy as she felt the power. Getting pain was his weakness and she could use that. Something his sweet Mercy wouldn't do.

She gave a deep groan and bit harder on his cock. Sade slammed his palms against the wall before him with a sharp gasp.

"Fucking suck me hard. Just like that." He looked down again and finally, his eyes locked to hers. "Bite my cock, God yes, fucking bite it, baby." He growled long and hard as he forced himself in and out of her now vicious grip. When she saw impossible pleasure threatening in his hot gaze, she clamped down harder.

Sade roared, and hot cum immediately shot against her throat before Mercy could worry she'd gone too far. She held her bite as he grabbed her head in both hands, fingers pulling her hair like he'd rip it out. She held tight, screaming on his cock and swallowing when his cum demanded passage either down or up.

When she'd taken every drop as he demanded, she trembled as his body heaved with his head back. Shock edged his strained groans, filling Mercy with pride. She'd given him that. Not his sweet Mercy. Her.

## Chapter Twenty-Three

Sade growled and shot off the bed, literally jerking his still hard cock out of her mouth. She watched him pace next to the bed, holding his head, his entire body heaving as the music continued to play. His head dropped back with his hands on his face, and he began to let out a growl until he turned and roared right at her.

She clenched her eyes shut tight, bracing for impact. But he just kept roaring in her face. Mercy screamed back, turning away from him, not understanding, not able to take the sound of agony he blasted at her.

He was on her again, his body pressing into her, mouth hot on her neck, tongue sliding up in loud grunts. She fought to reach his mouth with hers, desperate for him again. His fingers grabbed her head in a vicious grip and he kissed her hard, their teeth scraping and cutting until she tasted blood. She was dizzy with the pain, need and desire, fighting to keep up with him. Pain. She could take it. Somewhere in her mind, she knew she could take it.

And give it.

She bit at whatever her mouth could reach, making him growl and gasp. When he pulled out of her reach over and over, she growled back.

"Fucking kiss me," she gasped. "Untie me. I want to do things to you. Things I've never done before." He stared down, a haze in his silver eyes. One hand stroked her face, his touch so very delicate and restrained. The storm brewing in his eyes should have scared her, but fear was not something she fathomed in that moment.

Blood dripped from his mouth onto her chin, and he angled his head before lowering to lick along her chin then across her lips. He did it again but this time when he licked her mouth, his tongue plunged with a fury. They kissed again, a war of teeth and tongue, bruised lips fighting to devour first—consume all.

She didn't understand why, but she knew they were fighting. For her, she fought to find a ground to stand on. In her life, her mind, in that bed, that room. That moment. A fight to exist, a fight for rights to be. Somebody. Anybody. She needed to be his, she fought to become that. And she fought to understand what he was fighting so she could kick its ass and take back what was hers. Make him give up the ghost so that she could live.

Again he left her, storming to the kitchen area and yanking open a drawer. He turned with a dark fury, a knife in his hands.

Panic shot through her, fought to scatter her determination as he made his way back, his gaze on her body. She shut her eyes as he grabbed her top and sawed it off of her. Fear and desire warred as the air hit her naked breasts. Next he cut her panties off and then her skirt.

The pacing began again. He pressed the heel of his palms to his eyes, the knife flashing at every pivot.

"Talk to me, Sade," she gasped. She wanted to reach him in the dark place he was in, fighting alone. Fighting that something she didn't know.

The pacing suddenly stopped. He slowly turned until his slitted gaze locked with hers. Pain stole her breath at what she saw. Confusion and devastation. He turned and faced her, walking to the bed. When his body blocked out everything, his words whispered out. "Where… is Mercy?"

Pain suffocated her until she fought for air.

"Where... is my MERCY!"

She shook her head and let out a sob as he dragged the knife from his shoulder to hip, blood flowing down his body. "Stop," she barely cried.

He drew the knife from his other shoulder to his hip. "WHERE IS SHE!"

"STOOOOOP!" she screamed.

He was on her again, heavy and pressing. His mouth was hot over her breasts, teeth scraping the sensitive nipples while his chest rumbled with a hungry growl. "Where is she?" he gasped, his hands squeezing the mounds until she arched off the bed. "Tell me you remember," he rasped, devouring mouthfuls of her wherever his lips landed.

"Please fuck me," she begged hoarsely.

His breath shuddered at her mouth and his cock pressed at her opening. He slid in deep, his mouth on hers again, kissing as he moved in and out of her with near vicious strokes, growling in her mouth. Heat shot through her body as he rammed a place inside her that made her dizzy and confused and lost to everything but that. She stared at him through a slitted gaze as he drove into her.

"Remember me," he hisses harshly.

His kissed her again, like he was giving her mouth to mouth. The idea that he was fucking her to resurrect another woman shattered her heart until she began to wail and scream in the agony of not being enough. Not being the one. The one he loved, the one he was crazy in love with, desperate for.

"Untie me! I don't fucking remember you, I don't remember! I'm not your angel! I'm not your angel!" she sobbed. "Untie me, I don't want you! I don't fucking want you!"

He collapsed on her body and she continued to wail, "You fucked me! You fucked me because you don't love me! Love makes your dick not work, you told me, you don't love me!" she sobbed.

"You're not her!" he roared getting off of her.

Mercy clenched her eyes tight, wishing she could shut her ears and heart.

"Mercy fought my demons, and you!" he rammed a finger at her, "You fucking *feed* them! You don't have a clue about what we had, the love we had! She would have kicked my ass for doing what I did to you!"

Mercy wailed. "I thought you wanted it!"

"I do fucking want it!" He slammed his hands over his chest. "Don't you fucking see!" he roared. "I hate myself, I hate this fucking body! I want to fucking die and Mercy," he gasped. "Mercy taught me… how to live. God, I need her *back*," he finished in a hoarse voice that shattered Mercy. "I don't know how to live without her!"

"Untie meeeeeee!" she screamed, kicking and thrashing. "There is NO MERCY! There is NO FUCKING MERCY!"

****

Fury and pain roiled in Sade like a bomb in his blood. He looked around for the knife and grabbed it off the floor. In two steps, he was at the bed, ripping through the material holding her. One, two, three, four. Fucking done and seconds from doing things he'd regret eternally.

Mercy wasn't done. His blood smeared all over her, she flew at him in screaming rage, nails, feet and fists slamming his body and igniting his sadism's very short fuse.

In one move, he grabbed her and threw her on the bed, only to have her scramble up and attack again. "I hate you! I never loved you, you bastard! You're a liar, I never fucking loved you! I would remember! I would remember that, how would I forget! You're lying like you lied about my dad! You're a liar!"

Every word came with a kick or a punch. Some he blocked, some he gladly took. He was inches from letting her beat him into ecstasy except the pain her words caused demanded his sadism, demanded his anger. Because that was the kind of pain he couldn't stand under, that was a monster only his sadism could stand up to. But she couldn't stand up to his fury. And God help him, he was slowly slipping under its wicked oblivion.

"Open the door Sade!" Bo pounded on the door. "Open the fucking door! What the fuck is wrong with you, open this fucking door or I'll fucking kick it in! You're fucking up! You hear me?"

Sounded like he body-slammed the door and Sade stormed to it, glad for the intrusion. He jerked it open and walked into Bo until he was up against the wall. "You here to stop me?" he muttered through a furious adrenaline spike. "Are you? You better fucking get busy, man, you getting me? You getting me?"

"I'm getting you, man" he gasped. "But not fucking right here, we'll do it someplace else."

Sade stared down into Bo's face. The fury there didn't give a fuck about size or strength, it only cared about giving all you fucking had to it, didn't matter how it ended. And in that second, Sade hungered to oblige.

"Nobody's doing shit anyplace else." The click of metal sounded on his right, and he turned his gaze slowly to Liberty with a Glock aimed at his head. "I know how to graze really well, don't try me or I'll shave your ass down until you're on the floor. We are done fighting," she gasped. "This is not doing a fucking thing for anybody."

Sade turned a little to see Mercy standing in the doorway behind them, wearing his t-shirt. The sight of her disheveled appearance slowly brought him back to reality. Like she'd been used as a chew toy by a fucking monster. Her hair stuck up everywhere, black streaks of makeup covered her cheeks, his blood smeared all over her arms and neck, her lower lip cut and swollen from that great fucking sadistic kissing.

Burning shame slowly filled him until he clenched his eyes shut in self-disgust, ready to vomit.

"Now, what we're going to do," Liberty began, "is go in the living room and—" Liberty jerked her gaze to the living room. "Everybody to the safe-room! Now!"

Panic slammed Sade, and he grabbed Mercy's hand and ran with her, then spun and lifted her in his arms, sprinting to the room with the tunnel leading out.

"Okay baby, we need you to remember the code to get out of here," Sade gasped as he went.

"Oh God, I don't know a fucking code!"

"Hint is 'No More Nightmares,'" Liberty said as they made it to the room. "Have her try until we get it, I'm going to the gun room for weapons." The sound of an explosion rocked the air and Liberty slammed the door and locked it. "Cancel that order."

"Where is it," Sade said, looking around with Mercy in his arms still.

"There!" Liberty pointed to a silver door at the back corner of the room.

"A rhyme," Sade said, hurrying her over and setting her down. "You know any rhymes at all?"

Mercy began stuttering through syllables, trying to think.

"Maybe it's like a nursery rhyme," Bo offered, breathless. "Like, Twinkle Twinkle Little Star or something.

"Try it," Sade ordered.

"How, what do I do?"

"Press the button," Liberty called out, "and speak. Sade, help me barricade the door. Everything against it. Bo, look for anything that can serve as a weapon or defense."

Mercy pressed the button. "Twinkle Twinkle Little Star."

"Error... please speak clearly into the microphone." She leaned and repeated it louder into the mic. "Good try, Button," said a female computer voice. "Hint: No More Nightmares."

"Who's Button?" Mercy gasped.

"You must be," Bo hurried, stacking up items on the floor by them. "Try again, try to think. What nursery rhyme stopped your nightmares?"

"I don't even remember my nightmares!"

"Just call random nursery rhymes out," Liberty said. "Help her out, Bo Peep!"

"You watch the door, Iron Maiden," Bo shot back.

"I got your back, baby, don't you worry about that," Liberty said.

Sade hauled the other desk in the room near Mercy in case they got through. "What are the odds of them getting in?" Sade asked.

"They could blow the door," she said with a grunt, shoving a bookshelf over. "We can use these books," she said. "Keep trying, Mercy!"

"Books," Bo muttered. "Gonna read them to death?"

"I heard that," Liberty said.

"Hey Diddle Diddle," Sade yelled, "Come on, Mercy! Humpty Dumpty Sat On A Wall, Little Miss Muffet, Row Row Row your... fucking boat," he yelled, throwing the grandfather clock onto the desk. "Hurry!"

"Slow down!" she yelled, repeating them into the mic only to get the same message over and over. "I think if I knew my nightmares it would help."

"Wee Willie Winkie," Bo suggested. "The Itsy Bitsy Spider!"

Mercy tried again. "Good try, Button. Hint: No More Nightmares."

"No more nightmares, no more nightmares" Mercy muttered, clenching her eyes. "Just call more out, nothing is coming."

"Uhh, uhh," Bo snapped rapidly. "Humpty Dumpty Sat On A Wall."

"Good try, Button. Hint: No More Nightmares."

"They're at the door," Liberty whispered, signaling for them to be quiet, and then pointing at Mercy to keep on trying. Liberty signaled Sade over. "We have one weapon. That's not good. We'll have to be creative."

"Fuck," Sade whispered, looking back at Mercy. "Is there no way to contact her fucking father in here? Is there any other way out?"

"Yes, if we can get out of here alive," she muttered, "we can walk out the front door."

"Why didn't we just do that instead of coming in here and trapping ourselves?"

"Because it seemed like our best chance, and I wasn't exactly ready for them!" she hissed.

"I got it!" Mercy screeched. "It was Mary Had A Little Lamb!"

Sade and Liberty jerked around to find the door opened. "You're fucking kidding me!" Sade and Liberty hurried into what looked like an elevator.

Liberty tapped the button and the door shut at a snail's pace. Once moving, Sade looked around. "We going up or down?" he asked, putting his arm around Mercy, noticing she didn't return the gesture.

"Seems like up," Liberty said.

The floor beneath them shook. "Fuck," Bo gasped, arms flying out at his sides.

"They blew the door," Liberty said. "Come on, hurry hurry," she muttered.

They finally stopped, and the door opened in a garage where a black SUV sat. They quickly hurried into it, Liberty and Bo in the front, Sade pulling Mercy in the back with him.

Liberty lowered the visor and keys fell into her lap. Bo gasped in awe, and Liberty started the vehicle. "Everybody buckle the fuck up, everything is going just a tad too good to celebrate."

Exactly Sade's thought. Nothing went this good in his life, ever.

## Chapter Twenty-Four

It was like the fucking Twilight Zone as Sade stood in the shower at the next safe house, palms braced on the wall. They'd made it there with zero problems, and he could almost feel Karma smiling at him. *Go ahead and relax. Take a break. Kick your feet up, that way when I come and kick your ass, you'll really feel it.*

And he was pretty sure it was coming in the form of a little someone named Mercy. She'd been acting weird with him since they got there. The day of, she totally fucking dissed him on every hand. Then the next morning, she stared—no, glared at him the entire day. And now she wanted to talk to him. He was sure Karma had settled to get him this way—the one way that meant everything to him. Mercy.

To further add to the Twilight Zone effect, the new safe house was a mini-mansion on a remote part of an island in the Philippines. Population two-hundred-twenty if you counted them, with gorgeous blue-green ocean all around. They'd driven to the PO Box and gotten two sets of keys—one for the small private plane, the other to this remarkable place. All that was left was waiting for Kane's return, which they found out would be that evening. That would be the other Karma cookie in the oven—something happening that would prevent that, and break Mercy's heart all over again.

Sade dressed in jeans and a black t-shirt. A small part of him hoped that he still had some sexual effect on her. He knocked on her room door, and she called for him to come in.

Opening the door, he stifled a painful groan at finding her facing a desk in what looked like a fitted white t-shirt that stopped right at matching panties. Or was that a bathing suit? His mind decided panties.

The double doors leading to a small private balcony stood open to the ocean breeze. She turned from the small table next to it, and Sade's eyes zeroed in on her pussy, so perfectly outlined in that smooth white fabric. He finally raised his eyes and took in her bare stomach and breasts showing around the single button holding her top together. Fuck.

"It's not nice to stare, Sade."

Her near bored tone stung him as he shut the door. "It's not nice to look so edible."

"I want you to let me try something with you." She crossed her arms, all business.

He regarded her, his heart racing. "Like what?"

She reached behind her and lifted several white straps. "Tie you up."

His dick jerked as he angled his gaze at her, walking further into the room. "Why are you doing this again?"

"I had a dream." Her shrug matched her simple tone. "You were tied up and I want to see if it helps with my memory."

He held his arms out to her. "In that case…"

She eyed his offer then turned to the table, not seeming very happy about any of it. "You were naked in the dream," she said easily. "And on your back."

Sade was speechless and breathless as he removed his shirt and watched her get busy with the ties at the table. Almost felt like a dream. But he found it kind of funny how she stayed busy until he was on the bed, naked and ready for her little game. He didn't give one shit what she did to him, but more why she did it. That's what held him spellbound and obedient, and maybe a little nervous.

She tied his legs first, still being careful not to look at him, not even when all four limbs were nicely secure.

"I wanted to show you something before I get started."

Again his cock jerked and he had to smile at that one. "Get started? How long will this take and will I survive it?"

"I'm sure you'll survive." She went to the table and picked up a remote and pressed it. He watched her ass while she stood with her hip cocked, facing away from him. His heart hammered in his chest with curiosity and his stomach clenched when the song she'd danced to suddenly started playing. She made her way to the bed and sat on the edge next to him, feet on the floor and looking down.

He waited, watching her. "I talked to my dad last night," she whispered. "He's coming back."

Sade's stomach knotted more. "Look, I'm… sorry I had to lie to you about him. You have no idea how badly I wanted to tell you, so many times."

She kept her head down before she gave one of those lying shrugs. "It's okay."

"What's up with you, Angel? Why you got me tied up like this?"

"I wanted to try one last thing," she whispered. "Give you one more chance."

"One more chance for what?"

She stood and undid her button and turned around. In a nice slow seduction, she removed her top and bottom next, her hips swaying gently. She climbed onto the bed, kneeling between his legs. She took his cock in her hands and began stroking him, her inexperienced fingers making him hard and eager, her courage bringing a slow roll of his hips through her too delicate grip.

"Am I doing good, Angel?"

He watched her lips part and she laid along one of his legs. She held his cock at her mouth, staring at the head until he reached for her with a grunt.

"You want it?" she whispered.

"Put your pretty lips on me. Lick me 'til I'm on fire." He recalled the way she'd fucking bit him and brought him to orgasm in an instant. He twirled his hips with a hiss as he thought about how fucking good that felt. At first he'd thought Mercy wouldn't have done that. But he remembered how she'd given herself in that sexorcism and decided by principle, it was damn near the same.

"How do you want it?" she said, kissing softly on the top with her eyes closed.

"Deep in your fucking mouth," he grit, "with your teeth all over it."

"What about this?" She cupped his balls, her touch delicate then slowly getting firmer until he gasped on the promise of ecstasy that could bring.

"Tight. Fucking tight when I come," his hungry gaze followed her tongue along the length of his cock.

"I love your cock," she whispered, almost to herself. She angled her head and placed open mouth kisses from base to top. Then she flicked the very tip of her tongue on the slit until he was pulling hard on the restraints and bucking his hips for more. Torment. She was fucking tormenting him, and he loved that agony.

"Is it hot," she asked, flicking still.

"Fucking burning. Suck me. All of it."

"Not yet," she whispered, licking the ridge until he bowed off the bed in frantic moans.

"Fuck, baby, please."

"Please? Did you ever beg like this before?"

"I don't know," he shook his head. "I don't think so." Not out loud.

"I like it," she whispered, taking the head of his cock into her mouth for leisure sucking. "You look so good when you beg. I like to see your body out of control." She swirled her tongue all around the top. "I like to see you at my mercy."

Insane heat soared through him as all his dark kink raced in, begging for pain and torment. "Make me beg," he gasped.

Her hand kneaded his balls, promising naughty things while her other hand choked the base of his cock tight. Her lips and tongue remained delicate flames on the head with an occasional suck, just enough to drive him crazy.

"God, I want to make you suck me," he grunted, pulling harder on the restraints, feeling them give. "I love to make you suck my cock." That other desire began to trickle in, the new one. She gasped on his cock as though reading his mind, remembering.

She gave a little whimper that called it forward, then rolled her pretty green gaze up to his. "I hate it when you make me while I'm scared."

Oh fuck. He gave a half roar at hearing her little lie followed by her delicate kisses to the top of the head. She was teasing him. Showing him she liked his little dark game, but willing to pretend she didn't. The hunger to have it again spiked through his blood. "I want to play," he rasped. "Fuck your pretty ass while you're blind and helpless."

She gasped and flicked her tongue relentlessly over the slit then sucked eagerly over the head, letting her teeth play now.

"Fucking... *God!*" He hissed several times, looking down at what she was doing. Her hand squeezed harder at his balls.

"You fucking like getting your pretty ass fucked? Is that it? Is that what you're telling me, Angel?" He let out another half roar when she dove on his cock until the head hit her throat and she pulled up slowly, dragging her teeth. "Oh my fucking *God,*" he barely managed, bucking his hips hard.

She turned her body so that her pussy was in his face, adding another pleasure to the mix. "Jesus Christ," he gasped, leaning for it. "You're fucking dripping, baby."

She looked back while holding his cock, putting herself right on his mouth.

Sade was in another heaven now, another playground as his tongue and lips devoured her. She got back to sucking him, her moans and gasps adding to the ecstasy while she teased the head of his cock and squirmed her pussy all over his mouth. He growled, wishing he was free to force her to be still while he fucking sucked the orgasm from her body and fingered her pretty ass.

"Sade," she gasped, bucking her hips on his mouth, then devouring his cock. She was suddenly coming, squeezing his balls hard as she squealed on his dick. Her mouth became a hot, sharp ecstasy as she raked him with her teeth, bringing his orgasm instantly again.

His breaths strained against the agonizing pleasure, gripped in the vice until he was completely subject to it, moving to its demand.

Mercy's mouth slowly turned to a soft, delicate heat, kissing and licking in the violent aftermath. At hearing her soft moans, his heart hammered. That was one element he'd never had with painful pleasure. That, right there. He'd never wanted it. But now, feeling the press of her face against his leg and gentle lapping of her pussy on his chest, Jesus God, yes. Yes, he fucking loved it, and he didn't give a fuck why anymore, he was just glad he did.

She slowly climbed off and sat on the bed next to him. At seeing she wasn't happy, all that hot joy slowly evaporated until there was only the cold haze of *what the fuck?*

"Mercy..."

She shook her head, holding her arms.

"What did I do wrong?"

"You *came,*" she whispered.

"I came? I wasn't supposed to?"

"Not if you loved me."

"What?"

"You can't come when you love, remember?"

"I never said that, I said when I think about… fuck, Mercy—"

"Don't call me that."

Sade eyed her, his anger slowly rising. "And what the fuck am I supposed to call you, that's your fucking name!"

"I don't care, just not that, I want to forget I ever heard that name."

"Well, you can give that one up, nobody is forgetting anybody."

She jerked to him. "Oh yeah?"

"Oh yeah."

"Well, you know what? I'm leaving if you don't."

He stared at her, dumbfounded. "And where the fuck are you going? You're on an island!

Her jaw dropped and her gaze narrowed. "So you'd just let me leave because I can't remember who I used to be?"

"I never said I'd let you leave, but you can't make me forget who you are Mercy, sorry. Does this fucking mean you've given up on remembering?"

"I never said that, but I'm sick of trying to."

"Then take a *break*!"

"Take a break! And have you mope around mourning a ghost right in front of me? No fucking thank you." She jerked away from him again.

He thought about that. He didn't *mope*! "I'll do better."

"You'll do better," she muttered.

"I know this may sound weird, but, the more I go? The more I think you don't want to remember."

She spun with wide-eyed incredulity. "How can you fucking say that? I can't believe you just fucking said that! I cannot believe you just said that!" She smacked the bed and her face crimped just as tears rolled down.

"Oh my God, I'm sorry," Sade said, feeling like shit. "You just... act a lot like a jealous woman."

"Well I wonder why!" she yelled, standing now.

"Mercy—"

"I said *don't call me that!*" She glared at him, wiping her eyes. "There's no Mercy here, and... you know? Sade? I'm sorry about that. I really am," she gasped, crossing her arms over her breasts. "I know how much you love her, and... I once admired that. At first when I read that journal, I thought wow." She smiled that sweet smile. "This is like... Romeo and Juliet or Cinderella. I remembered those stories," she nodded, her voice soft with irony. "I'd never seen anybody with so much love for somebody and I thought... this person I was, she was fucking something really great, you know?" Tears spilled down her face again, and she laughed a little. "I was proud at first. I really liked how you thought of her. Of me." She nodded, looking down with a gasp. "Like a queen almost. It was beautiful." The barely squeaked words came with more rolling tears that stabbed Sade. "And then... as I went on, as I tried my best to remember who I was. I...I got so frustrated. And yes," she said, nodding and looking right. "Jealous even. And I was hoping..." She gazed at the bed like she couldn't look him in the eye. "That you might love me," she whispered hoarsely. "I mean the person that I'm not. I don't know who I am, I don't... remember who I was but... I still am." The words shot out on a broken gasp. "I still am, I'm alive." She wiped her face on her shoulder.

"And I realized something, Sade." She finally looked at him now. "I realized that..." her mouth trembled and it stole his fucking breath. "Realized that if I ever did remember you... I might just die because..." She gave a small sob before gushing, "I can't love you more than I already do. And I'm done trying to win your heart when it belongs to somebody else."

Sade watched her as she walked to her closet and opened it. She pulled out a suitcase and panic hit him. "What are you doing?"

"I told you," she mumbled. "I'm leaving."

"To where!" he cried.

"Back home."

"Home? There is no fucking home, Angel, nothing is safe."

"I don't care. I'll find a home, I'll relocate. If I'm supposed to die, then oh well."

"Oh well? Un-fucking tie me, Mercy. Right now. Why did you ask me to come here, why did you do all this and put on that fucking song?"

"Because I *remember* it!" she screamed. "One of the few things I remember and I don't want you following me, that's the ultimate reason you're tied."

"You're soooo fucking crazy if you think I'd let you leave."

She narrowed her gaze while pulling on shorts. "You can't stop me."

"Mercy—"

"I said don't call me that."

"What the fuck am I supposed to call you, that's your name!"

"I'll change it! Too many bad memories around it," she sobbed, putting on her shirt now.

Sade's fury shot up, and he yanked and growled until he got free and stood, staring at a startled Mercy. She eyed the door. "Don't even think about it, Angel."

"Don't call me that either," she seethed.

"Angel. Mercy. Baby," he said, walking toward her. "You brought me in here, made me get naked, gave me the most amazing orgasm of my fucking life, and you were going to leave me? Just like that?"

She swallowed, and nodded a little. "That's right."

He shook his head, his heart racing still from her confession just before. "Not even a goodbye kiss?"

"That's close enough," she gasped when he continued toward her.

"Oh no, baby. It's not nearly close enough."

She glanced around then back at him. "Stop. Don't come any closer, I mean it."

"You stop. I'm taking what's mine."

She was back against the table now, holding on. "I'm not yours," she shook her head.

He nodded. "Yes. You are."

"I won't be second," she whispered desperately.

She gasped when his body met hers, his cock pushing into her. But she held his gaze, making Sade's heart hammer. He took her face between his hands and lowered his mouth, kissing her lips softly. "You will never... be second." He slid his lips back and forth over hers, inhaling her sharp breaths.

"But you don't..."

"I do," he said. "I thought only Mercy could love me." He stroked her face with a hunger, nipping her lower lip. "I thought only Mercy could save me from myself."

"I can't save you," she gasped. "I don't... remember how."

"I'll fucking teach you," he said heatedly. "The way you taught me." He kissed along her jaw, his breath ragged with need, his cock hard for her again. "I'll fucking help *you*." He nuzzled at her neck and her fingers clawed in his hair. "Are you listening to me, baby?" He moved back to her mouth, plunging his tongue deep for a thorough taste, then pulling up. "Are you listening?" He looked deep into her tear filled eyes. "Broken or whole... you're all mine. You... are all mine."

She cried out with a gasp. "I remember that! Oh my God, I remember that, I told you that!"

"That's beautiful, baby." Sade lifted her in his arms, carrying her to the bed and laying her down. He began undressing her again.

"You don't seem excited," she whispered.

"Oh, I'm fucking excited." He yanked at her clothes, and she gasped, finally helping him. "I'm excited because I have you back."

"But I—"

Sade pushed her down with his mouth on hers, shutting her up. "You are. You're mine. You were mine whole, you're mine broken. God, I need to fucking show you." He held her neck and kissed her with desperation. She finally let go of her resistance and grabbed his face, kissing him back.

"Make love to me," she whispered.

"That's my plan."

"You think you can?" she asked.

He smiled along her neck. "I think so."

"'Cause if you can't," she whispered, her fingers digging into the muscle on his ass. "I'll understand, it's… okay."

"Would you?" He growled and kissed her lips, putting his cock at her entrance. "So fucking sweet of you."

She arched her back and cried out when he thrust his cock deep inside her.

"Oh God, yes. I just… thought if you loved me you couldn't…"

He rammed in and out of her until her words were barely audible in her gasps. "Let me fuck you," he growled, slowing and rolling his hips. "If you're going to talk," he sucked along her neck, flicking his hips until she screamed. "Say something sexy."

"Sexy," she cried.

"Yes, sexy." He kissed and fucked her with hunger again."

"I love you," she whispered in his ear.

"Oh fuck," he gasped. His orgasm suddenly rushed up from her words. "Again," he growled, "say it."

"I love you!"

Sade roared and thrashed, every thrust bearing a guttural growl until she screamed from it.

Sade collapsed on her, still in shock. "I fucking did it," he whispered.

"You did," she whispered, breathless. "Boy, did you ever."

He laughed in her neck, so thrilled. "Do you realize how fucking amazing that was?" He lifted his head and looked down at her. "To have an orgasm while… feeling?"

She gave him the prettiest smile and stroked his lips. "I did that?"

Her sweet question sent a wave of love that overwhelmed him and he devoured her mouth. "You did that," he whispered on her lips. "That was all you. Thank you."

She let out a sob and Sade pulled up, staring at her. "Baby, what? God don't cry, I hate it when you cry."

"I'm sorry," she gasped, turning her face to the side. "It's just…" Her breath gushed several times as she fought to stop the tears while Sade kissed her cheek repeatedly. "I had been praying to know how to help you. And I'd given up."

He grabbed her face between his hands and kissed her lips, his body shuddering. "My dick is hard again."

"It is?" she gasped like she'd not expected the miracle to happen again.

Sade knelt between her legs, needing to see her orgasm while his cock was in her. He lifted her hips and placed the head at her entrance and stared at her while he slid in, watching her body come alive. She gripped the covers and looked down. "Play with your pussy for me. Like you fucking did that night."

Shame and desire danced in her eyes, but what drew her hand to her clit was neither of those. It was that breathtaking love he'd seen in Mercy's gaze. It was in hers now. Almost like they both had fallen in love with him by some miracle. Like winning the lottery twice in the same month.

Sade cradled her ass in one hand and stroked over her fingers now touching her clit for him. And fuck, God, he was still hard as a rock while contemplating *love*. Soon she was squirming and her pussy gripped him tight. He began moving slowly in and out of her, growling as her hot muscles sucked him sporadically. He stilled when the pleasure pounded with a runaway hunger, wanting it to last forever.

Her squirming intensified, and her mouth flew open with sharp gasps and moans as she rubbed her clit. Sade took hold of her hips, his fingers biting. "Get fucking close so I can ram it hard and fast while you fucking come on my cock."

She shrieked and flew apart at his words, and Sade quickly jerked her on and off his cock as she came. Her fucking tits bouncing while she held on tight and screamed, sending him over the edge.

He fell on her, kissing her through half roars while his hot seed shot into her body for endless seconds.

"Oh God," she gasped as he slowed, his roars turning into groans now. "You did it *again!*"

He snuggled his face into the curve of her neck, gasping a light laugh while ready to fall into a deep sleep in her arms. "God, I fucking missed you baby," he whispered.

## Chapter Twenty-Five

Lying with her giant in her arms while he snored lightly, Mercy couldn't sleep, she was too happy. She wanted to run on the beach and scream and cry. She had Sade for herself, whoever she was, he was hers. That's all that she cared about, if she never remembered anything, she'd know that. And that was all she really cared about knowing.

She turned and glanced at the clock. Her stomach tightened with the need to get up and use the bathroom as well as get ready for her dad. He was coming. God, he was alive, she still couldn't believe it. She hated the fairytale feel of all of it, the too good to be true feeling. Once upon a time there was a princess and a prince who fell in love, and they lived happily ever after. She could almost remember when she had no problems believing in that kind of thing. Had she quit believing in it before she lost her memory? Something said no, or she wouldn't have been with Sade, believing she could help him.

She liked the idea. The fairy tale one, and believing in it. Why shouldn't she? Things could go right as much as they could go wrong, she'd rather hope for the best, and strive for it. If it turned out any other way, it wouldn't be because she didn't try or for lack of believing good things could happen. She didn't remember for sure, but she felt that wasn't the kind of person she was. She was a fighter. A survivor. She took opportunity with hope, not doubt. With confidence and determination, not fear.

A flash of an orange envelope came to her. She gasped, and Sade jolted awake.

"What?" he looked around.

"I remember an envelope!" she cried, sitting up.

He pulled her down into his arms and mumbled, "Nice."

"Nice?" she gasped. "Nice?"

"Mmmm, yes. So very nice." He slid his legs all over her and she felt his cock growing.

"My dad is going to be here in an hour, you realize. I was hoping to—"

Sade bolted up in bed. "Shit, an hour?" He flew up out of the bed.

"Where are you going?"

"Anywhere but in here," he said.

"Why? Doesn't he know we're..."

"Yes, but I am *not* disrespecting him by being in your bedroom when he arrives." He searched for his clothes and looked at her. "What's so funny?"

She covered her mouth and shook her head. "Just seeing you scared is funny."

"When I tell you what your father does to people like me, then you might understand my fear."

"Really?" she squealed, so hard to imagine of her dad.

"Really! Not to mention he's like my childhood superhero. I don't want him to think I'm—"

"A sadomasochist fucking his daughter?"

He eyed her and nodded. "God, that sounds bad."

"I'm sure he knows you like I do."

"Maybe, but still." He worked his t-shirt on and Mercy bit her lower lip, desire throbbing between her legs at how gorgeous he was.

"You should get dressed too. Maybe we can cook something, I don't know."

"Awww, you want to make it special?" How adorable!

"Very. The man saved our life quite a few times. A little gratitude doesn't seem out of order."

"Not at all." She flew up and hurried to the closet.

"Fuck, I should leave before I don't give a shit."

She looked over her shoulder and found agony on his face and a huge bulge in his jeans. "No fair," she gasped. "I'm just as weak!"

"I'll get started downstairs while you finish in here. Want to go for a swim tonight? I've been fantasizing about fucking you in the ocean under the moonlight." Her womb jerked and heat flooded her face. He nodded and smiled. "I take that as a yes."

She smiled and nodded, too happy to speak as he hurried to her and gave her a kiss that stole her breath and left her shaking as he walked out, winking before locking the door from the inside and shutting it.

He didn't want anybody walking in and seeing her. For some reason that made her happier than anything. She found a cute, red sundress to wear and danced around her room with it like Cinderella before the ball. Her dad was coming home. And she was madly in love with her prince. Wonder if he'd marry her?

She was so happy she could fly.

\*\*\*\*

"Who the fuck walks around with no hand when they have a perfectly good mechanical one?" Liberty said, stirring in the pot. "Find me some garlic, pretty boy and quit trying to peek at my nub."

"I don't want to peek at your *nub*. Oh my God, you're sick! Unless you're doing something sexy with it."

Sade quirked his brow at Bo before smiling and winking at Mercy across the table where they laid out the resident's fine china from a fancy curio cabinet. Mercy smiled, knocking over one of the glasses. "Oops."

Sade made his way around the table to her while Bo and Liberty argued about silly stuff. "I see I'm making you nervous," he muttered to her.

She laughed. "I'm just a klutz. Was I always a klutz?" She shook her head and rolled her eyes. "Don't answer that."

He put an arm around her shoulder and pulled her against him. "I promise not to tell you about any bad habits you had. Only the good ones."

"How sweet," she said, jabbing her thumb into his side, making him jerk away with a grin.

"Yeah, and the only man who's going to see my nub is my husband," Liberty said, making Sade and Mercy raise their brows.

Sade sang a wedding march tune and Mercy joined in with him.

"Oh, what, you two getting married now?" Bo said.

"God help us," Liberty muttered. "They'd need to staff a doctor with the way those two go at it." Bo and Liberty laughed.

"At least you won't see me wearing my woman's clothes," Sade laughed.

"What?" Liberty looked at him from the stove. "What's he talking about, wearing my clothes? Please don't tell me you're into that."

"You *made* me, you don't remember?" Bo put his hand to his chest. "I'm all hurt you forgot that special night when you made me your bitch!"

Liberty shushed him, holding her mechanical hand in a threatening fist.

Bo laughed and rushed in and kissed her. Mercy noticed she didn't resist him and couldn't help smile at seeing them play in the open like that.

"So I have to marry you to see that nub?" he mumbled, kissing her.

"Yep."

"When's the date?"

She giggled. "You'd marry me just to see my nub," she said, dryly.

"Noooo," Bo said, putting his mouth to her ear and saying something that made her turn red and blush.

"You're full of it," she muttered, pushing hair behind her ear and busying herself at the stove.

"I'm dead serious," he cried. "I do."

"Stop," she mumbled.

"I'm glad I'm not an intruder, you'd all be dead."

All heads jerked to the door where Kane stood.

Mercy stared in silent shock, her heart hammering. She'd gone through this scenario in her mind, how she'd act, what she'd do, how she'd feel… and now she stood rooted to the floor, staring into the face of a dead man. When he opened his arms, she flew around the table and launched into them with shrieking sobs of relief.

"Oh my God! Oh my God!" she cried.

"Button," he whispered in her ear. "My God, I missed you." He pressed a large hand to her head, cradling it. "I have a lot to explain sweetheart, I promise I will."

"Don't apologize!" she gasped. "I'm so glad you're alive, that's all that matters!"

"How are you baby? How's your head?"

She couldn't let go of his neck as she whispered. "I lost my memory, Dad. Did you know?"

"Don't worry, it'll come back."

She kept her eyes clenched tight as he stroked her back and rocked her while holding her off the ground in his arms. "I have a notebook," she squeaked. "I've been writing things down, to keep track. You can tell me what I'm missing, maybe?" Her tears streamed again. "I do remember that you were an amazing father," she whispered. "I didn't forget that."

He hugged her tightly, his whisper heated, "I'll help you get those memories back. I know a few tricks."

She laughed and he set her down. "So I've been hearing." She wiped her eyes and saw he was looking at Sade.

****

Mercy slipped her arm around Sade and he pulled her close to him as Kane opened the screen door and stood in the doorway. He looked out at something and gave a small smile with a nod.

A bolt of fear struck Sade as a shadow approached the doorway. She finally stepped up and Sade heard his breath leave him in one gasp as his knees nearly gave out.

A woman that looked just like his mother, stood there, staring at him with fear in her silver gray eyes and a small smile on her face. "Hi, baby," she said softly with a small wave.

Sade's body and mind locked up with things he didn't recognize ever feeling as he stared at the woman of his distant dreams and ever present nightmares. He fought to tear his eyes away, but he was afraid the apparition would disappear. But he had to know, understand. "What... what the fuck Kane," he finally managed, his voice barely working, still not taking his eyes from her. "What-what are you doing?"

"I had to hide her to keep her safe," he said quietly. "It was the only way to make a clean cut."

"I wanted to tell you," the woman suddenly gasped. The fear in her eyes like a spear in his heart. "Tell him how many times I wanted to tell him," she cried, looking to Kane and back at him, like she'd die if he didn't believe her.

"Many times," Kane said. "You have no idea how hard it was to keep her away from you. I promised her this day would come."

Tears streamed down her face and she nodded. "He did! Because I needed to go to you, I needed to tell you that I was okay, I saw you hurting," she gasped, both hands clutching her chest. "I saw, I knew, I felt you, always. In my heart!"

Sade felt his head shaking. She couldn't be real. "You died." He wanted to say he saw her but he hadn't. "They didn't let me see you. I wanted to see you and tell you."

She covered her mouth.

"She died," he told Mercy. "You remember, I told you?"

Mercy's tears fell and she shook her head. "I'm sorry, I-I don't remember, baby."

Sade looked around and found Bo. "She died, tell them."

"Yeah, man," he said, hurrying over. When Bo got close, he grabbed him and pulled him in his arms, scared. "She died, right?" he whispered to him. "She died, I was four. I killed her, remember? Remember man?" he strained before setting him before him. "You fucking remember?" he roared, pointing at her. "She! Died!"

"I remember, I remember, Sade. She died. You're okay man," he whispered, tears in his eyes. "I was with you, I remember."

Sade moved out of his hold and rubbed his head with both hands, turning in several directions. He looked over at her. She couldn't be real. God, she was still just as beautiful as he remembered her. He wanted to tell her, but he couldn't use his throat, it was locked up.

Sade suddenly couldn't breathe and he covered his face. "I-I'm having a hard time with this," he gasped before looking at her, terrified she'd disappear. "You're…you're supposed to be dead."

She let out a bitter sob. "I had to hide," she said, angling her head with regret. "I had to hide really, really good baby, so that he could never find me. Mommy would have told you so much sooner but things kept getting in the way," she said, her breaths coming in constant gasps now, her hands tight at her chest. "I have this huge memory book of everything you ever did, I followed my precious baby every day," she barely managed. "I was there the best way I could be, tell him Kane, tell him I was there the best way I could fucking be!" she screamed at him.

"She was there, Johnathon. Every single day for twenty years," Kane whispered.

"I'm sorry!" she screamed in broken bitterness. "I'm such a bad mother!"

Her scream and pain sent Sade flying to her, wrapping her in his arms. He lifted her off the ground, cradling her head. "Shhhhh, don't cry, don't fucking cry! Oh my God don't you cry, don't you fucking cry! Mom? Are you fucking real?" he sobbed on her shoulder. "Oh my God, you feel fucking real, you're fucking real, you're so fucking real!"

"I'm real," she sobbed. "I'm real baby."

"I missed you!" he gasped, not wanting to let her go. "I'm sorry, I didn't mean for you to get hurt! I fucking promise!" he sobbed. "I tried to be good, I tried to be a good boy every day, every day I tried so hard and I never could! I never meant to hurt you mom, I just wanted to protect you, that's all!"

"Stop it, stop it," she sobbed. "It wasn't your fault! It wasn't your goddamn fault," she wept bitterly. "Tell him Kane!" she gasped. "It was mine! I chose that life, not you!"

He finally set her down to hold her face, stroking it. "Oh my God," he whispered heatedly. "Look at you. Just look at you. You're so fucking beautiful, mom" he rasped, touching her trembling mouth with awe. "Oh my God, your teeth."

A sob burst from her and she nodded. "Mommy fixed her teeth." She stroked his face and Sade hugged her tight to him again.

"You fixed your teeth," he gasped. "They're so pretty."

"I did," she cried back, holding him. "Mommy's all fixed up, all better now."

Sade became aware of several arms hugging him, them.

"We're a family now, baby," Kane said kissing her head.

Sade looked at them and his mom gave the prettiest smile he'd ever seen. "We're married, baby. I married him after he saved my life. They were going to kill me and he saved me."

Sade gasped, looking at Kane. He grabbed his head and pulled it to him. "You saved her?"

"I did, son. I forgot to mention I'm madly in love your mother."

Sade let go a shocked breath, dumbfounded as he looked at his mom. "You married my childhood hero?"

She laughed for the first time and the sound brought Sade's sob. "I sure did, baby. Mommy married the Vigilante."

"That's so good," he cried with a gasp. "That's where you belong, with somebody who cherishes you. You cherish her?" he asked Kane.

"With all my heart," he said.

"The way I feel about Mercy?"

"Yes, son. Just like that."

"Thank God," he cried, hugging her again. "Thank you God."

****

After Sade was over his initial shock, they ate dinner. And fuck it felt like his very first Christmas where he got everything he could possibly ask for. He held Mercy's hand on his right and his mother's hand on his left under the table, never wanting to let them go. He couldn't even talk through the meal, and was glad everybody else carried the conversation. What he really needed to do was hide in a closet with Mercy and just cry for fucking hours. Enough hours that would equal all the years of pain and agony of not having his mom. Thinking he'd killed her.

"How about we break in the den," Kane said, getting up from the table.

"Sounds good to me," Bo said, looking at Liberty. Sade grinned at catching his tongue flick at her and it immediately made him think of Mercy's tongue action she was so fucking amazing at.

He angled his gaze at her then leaned and kissed his mom on the cheek before getting up and pulling Mercy with him. Everyone followed them to the den where they talked about everything from the weather to the size fish you could catch in the bay. Sade couldn't stop smiling, listening to Mercy and his mom plan parties and do girl things while Bo and Kane talked fishing expeditions with Bo's voice booming like a kid.

Fuck, he was breathless with joy.

"Check the weather," Kane said. "There's a storm headed this way. Just want to make sure it's nothing we need to hunker down for. Where's the remote for this ancient contraption?"

Liberty walked over to it and flipped a switch with one of her iron digits. "There's your remote."

Bo shot out a laugh while Liberty manually found a news station and returned to sit next to Bo who pulled her onto his lap.

Sade leaned to Mercy and whispered, "You still up for that midnight swim?"

She angled her pretty green eyes up at him. "What if there are sharks?"

He lowered and snapped lightly at her ear, smiling at how she drew her shoulder up.

"What the fuck?" Bo said, hurrying over to the TV to turn it up.

"…You heard right. A bullet to the head. Authorities say what saved the priest's life was the titanium plate in his head from an accident at the age of sixteen. Father Abraham was released from the hospital after telling authorities he'd been abducted, shot, and left to die. Check out live footage of a brief interview obtained as he was escorted to the local church where he claims he was abducted from."

Sade's heart was trying to beat out of his chest as he became aware of Mercy's nails digging into his arm.

"Father Abraham, do you have any comments or messages you'd like to give to your captors in case they're watching?"

Mercy gasped when the bright blue eyes turned to the camera and looked right into it. "God has protected his anointed. And the wrath of Purgatory is certainly coming for those who run and are in need of its cleansing fire." He shook a long finger at the camera. "You can run," he said with a smile. "But you can't hide. The eyes of the Lord are everywhere. Seeing." He pointed to his eyes. "Listening." He pointed to his ears with a secret smile. "And knowing." He pointed to his temple with raised brows. "Johnny."

To Be Continued…..

Click the links to purchase an autographed paperback copy of Mercy~A Dark Erotica or No Mercy~A Darker Continuation

Stalking Links:

Facebook Author Page

If you go there, you'll find my other stalking links.

I hope you enjoyed.

6248453R00185

Printed in Germany
by Amazon Distribution
GmbH, Leipzig